Susan has been an avid reader as long as she can remember. More recently, having been inspired to write herself.

If not writing, she can usually be found immersed in messy play with her young grandchildren.

However, once they and her work are put to sleep, she can be found dancing the night away – either on the dance floor or in the kitchen!

'It's better to have loved and lost, than never to have loved at all'

                      Ernest Hemmingway

Susan Hunt

THE HOUSE ON TOP OF THE HILL

Susan Hunt

Copyright © Susan Hunt (2025)

The right of Susan Hunt to be identified as author of this work has been asserted by her in accordance with section 77 and 78 of the Copyright, Designs and Patents Act 1988.

All rights reserved. No part of this publication may be reproduced, stored in a retrieval system, or transmitted in any form or by any means, electronic, mechanical, photocopying, recording, or otherwise, without the prior permission of the publishers.

Any person who commits any unauthorised act in relation to this publication may be liable to criminal prosecution and civil claims for damages.

A CIP catalogue record for this title is available from the British Library.

ISBN: 9798288323164

First Published (2025)

Thank you to my husband Martin for your valuable support

And Martin Cox, a wonderful artist who created the front cover

Although this book has only been published in 2025
It was actually started several years ago now
And is set in 2014.
As we all know, a lot can change in eleven years;
But that's another story!

Chapter 1

Separate Lives

'Are you sure you've thought this through?' Adam asked.

'I've thought of nothing else since Freya left,' I said, with conviction. 'You're not going to change my mind.'

'But you've already said, you've nowhere to go,' Adam argued.

'I can't let that stop me. At least now, when something does become available, I'm ready to move. I'll find somewhere to rent in the meantime. I won't be homeless! Like I said, you're not going to change my mind,' I continued. 'Besides what's it got to do with you now anyway?'

'It'll just be odd driving past and not seeing your car parked outside, or the lights on.'

'I'm sure whoever moves in will switch the lights on!'

'But it won't be you,' Adam tried explaining.

'It's a bit late for sentimentality now,' I considered. 'Besides, the girls don't live here anymore. You've all moved on; I need to do the same,' I continued, not that I needed to explain my actions to him anymore.

'I take it you've discussed this with the girls?'

'Of course I have,' I said, failing to inform him of a similar conversation I'd had with our daughter, Beth. Her sister had welcomed my decision whole heartedly, having already relocated back to Cornwall herself six years ago. But Beth had always been more like her father, enjoying all her creature comforts. And why Adam would think I would consult him before the girls, let alone consider his opinion anymore, was ridiculous after all this time! I'd loved making here home and by the sounds of things, seemed to have done a good job: the lights always on, the groceries bought, clean clothes ready for the next day, everything as it should be. But, once the girls had both left and Laura had turned Adam's head and he'd opted for a new life with her and her two relatively young sons and all that that could offer, that chapter was over. There had been a time when I had always respected his opinion – even moving here, away from friends and family and everything I'd known, so he could further his career. But ever since Freya had left, I'd wanted to follow her. Freya had always followed her heart, and she'd never looked back.

'You'll still have Beth,' I reminded him. 'I doubt she'll ever move.'

'I suppose, and Freya needs you,' Adam surmised. 'And I suppose it also means you'll be able to help her with all her wedding plans.'

'Yes, I'm looking forward to that. Anyway, I'm going to have to go and get on,' I told him, having said what I'd needed, promising to keep him updated on my situation.

I decided to take a well-earned break from unearthing all sorts of paraphernalia, that didn't even belong in the back of a wardrobe. Perhaps once I'd finished, the removal firm would be able to amend their recent inventory and astronomical quote!

I sat down with a cup of tea and a bar of chocolate to replenish my depleted energy levels. Despite it being weekend, I had been up since six-thirty, working to complete an order of wedding invitations, having promised myself and Poppy, the bride to be, that I'd have them completed by the end of next week. The materials I'd been waiting for had arrived yesterday, so it wasn't going to take me too long to finish them. I'd also had a couple of enquiries for samples to send out, both for weddings next spring. Typically, this time of year was quieter; the majority of couples preferring to choose the spring and summer months to marry - the invitations having been sent out months ahead. My business of supplying wedding stationary had all started after Beth had been unable to find what she'd envisaged for her own wedding. I'd practiced her ideas and managed to produce forty-five invitations and ninety order of service and place card settings, delighting my daughter and surprising myself – not only on my achievements, but as to how much I had enjoyed creating something so beautiful. I hadn't expected to ever have to tie another ribbon, or at least not until Freya decided to marry, keeping one for myself as a memento of what had been a magical day. So, when Emma, Beth's bridesmaid, had enquired as to the possibility of something similar for her own impending wedding, I had jumped at the chance to get creative again. Word had spread and the dining room table had soon become a permanent workstation and my business was born. That was a year ago now, and I now had enough work to keep me occupied full time. I had previously worked at the local stables, but could now enjoy riding instead of teaching. It also meant I could take my work with me wherever I went. And now, a designated workspace replaced the dining room table.

I switched on my iPad to check if anything new had come onto the housing market since I'd last looked, and to my surprise there was one; a very charming looking detached cottage and with what appeared to be the perfect floorplan, and surprisingly - within budget. Although I was familiar with the village, I couldn't exactly place the property, imagining it to be tucked away down one of the higgledy-piggledy, narrow back lanes.

So, as soon as I'd finished enjoying my moment of indulgence, I decided to give the estate agent a call to arrange a viewing for the following week. Something this good, wouldn't be around for long, especially at this time of year, and going by the information I had, it seemed to be just what I'd been looking for.

Chapter 2

Appearances can be Deceptive

I had cleared my work and made an impression on the house as well, surprised at just how much accumulated material I'd managed to acquire, whilst realising we had lived in this house for almost twenty years. The garage and garden had been Adam's domain, so when he'd left, he had taken practically everything that had resided in there, with him. We had also emptied the loft of all our treasured memories, that he'd so quickly forgotten or chosen to ignore. Beth had been a very methodical child, reflected in what remained of her life in the place she still called home. Whereas Freya's bedroom had always resembled the opposite, I doubted if she would even be able to recall what was stashed under her bed! Assuming it would be left for me to discover! But, for now, I had to prioritise and find myself somewhere to live.

I was already suitably impressed as I arrived outside the property, parking my car in the driveway, alongside what I imagined to be the estate agent's vehicle: a rather impressive Land Rover.

'It is you!' I declared, extending my hand to greet the gentleman in question, as I walked over to meet him emerging from the front door.

'Mr Gillibrand,' he offered, a bemused expression across his face.

'Felicity. Felicity Stevens,' I finished.

Mr Gillibrand remained motionless for a moment. Surely, he couldn't have forgotten!

'What, Felicity who ran over Mrs Cawthorne's cat?'

'The same!' I cringed, recalling the aforesaid. 'Well almost, a lot has happened since I last saw you,' I considered. 'So, how long have you been doing this?' I enquired.

'Ever since I left college. My father actually owns the business,' he explained. 'So, you're moving back?'

'That's my intention.'

'Well, you'd better follow me,' he suggested, leading the way inside.

'So, you couldn't keep away?' he enquired.

'Something like that,' I proclaimed, observing the cosy living room.

'So, is it what you envisaged?' Ben asked.

'It's certainly ticking all the boxes so far,' I commented, following him into the well-appointed kitchen; every bit as impressive as the photos had led me to believe.

Even the master bedroom had enough space for a large bed and came with built in wardrobes. Then, as we entered the back of the property, all my dreams flew out of the window and over the wall that had obscured the view from downstairs.

'The description didn't mention its close proximity to the local hostelry,' I commented, a little deflated.

'Hmm...' Ben sighed, joining me at the window. 'Though I imagine it'll be quiet at night.'

'Yes, but I'd hear them during the day when I'm in my garden. I want to be able sit outside and relax, connect with nature, not eaves drop on the local gossip.'

'So, would you like to see the garden?' he asked, perhaps realising we'd be wasting our time.

'I think I've probably seen all I need to see, thank you,' I replied, realising I'd had a completely wasted journey.

'So how about we go and check out what the neighbours are like,' Ben suggested. 'You look like you could do with a drink.'

'Is that even allowed?' I asked.

'I'm finished for the day.'

'Well in that case, I accept,' I said, following him down the stairs and out of the front door.

'Don't you have to drive somewhere later?' Ben asked, as we ordered our drinks.

'No, I've not far to go. I've actually booked a night upstairs!'

'I'm sorry the house wasn't exactly right.'

'Or that you'd failed to mention what lay beyond the garden gate!'

'We're only instructed to sell the property in question. Besides, I'm sure there are some who'd consider its appeal.'

'Like one of them over there,' I indicated, towards a small group of animated senior citizens, who looked like they'd just walked off the set of 'Last of the summer wine'!

'Do you not recognise the woman in the corner?'

'No,' I considered. 'Why, who is she?'

'Mrs Jones.'

'As in double history, Friday afternoon?'

'Well remembered!'

'Really! I thought you were meant to be selling this. We'd better sit over here.' I decided.

'So, are you retiring?' Ben began his interrogation.

'No, I've no intention of spending my afternoons sat over there.'

'So, what is it you do?' he continued.

'I make wedding stationary.'

'Oh, I didn't have you down as artistic!'

'It's quiet a lucrative business, I'll have you know.'

'That sounds more like the Felicity I remember!' Ben smiled. 'So, what brings you back?'

'Well, my work allows me to work anywhere in the country and my youngest daughter has already settled here. I just feel it's where I belong.'

'So, where do you live?' I asked.

'In the village, at the top of the hill.'

'So, are you married?' I continued my own interrogation. 'Don't worry!' I quickly interjected, when he didn't automatically respond. 'I'm not suggesting I move in with you or anything!' I said, picking up my glass trying to hide my embarrassment.

'I remember now, you always were quite forward,' Ben recalled. 'Wasn't it you who asked me to dance?'

'Forward thinking,'

'Let me get you another drink,' Ben suggested, as I finished my wine. No doubt feeling guilty for wasting my time.

'Thank you, I think I could manage another,' I accepted, realising just how quickly I'd drunk the one in front of me and the added bonus of not having far to go to bed!

'I can recommend the restaurant,' Ben said, returning with our drinks. 'If you'd like to join me?'

'It'd be my pleasure, thank you,' I accepted, beginning to enjoy his company.

He returned with a couple of menus and we both began to relax, now blissfully unaware of Mrs Jones in the other corner, or anyone else for that matter.

The restaurant was busy and exceedingly good; realising I certainly wouldn't have far to come to enjoy a Sunday lunch.

'So, have you got any more viewings arranged for tomorrow?' Ben asked, eventually returning to what brought me here.

'No, I came all this way on the understanding this would be right!' Realising now, just how impetuous I had been.

'I'm terribly sorry you've had a wasted journey.'

'There's definitely room for improvement,' I replied, finishing my drink. 'Although, I have to admit, the cottage itself was just what I'm looking for. But I'd appreciate your honesty next time. The problem is, I'm not prepared to budge on location, so I'm probably going to have to consider renting somewhere short term.'

'You're probably right,' Ben agreed.

'Unless you know something I don't?' I asked, trying to read his face. 'I've done it again, haven't I? I meant, if you know of anything coming onto the market, inside knowledge,' I explained. 'Is that what happened?'

'Now you've completely lost me!'

'When you broke up with me?' I continued, finally asking what I'd always wondered. At the time, being so upset I hadn't waited for an explanation. Not that Ben had offered one. I'd just turned and run in the opposite direction – until all I could hear were the crashing waves. 'Was it something I'd said?'

'No, you were two timing me!'

'I was not!' I exclaimed, almost choking on my words.

'Well, that's what I heard.'

'So, exactly what did you hear?' I asked, unable to still quite believe what I was hearing.

'That you were seen kissing some other guy.'

'When?' I asked, still unable to quite comprehend his accusation.

'One lunchtime, in town, you were with that friend of yours and another lad, presumably her boyfriend,' he recalled with clarity.

For once, this evening, I was quiet, staggered to think that Ben had believed I would have done such a thing. I had, truly loved him. I had never actually told him as much, I was, still only sixteen and although I knew how strong my feelings were, it was still strange territory for me. So, instead I had kept quiet, accepting that Ben hadn't felt the same way after all.

'So, what's your take on the events?' Ben asked.

'I'd been set up,' I began, trying to reflect on something I had tried to forget at the time. Never realising the impact it could have had on my relationship with Ben, when it had meant nothing, as far as I had been concerned, at the time.

'I'd walked into town with a friend,' I began explaining, recalling the day in question. 'I'd known she was meeting someone,' I said, 'but that's all I knew. I swear,' I continued hurriedly. 'It was only when I got there, I'd realised the situation, and it was him who came onto me,' I finished, almost in tears. 'I'd made it very clear how I felt and that had been it, or so I'd thought!'

'I'm sorry,' Ben, now said. 'Perhaps we should call it a night,' he suggested. 'What time are you planning to leave tomorrow?'

'I haven't really given it much thought,' I considered.

'I'd really like to spend some more time with you, if you're not in a hurry to leave.'

'So, don't you work weekends?' I asked, considering the nature of his job.

'Occasionally, but I'm actually off tomorrow.'

'I think I'd like that,' I agreed. 'Where shall we meet?'

'Here I suppose is as good a place as any, that way I can collect my car in the morning.'

'You'll have me turning into Mrs Jones if you're not careful!'

'You could always drive up to mine if you like, and we can go from there,' he suggested. 'See what you think in the morning, just give me a call when you're up,' Ben said, once we'd left the table, giving me a kiss on my cheek before he left, igniting a little spark that had lain dormant for many years.

Despite the bed being very comfortable, I hadn't slept very well at all, tossing and turning, unable to stop dwelling on what had actually happened to destroy my happiness all those years ago, and how it could have all been so easily resolved, if we'd only sat down and talked!

I had given Ben a call before I'd gone down for breakfast, arranging to meet in an hour. I'd packed my case and loaded it in the boot of the car, though, was hardly relishing the drive home later.

'All packed?' Ben asked, walking towards me.

'Yes,' I replied, a little wearily.

'Cheer up, you don't have to leave just yet. How about we meet back at mine, we can grab a coffee and decide what to do then.'

'Sounds good,' I agreed. 'I'll follow you up there.'

His house stood, as he'd described – at the top of the hill, set back a little from the road, which was probably why I hadn't been able to place it.

'So, how long have you lived here?' I asked, admiring his home.

'Since it was built, about thirteen years now.'

'So, does your mother still live down in the village?'

'Yes, she's never moved.'

'Not many people do', I considered. My own parents had made here our home, remaining here until only recently, when they'd surprised us all and decided to relocate to the Isles of Scilly,– somewhere both of them were very fond of, having holidayed there ever since I could remember, falling in love with not only the dream, but the warmer climate; an important consideration I'm told, at their age. They now had the best of both worlds with time spent here on holiday each summer, especially now that Freya had made here her home, they'd always have some reason to return. Realising, Freya had perhaps put their dream on hold, having lived with them when she'd first moved down here.

'How are your parents?'

'Living the dream, it seems,' I explained.

'So, what would you like to do?' Ben asked,

'I'd like to go to bed. To sleep, I mean!' I added, quickly correcting myself. I really must learn to think before I speak.

'I didn't really sleep too well last night,' I explained.

'That makes two of us. How about we finish these and head down to the beach, blow away the cobwebs?' Ben suggested. 'It never fails to rejuvenate me.'

I remained quiet - afraid I might say the wrong thing.

I changed into my walking boots, my preferred footwear when not sat inside working. Either those or my riding boots. These days, my heels very rarely saw the light of day. We set off down the road, along past the big old house that I'd once imagined to be haunted, before its neglected appearance had been transformed into something truly remarkable, perhaps resembling its former glory, or as Ben would probably describe as, 'sympathetically restored'. Then past the pub, turning at the corner. The lane soon became narrow and winding, descending into a beautiful little hamlet with a cluster of charming little cottages once used by the slate miners. We opened the gate that led us to the footpath through a lush green valley, winding its way down past hedgerows filled with honeysuckle. Despite my lack of sleep, I had a spring in my step and felt so alive. Eventually the path became less trodden, revealing stunning views of the coast and beyond. The further we continued the steeper it became - only a few prepared to venture this far and negotiate the scramble down. But, without question, well worth the effort.

'So, is this the attraction?' Ben asked, eventually breaking the silence.

'It's one of the reasons. But I've always felt I belonged. It's who I am,' I tried explaining, as we reached the sand.

'I know what you mean, I can't say I'd ever consider leaving.'

'Even though my parents aren't here, it still feels like I'm coming home.'

'We just have to find you somewhere to live.'

We found a rock where we sat and relaxed, keeping an eye on the approaching tide, enjoying the warmth of the sun and our own thoughts; mine of happier times spent here as a child, exploring the many hidden depths of the caves and the craggy rockpools teaming with life, never tiring of what was on offer. Then, with my own daughters each summer, bringing a picnic with us when the tide was out. Freya had always loved the outdoors - here or at home, never happier than when on horseback. So, as soon as she'd sat her A levels, she'd returned, staying with her grandparents. She'd soon found employment, accepting a job at the local stables and a couple of shifts at the local pub - where, within a matter of days, had fallen hopelessly in love with Clether, not so much a local, but not so far away that they couldn't see each other again. He'd been playing his guitar at a gig at the pub the night they'd first met, six years ago. The rest, as they say, is history. Clether, had also found his dream job, building surfboards out of wood, either reclaimed, or harvested from other sustainable sources. They had moved in together when her grandparents had declared their intentions, and more recently announcing their engagement, after finding an almost derelict barn to convert further along the coast, a more attractive proposition I imagine, when carrying a surfboard down to the water!

Mum and Dad hadn't wasted any time in realising their own dream, accepting an offer on what had been the family home since they'd first married.

'We should have brought a picnic,' I said, realising the time, but reluctant to move.

'I was just thinking about lunch! How about we head back, I know the perfect place to take you. What time are you wanting to leave?'

'I never want to leave,' I admitted, grabbing Ben's hand as we climbed the rocky steps leading us back to the path. As a child I'd always longed to stay down here, relishing in the freedom it bestowed. Reluctant to return to the confines of home.

'Perhaps I could stay another night.'

'If you've nothing to get back for. Then why not.'

'Nothing that can't wait,' I considered, delaying the inevitable, whilst realising the sooner I returned, the quicker I'd be ready to leave. But surely, one more day wasn't going to make that much difference.

'What are you having to drink?' Ben asked, as we stood at the bar together.

'I'd love a cold glass of beer,' I mused, having worked up a thirst.

'So, you're staying?' Ben concluded.

'I don't know where yet!'

'That's easy,' Ben retorted. 'With me!'

'Are you sure?' I asked, a little astounded.

'Why on earth not? I have a perfectly good guest room; it has a cosy double bed and its own bathroom. Even its own balcony, and breakfast is included.'

'You've sold it!' I declared, accepting his invitation and following him outside.

'If only it had been this easy yesterday!'

'I'm not asking a lot.'

'I know, don't lose heart. I'm sure there'll be something soon. But in the meantime, you are going to have to consider renting somewhere.'

'I know, I'll give it a week and start looking,' I said, already resigned to the idea, prepared to wait for the right property.

'Well, no more talk about houses,' Ben concluded, as we found ourselves somewhere to sit.

After a leisurely lunch, Ben led me away from the noise of the families enjoying the sunshine to join the coast path between narrow banks of honeysuckle, brambles and prickly gorse - always seemingly in flower. The path soon widened; the banks now carpeted in soft heather. I followed Ben who deviated from the trodden path and down a steep bank that plateaued, from where we lay, watching the basking seals below.

We ambled back to Ben's, both now refreshed and relaxed, especially now I knew I didn't have to leave just yet.

His house suggested affluence, sitting proudly at the top of the hill on the periphery of the village. Although, once inside, gave little away about the occupant, other than he lived alone, no loved ones displayed on the walls or mantelpiece. Despite which, he was obviously very meticulous - the hall, devoid of any stray footwear and apparel to denote his pursuits. Even after Adam and the girls had moved out, my hall alone, could tell a story.

Ben led the way through the hallway and into the kitchen, the work surfaces clean and tidy, apart from a few necessary appliances, though he wasn't short of cupboards and drawers to stash stuff away in. Ben poured us each a large glass of white wine to take out into the garden to enjoy.

'This is lovely,' I said, sitting back and enjoying the late afternoon sun. 'Thank you so much.'

'It's my pleasure. I appreciate your company,' he replied, continuing to explain how monotonous life sometimes seemed, living on his own.

The rest of his house also described a bachelor existence, devoid of the occasional photographs of loved ones, sparse of many personal possessions. Despite which, he had obviously got a good eye for detail, making the space warm and luxurious, including an array of sumptuous fabrics in coordinating colours and textures to complement each room. Even the windows, seemingly positioned to take advantage of the light and view; the sun beginning to set as we relaxed in the comfort of the living room.

Ben's chivalry continued into the evening, taking me out to dine in a stunning restaurant in an opulent country house hotel, and although I limited my alcohol consumption in anticipation for the long drive home tomorrow, I still managed to relax and enjoy the evening.

Inevitably though, all good things must come to an end, at least for now.

'Thank you,' I said, wrapping my arms around Ben before I left, appreciating his hospitality. 'It was very kind of you to put me up.'

'My pleasure! I'll let you know if there's anything new comes on the market.'

I'd slept well, despite sleeping in my ex-boyfriend's house! Beginning to sing along to the car radio, smiling to myself, still quite unable to comprehend how the weekend had turned out – something I could never have imagined. It'd felt slightly odd driving away, leaving it all behind, although reassured, knowing that despite not having found somewhere to live yet, I could at least now envisage the future.

Chapter 3

All Work and no Play

By the time I arrived home, I was even more motivated than ever to accept the challenge that lay ahead, realising the sooner I packed everything away, the sooner I could attain my dream. So, after a trip to the post office to send off some invitation samples, I decided to tackle the bookcases, realising I should perhaps join the library rather than fill my shelves with books that I'd already read!

By the time I decided to take a break for lunch I'd accumulated more in my charity pile than to take with me! Although satisfied I'd earned a break, I hadn't yet felt any life changing euphoria that I'd been assured would happen when you decluttered. Though, I still didn't consider myself to be ruthless; I might be making a fresh start on my own, but I wasn't going to destroy all trace of my existence – it just wasn't in my nature.

Of course, it wasn't all work and no play, in between packing and making wedding stationary I made sure I found time to visit the stables and take Charlie out for a ride, especially as the weather was so glorious. Everything was on track with the sale of the house, all I had to do now, was find somewhere to live. I'd now resigned myself to the idea of having to rent somewhere, not that there appeared to be much choice in that department either. Ben had suggested I consider a property that had recently come to the market in the little hamlet, just outside the village; it wasn't so much the location that was the issue, more the fact it needed work doing to it. I'd agreed to give it some thought, though if I was perfectly honest, I just wanted somewhere I could move into and get on with life, and not have to spend time restoring some tired, old house, that probably needed bringing back to life.

Both Freya and Beth had been keen to receive an update on my weekend away, and if the property I'd viewed had met with my expectations. Freya had seemed a little disappointed that it hadn't met with my approval; the fact I'd chosen to live so far away was no reflection on our relationship, just that we both chose to follow our hearts. Unlike Beth, who had always strived to conform to expectations, not imposed by myself or her father, you only needed to look at Freya to realise that. Even as a baby, Beth had followed the book: smiling at six weeks, sitting up at six months and walking a week after her first birthday. Her early drawings had depicted a uniformed house with four windows, a door and a chimney. Then as she'd grown, she'd followed the same boy band as her friends, read the same books and magazines - followed the crowd, rather than expressing her own personality. Whilst Freya had preferred to listen to a more diverse playlist and read Wuthering Heights - a free spirit, letting no one dictate or influence her decisions, something I had always admired about her.

Beth had again expressed her concerns, hoping to persuade me to reconsider, reminding me of my age - perhaps concerned I was experiencing a mid-life crisis, or probably more concerned how she'd begin to explain my actions, when she couldn't understand herself. she'd probably report back to her father, who would no doubt sympathise with her. But I wasn't going to let either of them persuade me otherwise, I'd made the mistake of listening to Adam and moving here in the first place. I may not be able to turn the clock back, but I could change the future. Beth might belong here, but she would just have to learn to accept that life moves on and changes for us all. Of course, I'd failed to mention Ben to either of them, choosing to keep him under wraps, for now!

Orders and Requests for samples continued to arrive, providing a happy balance between packing and work, still able to prioritise, preferring to work in the morning before lunch, followed by another attempt at reducing the contents of what lay hidden behind closed doors and increasing the amount of brown cardboard boxes, that were becoming increasingly obvious in every room. Initially, the prospect had been quite daunting, but as long as I remained focused, I was confident I'd reach my goal, realising that meant eventually having to tackle under the stairs. Only today, I'd had an urgent request for a number of additional invitations, a number of guests having prior engagements and unable to attend; something I realised many couples failed to anticipate – realising that perhaps I should suggest this in future, to help me, if nothing else. Though, not exactly sure as to how I'd feel as the recipient, receiving an invitation so late in the day!

Ben, as promised, continued to keep me updated on practically everything new to the market, either for sale or to rent for my appraisal. I was very grateful for his help, although nothing, as yet, had met with either my approval or requirements. This morning's property was, as requested in the village of my choice, that not only came with an extortionate asking price, but five bedrooms and large gardens. Large enough, I shouldn't wonder, to build something to suit my budget. Then there was still last week's offering - well in budget, but in need of modernisation, something I still couldn't quite contemplate, but which Ben had obviously found an attractive proposition, having realised it's potential, whereas I struggled to get my head around the task of undertaking such a project.

Today, was Beth's birthday, even better it was Saturday. So, once the invitations were finished, I was free to go and wish her a happy birthday with a bunch of her favourite sunflowers and a bottle of her favourite wine to celebrate.

I was welcomed in and offered a coffee, which I enjoyed sat with Beth at her dining room table overlooking the garden where Lucas was working.

'It's looking lovely,' I commented.

'Thank you. So, what's the latest on the home front? Have you found anywhere yet?'

'No, not as yet.'

'So isn't it time you accepted defeat.'

'Certainly not!'

'But you're going to be homeless at this rate. It's bad enough I have a sister who lives in a shed!'

'It's not a shed,' I reminded her. 'It's a very nice shepherd's hut.'

'It's a glorified shed on wheels. And now, you're as bad. Even worse – you have nowhere to live! What am I going to tell Lucas's parents, I've been stalling saying anything, hoping you'd come to your senses.'

'Oh, I saw his mother just now, outside the bakery,' I informed her.

'What did you say?' she asked, alarmed.

'More what she said! She suggested I buy one on the new estate being built down School Lane.'

'There you go, what a brilliant idea. Are you going to look? I could come with you if you like?'

'No, of course I'm not! If I'd wanted to stay here, I wouldn't have sold my own house!'

'But things have changed, it's not too late. You could make a fresh start; it's a wonderful idea. Say you'll at least take a look.'

'You clearly still don't understand, do you,' I said, wearily. 'You seem more concerned about your own reputation, than my happiness.'

'But Mum, you'll lose everyone's respect around here.'

'Well, that's all right, because I won't be here!' I continued to explain. 'Now, what have you got planned for the rest of the day?' I asked, changing the subject.

'We're meeting up with Jack and Laura for cocktails and dinner later. Lucas has booked a table at the new Italian in town. It's very popular, he had to book it weeks ago.'

'And expensive, by all accounts.' No doubt the place to be seen. Expecting them to be checking in and posting various updates as to their location for everyone to see on social media later.

'Right, it looks like Lucas has finished,' I commented, noticing him locking the garden shed. 'I'll just say hello and then I'll be off, I've got some invites to finish. Have a lovely day Beth,' I said, standing to give her a hug.

'It's looking lovely,' I commented, as Lucas entered, leaving his shoes outside.

'Thank you, we're expecting Mum and Dad later.'

'I'm sure they'll appreciate the effort you've gone to,' I said, hearing another mower start over the fence! Imagining tomorrow, they'd all be out with their buckets of soapy water and shammies! 'Well enjoy the rest of your day, and your night out,' I told them, as I was escorted through the house and out of the front door.

I returned home rather frustrated, adamant I was going to find somewhere, anywhere! So, decided to call Ben and see if he had any other suggestions.

'I was just going to call you; I was worried you'd slipped into hibernation!'

'It's glorious here!' I commented.

'No, I was just thinking about Freddie, our tortoise. We used to keep him under the stairs in the winter.'

Then, when I failed to register, he reminded me I'd been delaying clearing under the stairs when I'd last spoken to him!

'Anyway, you called me.'

'Just for an update really.'

'There's still the renovation project and there's an old chapel a few miles away, but you'd have to have a lot of imagination to take on something like that.

'What are you saying? I'll have you know, I've a very good imagination!' I added, realising I'd have to show him some of my work.

'I meant in redeveloping an existing property, that's all. Don't take it personally.'

'I'll accept that as an apology. I'm looking for somewhere to live primarily, then I'll add my own stamp on things. Remember you haven't seen my existing home.' Realising, it no longer resembled a home, devoid of memories, now more a warehouse or sorting office. The only room still completely intact was what used to be my old bedroom, now used as my workspace, having a beautiful outlook over the garden and fields beyond. Somewhere I could gaze out and gleam inspiration. I now slept in Beth's old room at the front of the house, perhaps not as tranquil a space to gleam inspiration at the start of each new day, but I was more of a get up and go sort of person than linger in bed, and once the curtains are closed and lights out, I could be anywhere. All that really mattered was that I had a comfortable mattress, clean bed linen and a good book to lose myself in at the end of the day; preferring a minimalist look, having learnt to put my clothes away rather than throw them over the back of a chair or leave them strewn over the floor. I let my imagination run wild across the landing, in my work room: the walls pasted with inspiration. I didn't have a desk as such, just several old tables of varying size, although often littered with tiny wooden hearts, post it notes and bits of string and ribbon. There was method to my madness, as on one desk lay all the completed piles of stationary ready to be despatched to the happy couples on the start of their fairy tale - all very different - not everyone wanting to conform to tradition. Only this morning, I'd received a request from a couple who were planning a nautically themed wedding, having met aboard a ship; my mind already working overtime on ideas. My sewing machine sat open and ready for action under the window, beside my despatch station, reels of ribbon, string, lace and pretty bunting, all ready to adorn the requests of stationary. Adam had never been able to understand how I could manage to produce such wonderful work in such chaos - but it's just how I worked. Even the kitchen looked like a crime scene after I'd finished preparing a meal! Only at the end of the day did I insist on serenity. Adam of course, had been the complete opposite, everything behind cupboard doors or the inside of a drawer in his study, only the bedroom and bathroom had told a different story. Though now he's living on Beech Tree Avenue, I imagined he'd be expected to conform to a far stricter regime.

'So, where's the chapel?' I asked, not that I'd ever considered living in such an unusual abode.

'It's rather isolated, between Tremillock and St Cuthberts,' Ben explained.

'I imagine It'll be haunted!' I said, already getting goose bumps.

'So, you wouldn't be interested in the little house in the church yard then?'

'What, has it come on the market? I must have missed it.'

'Well to rent. It was up for sale last year, I'm sure they'd accept a reasonable offer if you were interested,' he said, enthusiastically.

'I've always considered that house, odd, surrounded by gravestones. Can you imagine waking up there each morning? Worse still, at night!'

'I'm sure that's why it hasn't sold. It's not everyone's idea of; I was going to say Heaven! I can't imagine you'd get a Sunday morning lie in either.'

'Have you ever been inside?' I asked.

'No, one of my colleagues is dealing with it.'

'No, I meant to a party or something.'

'I don't really think it's a party house.'

'Oh, I don't know, no one's going to complain about the noise. It might even get interesting on Halloween!'

'Anyway, when are you next planning to come down?'

'It's a long way to come when there's nothing really suitable. I suppose I'm going to have to consider something to rent a little further afield, aren't I?'

'It's looking that way, and it would only be temporary. How about I have a look at what's available and I'll get back to you?'

'Thanks, I'd appreciate that.'

'Leave it with me,' he said, leaving me to get on with producing the table plan and order of service for Lewis and Isabella's wedding, now they'd received all their acceptances. Of course, it wasn't left to me to organise where Aunt Edith or Grandma sat, all that had been decided. All I had to do was make it as appealing as possible. Their wedding was to be conducted in a village church in the heart of their local countryside in Leicestershire, followed by a reception at the local pub. Their guests had been well informed as to every detail, including where to park their cars and to the abundance of confetti that would be available to throw; no doubt blue, to match the sapphire in Isabella's ring, her nails and the ribbons on the car, just like I'd been instructed to consider when producing their stationary. At least as a guest, you'd know exactly what to expect, unlike another couple's order I was working on, leaving a lot to the imagination! Freya's wedding was still in the initial planning stages, concentrating on their home first and foremost, so it would be ready to move into once they were married. Though they were both quite adamant they wanted a more spiritual wedding rather than a traditional religious ceremony, conducted in an ancient woodland beside a babbling brook, their first night as a married couple spent sleeping under the stars - weather permitting!

Ben had kept his word and got back to me later in the day, just as I'd taken a break and wandered outside into the garden with a cool drink. Unfortunately, he hadn't been able to come up with anything other than what I'd already seen online, all of which to rent and further from my chosen area.

Though, I'd let him persuade me to take a look at a couple, especially as the invitation extended to dinner, bed and breakfast, in his beautiful house, and time was running out. I'd also agreed to take a look at the renovation project, if only to satisfy his curiosity, if nothing else. Though with time running out, I hadn't a lot of choice. I was very fortunate to have Ben and his inside knowledge and somewhere to stay.

Sure enough, Beth had checked in to the restaurant on Facebook, already attracting a lot of attention. No doubt there would be updates throughout the evening!

'Hi,' I said, picking up my phone to Ben.
'Hi, it's not too late, is it?'
'No, I'm still up. Why, is everything all right?'
'Yes, I just wanted to alert you to another property I heard of this afternoon. I drove by this evening to check it out and it looks okay from the outside, I'll send some photos across to you, it won't have uploaded online yet.'
'So, no unusual neighbours?'
'No, and as far as I can tell, it doesn't overlook a graveyard or beer garden, it's even in the catchment area for Saint Bartholomew's.'
'Well, top marks! Although, a school wasn't actually on my list,' I informed him, considering how much more difficult the task could be. 'Were the children all tucked up in bed?' I questioned, considering the proximity to the aforesaid.
'It was only seven o'clock!'
'So, how come you've only just called?' I asked, realising it was now nearly ten.
'If you must know, I've been home all evening, but I must have nodded off.'
'Sorry,' I apologised, realising it was none of my business. 'But you didn't see anyone loitering on the street corner?'

'No, they were probably all inside, diligently doing their homework! You'll be able to take a look for yourself soon enough,' he informed me.

'I'm sorry, I'm very grateful,' I said, realising just how much he seemed prepared to do to find me the right property.

'Well, I'm going to set my alarm and get to bed. I've a lot to do before Friday.'

Although I had the luxury of managing my own hours, I was also conscious I couldn't be away from my desk for too long, especially at this stage of proceedings with a move on the horizon, which would obviously cause some disruption.

Chapter 4

That's What Friends are for

As often is the case in life, or at least as far as I was concerned, everything always seemed to happen all at once; just as I thought I'd cleared my desk of all immediate requests - I got more! But nothing I considered couldn't wait until my return. I'd had to learn to prioritise over the years, even if that sometimes meant saying no, not only to orders, but any request. Though, right now, my thoughts were focused solely on finding a suitable property to live and work from, until a permanent solution could be found. Or at least, once I'd decided on what shoes to pack for dinner tonight! Only after accepting Ben's kind offer, had I realised I was probably just as nervous about what to wear as I had been on our first date! Back then it had only been to the cinema, but I could still remember how special I'd felt when his eyes had lit up when I'd opened the door. Not that I was expecting a repetition of those events, appreciating his intentions were purely amicable. But I was enjoying his attention and help in finding a property.

Ben, as agreed was waiting outside the station, having offered to collect me in time for my first appointment, which he'd insisted on viewing together.

'I thought we could grab lunch after,' Ben suggested, as we neared the first property.

'Great, as long as it doesn't interfere with any of your other appointments.'

'No, I've arranged my appointments to suit. Though, I'm afraid I'll have to leave you to your own devices this afternoon. But I should be done by five.'

'That's fine, I didn't expect you to take time off. I really appreciate all you're doing.'

'Right, it's just round here,' he said, turning the corner and glancing towards me for a reaction.

Unfortunately, I realised my face must have said it all. The property itself was well presented: the garden mown and windows clean, even flowers in the window, but it didn't make my heart sing or even warm, and I couldn't imagine arriving home here. I had always been a firm believer in first impressions, but decided to at least take a look, if only to satisfy Ben's curiosity.

The owner, a middle-aged woman, was very quick to open the door, not that I was planning on running away, or that there was anything derogatory externally, that I'd had chance to notice! The hallway, I noted, was quite narrow as we followed Gemma into the living room: a very pleasant room with a view out to similar properties. Ben, I noticed, was still trying to gauge my reaction, whilst at the same time, noting all the key features that obviously came naturally to someone in his profession.

'My husband and I bought the house from new, twenty-five years ago, before our Sam was born. Even he's moved out now.'

I wasn't quite sure what to say to that, having never met either of them before!

'So, have you tried selling it?' Ben enquired, knowing exactly what to ask in these situations.

'Not as yet,' Gemma continued. 'You see, my Harry, has already accepted a position at his new office in Cheltenham, and although I'm going to follow him, I wanted the option to return one day. It was our Rob who gave us the idea. He suggested we might be able to let it out over the summer. His wife often comes down here with the children. It might not be your typical holiday let, but it's not too far down to the quay and there's plenty of holiday lets down there that command a fortune. Then Harry, my husband, decided we could afford to let out here and have somewhere in Cheltenham.'

'The best of both worlds,' Ben continued.

'Would you like a drink?' she asked, as we entered the kitchen.

'No thank you,' I replied, without consulting Ben. 'We've got a busy schedule.'

I had to admit, the kitchen, which we'd been informed was only completed six months ago, would be a pleasant place to prepare one's breakfast and dinner, even lunch, being able to carry it through to what Gemma described as, "the family room" or out into the garden.

'So, will this be your first home together?' Gemma began, I assume after having noted the absence of a wedding ring.

'I'm just here for support, as a friend,' Ben quickly retorted.

'So, you'll be moving in on your own?' she addressed me.

'That would be the plan.'

'So, are you familiar with the area?' Gemma asked.

'Ben assured me it's a very respectable area with an outstanding school.'

'I'm sorry, I thought you said you'd be on your own?' Gemma quizzed. Wasn't it meant to be us asking all the questions!

'Is that a problem?' I asked.

'No, there's another young woman next door with a little one on her own. Her husband left before the baby was born! Rumour has it, he wasn't his!'

I looked at Ben, who just raised his eyebrows.

'Do you want to have a look upstairs,' Gemma asked.

'I think I should,' I replied, considering I'd need somewhere to sleep. Again, looking at Ben, who seemed to share my astonishment.

Gemma led the way up the stairs and across the landing into what she described as the master suite, though there was barely enough room for the double bed!

'We had the wardrobes built in,' Gemma boasted proudly.

'It isn't en suite,' she disclosed. 'But the bathroom is only next door. When my mother was a child, she had to go outside!'

Unfortunately, the bathroom suite didn't meet with my expectations. Something they had overlooked or hadn't yet got round to updating.

The other bedrooms were both adequate, though the view from the window was uninspiring, with next doors laundry hanging out, leaving nothing to the imagination!

Ben and I thanked Gemma for her time and waved her goodbye as we drove away.

'Well?' Ben asked. 'Though, I think I already know what you're going to say.'

'Go on then.'

'It wasn't really you.'

'It most definitely wasn't me!'

'Not even the built-in wardrobes?'

'Especially the bedroom, there wasn't much room in there.'

'I suppose it all depends on what you've got in mind!' he laughed.

'Don't you find it odd looking around someone else's home?' I asked.

'I'm only ever there in a purely professional sense though,' Ben explained. 'I'm never imagining showering or boiling the kettle.'

'I suppose, but do you ever see somewhere you could imagine yourself living?'

'Occasionally, I'm actually going looking at two new houses tomorrow, on the cliff overlooking the harbour at Merling, they should be pretty impressive, come along if you like.'

'Have you not listened to a word I've been saying,' I replied, a little too harshly.

'I wasn't meaning with the intention of buying one, I expect they'll be well out of your league. I was just suggesting you might like to see something special, that's all.'

'Sorry, I am really grateful for all your help,' I apologised.

'We'll find somewhere soon,' Ben sympathised, as we pulled into a parking space.

'We're going to have to!'

'This is nice,' I said, lightening the mood, as we entered the village pub.

'Have you never been in?'

'No, I can't say I have.'

'There,' Ben indicated, as a couple got up to leave. 'You grab that table, and I'll get us something to drink. What would you like?'

I wanted to say a bottle of something red, but refrained and just asked for a glass, though it seemed even Ben considered a large one necessary.

'So, are all owners as inquisitive when selling their homes?' I asked.

'I suppose it's an unusual scenario, inviting someone strange into your home,' Ben explained, especially when it's still going to belong to them.'

'Can you imagine her as a landlord? Though I expect there's a healthy neighbourhood watch!'

'What are your neighbours like where you currently are?'

'Great, though I've known them for many years.'

'I expect they'll miss you then?'

'I suppose, it'll be strange seeing someone else's car parked on the driveway,' I considered, recalling what Adam had said. 'Though they've never seen my smalls!'

'Yes, I noticed that as well! I could tell you a few tales myself!'

'Go on then,' I asked, taking another sip of wine.

'Not here, I have a reputation to maintain, remember.'

'I feel like going to bed now,' I commented after finishing my wine and devouring my lunch.

'Would you like me to take you home?' Ben asked.

'No, just drop me off in town,' I replied, realising what I'd just implied.

'It's no problem.'

'No, I need to stretch my legs and get some fresh air,' I said, standing to leave.

'I'll let you know when I get finished, it shouldn't be too late.'

Chapter 5

Down Memory Lane

I wandered along the harbour towards the path that eventually reached the coast, unable to resist stopping outside an estate agent's window along the way, only to be disappointed. I'd perhaps have a look inside on my way back. Then, as I turned, I noticed a familiar face approaching.

'I thought it was you, what are you doing looking in there?'

'Hi Stella!' I greeted. 'Oh,' I sighed. 'I've sold my own and have nowhere to go, I'm moving out in a few weeks, I'm looking to move back, but as yet, haven't found anywhere! So, I'm having to resign myself to finding somewhere to rent for the short term. Only that seems to be proving just as difficult!'

'Really? Well, I might just have the perfect solution. How about we grab a coffee in here,' Stella suggested, turning to the little tea shop next door.

'After you,' I gestured, following her inside, intrigued to hear what she had to say.

I'd known Stella since we were at school, but hadn't really kept in touch over the years, just bumping into each other occasionally when I was down here. We had been friends through school, sharing the same classes and bus home, but were never really soulmates, as such - that had been Sarah's role. Though when I thought about it, we hadn't caught up in years, apart from Christmas cards and the occasional posts on Facebook.

We ordered our drinks and despite having only recently finished lunch, a piece of cake - unable to resist the lure of softly spun buttercream.

'So, let me explain,' Stella began. 'My house is going to be empty over the summer; I'm going to take advantage of a residential summer course whilst Ruby is away on one herself. I'm a little reluctant to leave it for so long, but didn't know when I'd ever get another opportunity. So, you'd be doing me a favour really.'

'Do you still live in Tresgilly?' I asked, trying to remember exactly which house she grew up in.

'No, I'm in Tremillock now. Come and have a look once we've finished these, see what you think.'

Only if you're sure,' I managed, between mouthfuls of carrot cake.

'Honestly, it could be the answer to both our problems.'

'It'd certainly be a weight off my mind,' I answered, starting to relax, having forgotten how stressful property hunting was!

'So, where are you staying whilst you're down here?' Stella asked.

'Well, you're never going to believe this,' I began, 'but I bumped into Ben Gillibrand last time I was down here.'

'Didn't you go out with him once?' Stella asked.

'Exactly! He was waiting outside the property he was going to show me around. He's an estate agent, did you know?'

'Yes, he's done all right for himself. Have you seen where he lives?'

'That's where I'm staying,' I explained.

'Wow! You don't let the grass grow!'

'So, how old is Ruby now?' I asked, changing the subject. Failing to explain I'd already checked out the guest suite!

'She's fifteen now, just one more year at school. What about your daughters?'

'Well, Beth's happily married and hasn't moved far. Whereas, Freya's already moved back down here, she's converting an old barn with her boyfriend, well fiancée, before they get married,' I explained.

'Where're you parked?' Stella asked.

'Oh, Ben dropped me off, he had to go into the office this afternoon, we're catching up later.'

'I'm not spoiling anything am I?'

'How do you mean?'

'Offering you somewhere to stay. It sounds like you've already got your feet under his table.'

'No, we're just friends,' I explained. 'We hardly know each other.'

'It sounds to me as if that's all about to change!' she said, grabbing her bags from under the table.

I realised, as we pulled onto Stella's driveway, that she hadn't done so badly for herself either; her home, an impressive modern property set at the end of the road, bathed in the afternoon sunlight, no doubt commanding a beautiful spot to catch the setting sun. If the outside was anything to go by, then she too, had landed on her feet.

Stella led the way through an open porch, trailed in beautifully perfumed pink roses.

'I hope you like it,' Stella said, dropping her keys in a bowl on the hall table. 'You'll have to excuse the dirty pots,' she continued, as we entered the kitchen. 'There is a dishwasher!'

'It's beautiful,' I swooned, trying to take it all in. If only it was for sale. But then again, I doubted if I would ever afford it.

'Come through to the living room,' Stella invited, leading the way.

'So how much would you want?' I asked, realising it wouldn't come cheap.

'I wouldn't want paying,' Stella explained. 'All I ask, is that you pick up my post and keep the garden tidy,' she said, opening the glass doors. 'And pander to Leo's needs,' she continued, scooping up an enormous, long-haired white cat. 'I do hope you're not allergic?'

'No, not that I'm aware of. I've never actually had a cat,' I considered. Not that I didn't like them, but had always loved horses. Beth had once had a rabbit, who'd constantly tried to escape under the hedge at the bottom of the garden and was now laid to rest there.

'There'll soon be an abundance of fruit,' Stella advised, as we began exploring the rest of the garden. 'Just help yourself. I usually make jam, there's so much. But you can always make smoothies or just freeze it.'

'Let me show you upstairs,' Stella said, leaving Leo to settle back down in the sun.

The upstairs was as lovely as the downstairs. The master suite having an impressive, vaulted ceiling, with a floor to ceiling gable ended window overlooking the magnificent garden and an uninterrupted view over the fields beyond; the bed itself, taking centre stage.

'There's an en suite through here,' she said, leading me to a cleverly designed space at the back of the room, accessed through a dressing area.

'All yours! Unless of course you have a friend over!' As I took in the size of the bath.

'Although there are another two bedrooms I'll show you, and another bathroom.'

'I'm sure this will be sufficient for my needs.'

'I'm afraid I'm only taking one case when I go, so you'll have to ignore all my stuff. But I think you'll find there's plenty of room in the wardrobes. It's not as though you'll be bringing much yourself.'

'No, just enough to see me through the summer I should imagine.' Though in truth, I had no idea how long it was going to be before I found somewhere to call home.

Realising, I should really start to consider what I might actually need, before it all got stored away.

'So, what do you think?' Stella asked. 'Is it adequate?'

'More than!'

'Great, that solves both our problems,' she said, leading me back into the kitchen. 'Drink?' Stella asked, opening the fridge. 'I've got an open bottle of Sauvignon Blanc needs finishing, if you fancy joining me,' she continued, retrieving a couple of glasses from the well-stocked glass fronted cupboard across the room.

'I think you'll find there's everything you need in here,' she added, as if reading my mind. 'There's even a bread maker somewhere. I keep all the manuals for everything in a file in the bottom drawer here.' she said, showing me. 'Though some are probably obsolete now! I'll try and amend it before I leave. Wine?'

'Yes, thank you.'

We carried our drinks back outside to enjoy in the sun, leaving Leo to sleep peacefully at the bottom of the garden, whilst I tried to take in what would shortly become my home, still unable to quite comprehend my luck. Stella continued to explain about bin day, the window cleaner and the neighbours, who she assured me, were all very friendly and approachable, promising to leave a list of names and anything else she remembered, leaving us to relax and catch up on old times.

'So, are you retired now,' I asked, considering her ability to take leave of absence.

'No, I still teach ballet,' she explained. 'But only term time. I start back in September. That's one of the reasons I'm attending this course; it'll keep me in shape!'

'So, did Ruby follow in your footsteps?'

'Yes, I suppose it was only natural. She's hoping to get a place at The Royal School of Ballet when she leaves school.'

'So, is it just still you and Ruby?'

'Always has been,' Stella shared, with a little sadness in her voice. 'More wine?' she offered, finishing her own glass as she got up to go and retrieve the bottle from inside.

'Why not,' I declared, deciding to celebrate my good fortune. Reminded of how Stella had always avoided discussing her personal life. Recalling the first time I'd heard about her daughter, was when my mother had told me she'd seen her, later on in her pregnancy, at a loss as to who the father was, imagining it to have been some sordid affair that she'd somehow missed! Not that my mother was a gossip, but I sometimes wondered what they'd found to discuss at all the parish meetings she'd attended. I had been living away at the time, so the next I'd heard - other than my mother's own interpretation of events, which were all based on idle gossip, had been from Stella the following Christmas, having slipped a beautiful photograph of her daughter inside a card, then almost a year old.

'So, are you still devoted to horses?' Stella enquired, returning with the bottle and having refilled her own glass.

'I am, I still ride as often as I can, but I think I mentioned, I now create wedding stationary.'

'Yes, I remember now. How's it going?'

'Very well.'

'You sound surprised?'

'I suppose, I just never expected it. It was never my intention to go into business, it just grew,' I explained, as I picked up my glass, still astounded at the success of what I'd created in such a short period of time and only three years after tying my first knot. Suddenly alerted to a message from Ben.

"Finished in 10"

'Is it all right if I ask Ben to collect me from here?' I asked. 'I was meant to be meeting him in town.'

'Absolutely!'

I texted Ben back with Stella's address, explaining how I'd met up with her in town, deciding to explain the whole story later, continuing to swap contact details with Stella, who gave me a key.

Naturally, when Ben arrived, he was eager to accept Stella's invitation inside.

'Hi Ben,' Stella smiled, extending her arm.

'Hi. Beautiful property,' he said, shaking her hand.

'Thank you. I'll take that as compliment coming from you,' Stella replied.

Ben looked puzzled for a moment, then realised I must have explained his profession.

'Well, thank you for everything,' I said, embracing Stella. 'I'll keep in touch.'

'I was hoping she might invite me in for a drink, I would have loved to see more,' Ben said, reversing out of the driveway.

'You'll never guess what,' I said, excitedly.

'In which case, you're going to have to tell me.'

'I'm moving in!'

'What, with Stella? That's very kind of her.'

'Not with Stella,' I corrected him.

'I don't understand,' Ben paused, trying to comprehend. 'You're not buying it are you?'

'No, don't be daft, I'd never afford somewhere like that.'

'I still don't understand,' Ben said. Surely, he hadn't given her the wrong impression. Though, who knew when it came to Felicity!

'She's going away for the summer and has asked me to house sit,' I explained. 'So, I'll be able to show you around myself.'

'Well, that was a stroke of luck!'

'I'll say!'

'So how do you know her?' Ben asked.

'We went to school together. Don't you remember?'

'What's her maiden name?'

'Walker, still is. She caught the same bus as us every day,' I continued, still unable to quite comprehend how he couldn't remember. 'She was even in our tutor group.'

'Yeah, I remember now, she's got a kid, hasn't she?'

'Yes, a daughter, though I've never met her.'

We continued our short journey in silence, Ben having suddenly become preoccupied since he realised who Stella was. Surely, he wasn't the father! I considered.

'You, okay?' I enquired, as we reached the top of the hill and pulled onto his driveway.

'Yeah, just been a long day, that's all.'

'I can see if there's a room at the Inn, if you'd rather be on your own?' I suggested.

'No, don't be daft, I'll be fine,' he smiled, lifting my case from the boot. 'I've been looking forward to tonight. Besides it'll take my mind off other stuff.'

'As long as you're sure?'

'Perfectly,' he said, leaning in to kiss my cheek.

'Let me help you prepare dinner,' I offered, as we entered his house.

'Are you hungry?' he asked. 'I was just going to rustle up a stir fry later.'

'That's fine then, I'm happy to wait.'

'Fancy a drink, we can take them out to the garden and relax a while,' Ben suggested.

'Sounds perfect.'

'You go ahead, I'll bring them out,' he told me.

I wandered out towards the bottom of the garden, drawn to the strategically placed chairs adorned with cushions.

'I see you've found my favourite spot,' he commented, joining me.

'I can see why; it's beautiful. I imagine you must spend quite a bit of time out here.'

'It's just so peaceful, especially in an evening just listening to the birds and watching the sun go down.'

'Thanks,' I said, accepting the glass of wine he'd just poured, considering what he'd just said and adding it to my already long wish list. 'So, do you have any children?' I asked, trying to ascertain more from Ben than he'd already divulged and to quell my curiosity.

'No, I was never that fortunate. But do you mind if we talk about something else.'

'Course. Sorry,' I said, struggling to think of anything else, especially after all the wine I'd consumed over the course of the day!

We sat in silence, whilst I tried to decipher his change of mood, until I couldn't stand it any longer.

'Are you sure you wouldn't prefer it if I stayed somewhere else?'

'No, I'm sorry,' he apologised. 'What would you like to do this evening? We can hit the town if you like, see if there's any live music on.'

'We can see what's on if you like, or I'm just as happy staying in,' I shrugged, having envisaged a relaxing evening together in the comfort of his beautiful home, though didn't want to appear dull.

'I suppose you've had a long day. More wine?' he asked, finishing his own.

'Better not, I had a couple of glasses with Stella earlier. I'll wait until we eat.'

'Why didn't you say,' he said, offering his hand to assist me up. 'Come and keep me company in the kitchen.'

'So, tell me, is Stella's house as impressive on the inside as it is outside?'

'It's exactly what you'd imagine. I still can't believe my luck. You'll have to come round for dinner, once I can navigate my way around the kitchen.'

'I'd like that. Don't forget you said you'd come with me tomorrow to look at those new homes by the harbour.'

'I haven't forgotten. I said I'd catch up with Freya in the morning whilst you're in the office, that way you can give me a lift in, if you don't mind?'

'That'll work well, then we can get off as soon as I'm done.'

'Here,' Ben said, passing me some cutlery. 'Can you set the table.'

'Sure,' I said, grabbing the knives and forks. 'Do you want me to top up your glass?'

'Thanks, help yourself.'

I poured some wine into Ben's glass and helped myself to a glass of water, before sitting across from Ben.

'You're not a bad cook,' I complimented Ben, enjoying the meal.

'I'll have to treat you to my fish pie, see what you think of that. Though I thought we could eat out tomorrow night, if you fancy. Unless you've got other plans?'

'That'd be lovely. Though my treat.'

'So where are you taking me?'

'You might have to recommend somewhere, but not the pub this time.'

'What's wrong with the pub?'

'Nothing, I just fancy somewhere different that's all.'

'I'll have to get back to you on that.'

We relaxed for a while before carrying our drinks into the lounge, along with a selection of cheese and biscuits and a bottle of port, something I was unable to resist with a wedge of stilton.

'So, who else is still around here?' I asked, not having my mother here to inform me anymore.

'There's still a few; I suppose more girls than boys,' he considered. 'Do you remember Megan Hill?'

'I do; she always had her head in a book!' I recalled. 'So, what happened to her?'

'She married James Hughes.'

'Both their parents farmed, didn't they?'

'That's right.'

'So much for opposites attract!'

'Ah, but Adam Medford is still married to Annie Harrison!' Ben informed me.

'Wasn't she head girl?'

'Precisely! You'd have never considered them to be a match. He spent more time outside the headmaster's office than in the classroom!'

'So, what happened to Jennifer Langley?' I asked.

'Oh, she teaches at a local primary school, has done since she qualified. She married a guy older than us who's a postman round these parts.'

'We should organise a school reunion,' I suggested, as we continued reminiscing. Then, just as I was about to declare my intention to call it a day, I noticed Ben's expression had changed.

'I'm sorry about before,' he began.

I remained quiet, waiting for him to continue, too tired to resume any conversation, afraid I'd say the wrong thing, having consumed more than an acceptable amount of alcohol since my head had last hit the pillow.

'There's no need to explain,' I eventually managed, when he hadn't volunteered anything else.

'No, I want to,' he paused briefly. 'It's just I find it difficult. I've avoided having to tell anyone this before, but I suppose it no longer poses a threat.'

I sat up, facing him across the sofa, waiting for his revelation. All notion of sleep having now eluded me.

'You've lost me,' I admitted, wondering if I'd missed something.

'I'm infertile!' he exclaimed, shocking us both.

'Oh!' I paused, unsure of a response. 'So, how long have you known?'

'It only became apparent when my wife and I couldn't conceive.'

'So, you were married?'

'Yes, to Chloe, until she found someone who could give her what she wanted. It was all she'd ever dreamed of, she longed to be a mother. We'd every intention of having a family,' he continued, hardly drawing breath. 'We'd even chosen names for our son and daughter and could even picture what they'd look like. We watched all our friends get married and start families, but for us, it just never happened. I remember the joy when she eventually told me she was pregnant, until I realised it wasn't mine. Then I thought it

could be the answer to all our problems, imagining it to have been a foolish mistake or the result of a one-night stand. But, unbeknown to me, she'd been having an affair, fallen in love with the father of her child. It was the most agonising time of my life,' he managed, before I caught him in my arms, wrapping them around him, cradling him against my chest while he sobbed and I tried to absorb the enormity of what he'd just told me, imagining the impact and devastation it had had on his life, that the majority of us take for granted. Never considering how it must feel to know you'll never cradle your own child, hold their tiny hand and kiss them goodnight; realise a love you'd never experienced before. Reminded of the euphoria I'd felt, the first time I'd cradled each of my daughters to my breast.
Ben quietened, remaining in the safety of my arms, while we both reflected on what he had kept to himself for so long.

'I'm sorry,' Ben said, eventually surfacing.

'Don't be ridiculous,' I told him. 'I'm glad you felt you could tell me. I'm so sorry, I can't begin to imagine what you went through.'

'You must be exhausted,' he said, realising the time.

'I'm fine, I'm more concerned about you. Let's go to bed and we can talk tomorrow,' I suggested.
So, with a heavy heart, Ben switched out the lights as we turned and climbed the stairs, Ben, still hold of my hand as we reached the top, embracing as I kissed the back of his head.

'It'll all seem better in the morning,' I offered, realising it was probably a ridiculous thing to say, but at a loss as to what else I could say, I turned, leaving him standing there alone.
Normally, after all that alcohol I'd be asleep as soon as my head touched the pillow, but I couldn't help thinking of Ben, imagining the consequences of discovering such devasting news. It wasn't long before my eyes began to surrender, only I could hear Ben sobbing. So, without a second thought I

wandered across the landing and climbed into his bed beside him, holding him tight against me.

'I'm sorry, I didn't mean to disturb you,' he whispered.

'Nonsense, I'm here for you. Close your eyes, I've got you.'

The next thing I knew, the sun was pouring into the bedroom. Despite having had too much to drink, I could still remember how I came to be waking up beside Ben, who was still sleeping like a baby.

'Shit!' I muttered, reminding myself to be more careful, which was easier said than done after so little sleep. I crept out of bed and across to my bedroom and into the en suite to wake myself up under the shower, before wandering downstairs to get a drink of water, promising to never drink that much again!

'I'm sorry, I must have disturbed you,' I said, joining Ben at the table outside. 'How are you feeling this morning?'

'Honestly?'

'You can be as honest as you like with me,' I told him.

'I've felt better,' he admitted.

'It must have been that port! How about I make us both some breakfast?'

'Thank you – for last night.'

'Anytime, that's what friends are for, right?' I told him, kissing the top of his head.

'I'm glad you're moving back.'

'At least I've got somewhere to live now,' I reminded him.

Ben joined me in the kitchen, unsure of what each other deemed suitable for breakfast.

'I can rustle up a full English if you like?' Ben suggested. 'I've got all the components.'

'What do you normally have?'

'It varies, sometimes scrambled egg or just a bowl of muesli. It all depends on how long I've got.'

'Well, we don't have to be out for at least another hour, so I think we should indulge ourselves. But just eggs, sausage and tomato for me please.'

'No bacon?' he asked, adding some rashers to the pan.

'No, I can't be doing with that streaky stuff.'

I poured myself a glass of fresh orange juice: an absolute must on my breakfast list, reminded for some reason of Adam and how he'd always insisted on porridge for breakfast, eventually learning to cook it overnight in the slow cooker, so it was ready in the morning. Realising, that perhaps it was just strange sharing breakfast with someone else, especially a man.

Never thinking to sit outside at home, I followed Ben's lead, carrying my breakfast outside to enjoy in the sunshine, making a mental note to utilise my own outside space more often, all be it a little late in the day!

'So, was there nothing that could be done to rectify your condition?' I asked, between mouthfuls.

'Apparently not, at least not then. I was basically told to go away and accept it.'

'Easier said than done,' I realised.

'It was suggested we look into adoption, but we didn't want someone else's baby. Besides there was more to it than that.'

'How do you mean?'

'Well, all the psychological affects it had on us. It still messes with my head,' he explained, resting his knife and fork.

'I'll not mention it again,' I told him. 'Unless you want to talk about it.'

'Thanks. It just hits me sometimes, when I'm least expecting it. Yesterday when you reminded me who Stella was, it just brought it all back. I remember she was heavily pregnant when Chloe announced her pregnancy. At the time, I couldn't help thinking how unfair it was that an unmarried woman was able to have a baby, when our inability had destroyed our marriage.'

I sat back, the realisation and extent of the implications dawning on me, having never really considered the psychological effect it could have on a person.

'I learnt to accept what Chloe did was right. But, at the time, it just added to my feeling of loss.'

'So, did you ever meet anyone else?'

'No, I avoided going there, knowing the outcome. I know it's not everyone who wants children, but it's not the first thing you want to address, either.'

I considered how I would have reacted to the news, had I been in Chloe's shoes, or even my daughters, if they were presented with the same problem. Something difficult to imagine, unless you're actually faced with it. Situations like this are always easier when they're happening to someone else. We never truly know what's going on behind closed doors or behind a smile, what difficulties the people we meet are facing, often drawing the wrong conclusion, when we couldn't be further from the truth.

'So, what's Stella's story?' I asked. 'Do you know?'

'No, she's just been a constant reminder of what I lost.'

'But you didn't recognise her.'

'Until you mentioned her name.'

I decided to clear the pots away, vowing to avoid the subject, unless Ben broached it and enjoy the rest of the day together.

I'd said goodbye to Ben as he'd dropped me in town to meet up with Freya, before he'd gone into the office for a couple of hours. I'd arranged to meet Freya at the little coffee shop I'd visited with Stella the other day, both familiar with it, having sat at Freya's favourite table in the window on many a rainy afternoon during the summer holidays. It had always had to be the table on the right, so she could catch people's expressions as they'd entered the cafe. Today though, was too nice to be sat inside, listening to other people's conversations. So, instead, we each ordered a coffee to take out with us, deciding to head away from the town and towards the track that led to the beach, leaving the crowds behind to enjoy their ice creams and watch the boats arrive in with their fresh catches, unaware of the beauty that lay just a short distance away.

'Can you tell me if there's a post office?' Someone asked, stopping Freya. No one could possibly mistake her for a tourist, especially in her jodhpurs and riding boots, having arranged a couple of hours off before returning to the stables. She looked well, despite working long hours at the stables and then on the barn in an evening, though she'd always been a hard worker, even when it came to revision, realising the satisfaction to be gained.

'So, what time did you get to bed last night?' I asked, reminded of a message Freya had sent at eleven-thirty last night.

'We'd just finished when I sent the message, we'd been repairing the stonework. Then, when the light had deteriorated, reviewing our plans and options for the sewage treatment plant.'

She'd never needed much sleep, even as a teenager, I recalled. The complete opposite to her sister, who I'd practically had to drag out of her bed whilst Freya would already be up, mucking out at the stables. Even as a baby she'd thrived on little sleep, leaving me exhausted! Then I was reminded of Ben, and what he wouldn't have given to have held a crying baby in the small hours.

'How's the house hunting going?' Freya asked.

'Well,' I began, continuing to explain my stroke of luck and my connection to Stella, and while I was about it, introducing Ben into the conversation, explaining our connection, where he worked and his generous offer of accommodation.

'Perhaps I'll take a look for myself!' she said, smiling.

'I haven't said anything to Beth yet,' I explained.

'Oh, well I shan't spoil your fun! I think she just realises how much she'll miss you, that's all,' Freya said, trying to explain her sister's behaviour. 'But at least now you can tell her you've got somewhere to stay. I think she was afraid you might have to pitch a tent in our coppice, or sleep in the byre!'

'Imagine Lucas having to explain that to his parents!'

We continued on our way, taking a fork in the path, Freya looking over her shoulder to check no one was following us, wanting to keep the location a secret. I had known about it since I was a child, my mother showing me, swearing me to secrecy. The track soon became untrodden, covered by a canopy of trees, almost a swamp underfoot; fortunately, I'd had the sense to bring a change of footwear, so I would look the part when I accompanied Ben later. Then, within minutes we could smell the sea as the sun lit our way to a large expanse of almost deserted beach.

Freya kicked off her boots and I followed her lead, running after her towards the sea.

'We thought, next autumn for our wedding. We think we'll have the barn finished by then,' Freya explained. 'I've got loads of ideas I can't wait to share with you. We've even found the perfect venue, tucked away in a secluded valley. It's got everything we've ever dreamed of,' she continued. 'I want to walk through the woods with Dad, to Clether waiting to lead me across the brook and under the tree where we'll make our vows and be showered in the falling leaves.'

'You make it sound romantic.'

'Exactly as it should be. We just need to decide on the actual date.'

I always knew Freya's wedding would be different than her sister's traditional ceremony, and that it would have to include some connection to nature. And like my mother had concluded - God had made the trees and leaves, so what better place to get married, than in the midst of God's wonderful creation.

'Have you mentioned it to your dad yet?'

'No, we've only just found it ourselves. You're the first to know.'

'So, when am I going to meet Ben?' she asked, keen to see him for herself. 'How about we all have dinner tonight?'

'I said I'd take Ben out,' I told her. 'My treat, for letting me stay. Though I've no idea where to take him.'

'Well, why not come over to ours?' Freya suggested. 'The weather's perfect for a barbeque. Where else can you sit in a dining room and gaze up at the stars? I'll be quite sad when the roof goes on.'

'I'm not sure it's quite what Ben would be expecting,' I said, imagining us all huddled around an open fire, balancing our plates on our knees.

'You're beginning to sound like Beth.'

'I didn't say we wouldn't,' I mused, considering her invitation.

'Then we'll see you at seven. And don't be late!'

All too soon it was time to say goodbye, at least until this evening. So, as Freya began to weave her way back through the crowded street, I sat watching the boats whilst waiting for Ben, unsure as to how he would receive the invitation, now able to contemplate a future here, if not how to tell Ben of our rendezvous later.

Chapter 6

The Price of Happiness

'Here we are,' Ben said, as we pulled up outside the new properties.

'They're very attractive,' I couldn't help commenting. 'How much are they?'

'That's what we're here to find out. Here, take a look at the brochure.'

'Have you produced it?'

'No, Emma. She met the developer yesterday, but wants my opinion before putting a price on them. They're pretty unique.'

'It says here, "These stunning properties represent an exciting opportunity to secure a state of the art, contemporary home, sat in a commanding position with far reaching views".'

'Pretty accurate, wouldn't you agree?'

'So far, so good.'

Ben unlocked the front door of the first property which opened into a well-lit entrance hall, leading into the open plan living area, incorporating the kitchen and dining area with bi fold doors, spanning the width of the room, leading out to the garden - which obviously still required some work!

'It states here that, "The kitchen is stylishly designed and finished to an extremely high standard with soft shut drawer units",' I demonstrated. 'And a "sunken stainless-steel sink"!' Wondering how else you'd incorporate a sink! 'Even I've got integrated appliances.'

'Kinky!' Ben remarked, whilst checking the quality of work.

'I thought they were pretty standard,' I commented, reminded of my own kitchen, not that there was much similarity. However, I'd never considered chrome to be opulent! '"A fusion of contemporary elegance and twentieth century opulence, blending seamlessly together to offer stylish modern living",' I quoted.

'You're quite good at this,' Ben remarked.

'I should be, the number of descriptions I've read!'

'And here,' I said, arriving beside the island, 'we have the perfect place to partake in a coffee, whilst your wife lingers in bed, making the most of her Sunday morning lie in, before walking into the shower, reminiscent of the rain forest, saving the luxury of the double ended bath for when you can join her to sit under the Velux window to watch the stars with a bottle from the wine chiller, before retiring to your thermostatically controlled boudoir, that has a balcony, encased in self-cleaning glass, reminiscent of the oven door!'

'She's never written that, has she?' Ben asked, snatching the brochure from me.

'I can't wait to see the bathroom with its "muted grey tones, enhanced by the spot-lit ceiling, reminiscent of a star lit sky",' I continued, referring to the brochure. 'I suppose she's referring to the bath when she describes the bathroom as "more than a place to wash!" And assume the star lit ceiling is to compensate for there not being any natural light?' I said, looking around. 'And why does it say, "glazed windows"?' I asked, entering the master suite. 'Is glass extra?'

'See, I knew it was a good idea bringing you.'

'Wouldn't it be good if you could try before you buy?' I suggested, taking in the view from the master suite, resisting the urge to jump on the bed.

'We could always try the local pub and its award-winning food,' Ben suggested.

'Speaking of which, Freya's invited us round for dinner.'

'I thought you said they only had a tiny shepherd's hut. Won't it be a little cosy?'

'I imagine it'll be alfresco.'

'Sound's fun!'

'I can always decline, if you'd rather not?'

'No, like I said, it'll be fun!' he declared. 'What's on the menu, did she say?'

'No, she didn't,' I replied, beginning to wonder myself, considering what they might deem suitable. Everything normally either barbequed or cooked in a cauldron over a fire pit.

'So, what's her guy like? Anything I should know or avoid?'

'I think I told you, he makes surfboards,' I explained. 'He's absolutely passionate about wood. I imagine he'd build his home from it if he could, but planning insisted it had to be built in local stone, I imagine he'll use as much reclaimed material as he possibly can internally though.'

'So, how far have they got with it?' he asked, enthusiastically.

'They've only had it a few months, so not very far. Freya was telling me, they're planning on it being finished about autumn next year. I've not seen it yet myself, just pictures. But it needs a lot of work from what I can see. You wouldn't catch me taking on something like that.'

'No, I'd gathered that!'

'Anyway, you'll be able to see for yourself, put a price on what they might hope to achieve once it's finished. Not that they've any intention of selling it. But I suppose they'd be curious to know.'

After lunch we strolled along the harbour for a while before a more strenuous walk along the coast path, the weather too nice to miss the opportunity. Having both grown up here, we were familiar with the best places to deviate from the path, and depending on the time of year, pick blackberries, sloes or Rosehips; or quite simply lie in the long grass overlooking the sea and watch the seals play below whilst listening to the chatter of the Corn Bunting as they explored the brambles and gorse, especially after neither of us had slept well last night. Although, the pressure to find a suitable residence was at least off for now.

'This is nice,' I said, relaxing.

'I'm going to miss you,' Ben declared.

'It won't be for long,' I commented, suddenly realising how soon I'd be able to call here home again and enjoy everything I'd missed.

Chapter 7

Back to Nature

After following the Sat Nav and my own interpretation of Freya's description of where their property exactly was, we arrived at our destination, parking Ben's car on what would one day be their driveway, retrieving our warm layers for later and a cool box filled with beers and a trifle for dessert from the back of the car. Ben, aghast, as to our venue for dinner; either that, or the work that was obviously going to be involved in transforming, what appeared to be just a derelict farm building.

'You're here,' Freya squealed, jumping up from where we'd found them sitting a little further afield. 'Clether, this is Ben. I assume you're Ben?' Freya corrected herself.

'Of course, it's Ben!' I announced.

Ben smiled, shaking their hands, thanking them for extending their invitation. Realising of course, they were probably as curious as he was.

'So, what's for dinner?' I asked.

'We've got sea bass parcels with green risotto. We've only just lit the barbeque, so we've got time to show you around first,' Freya announced excitedly, walking back towards the barn. 'What do you think?' she asked, as we were led through a door shaped opening.

'It's very open plan!' I considered, trying to think of something positive to say.

'Just here,' Freya turned, 'will be the sofa, looking out over the valley.'

'But we thought we'd eat through here tonight,' she informed us, leading us back through the imaginary hallway. 'In what'll eventually be the kitchen, dining room,' she said, continuing to light the candles that stood on the mantelpiece of an old, reclaimed fireplace surround that stood against a wall. And then above the table - which was draped in what looked suspiciously like bed linen, were more burnt candles in a chandelier, hanging from a rope, hooked over a branch, that had obviously, over the years, intruded in what will become their dining area.

'It's beautiful,' I commented, amazed at what she'd managed to create. Ben, I noticed, still very much in awe of everything.

'So, what's your time scale?' Ben contributed.

'Fifteen months and twelve days,' Clether informed us.

'That's very precise,' I added.

'Freya wants it ready so I can carry her over the threshold.'

'Clether's made a provisional booking for October for the venue I was telling you about this afternoon,' Freya explained.

'Oh, that's wonderful! Congratulations! I wish we'd brought Champagne now.'

Once the meal was cooking, Ben and I were shown the entirety of their estate, extending down through the trees and into the valley. Freya explaining it'd be ideal terrain for goats and hens; exactly what she imagined the purpose of the goats, other than a suitable playground for them, I'm not quite sure! Ben cracked open the beers and made himself comfortable beside the barbeque with Clether, as only men know how, whilst Freya added more stock to the pot of risotto hanging over the open fire, before lighting more lanterns as the daylight faded.

I too, began to relax, enjoying the solitude and simplicity of the evening and the connection to nature, just a few short miles away from the noise and pollution of everyday life, with only the occasional hoot from an owl to disturb the silence.

The food was divine, enjoyed all the more with the people I held dear. Precious time I'd missed with Freya. It hadn't mattered there was no ceiling or even roof above us – like Freya had said, where else could you dine and look at the stars.

After enjoying the last few embers, Ben and I reluctantly left Freya and Clether to retire to their cosy little abode, thanking them for a wonderful evening, promising to return in the not-too-distant future.

Ben and I awoke beside each other, feeling fully rejuvenated after the best night's sleep either of us had had in a long time. Realising, perhaps why Freya and Clether managed to achieve all they did.

Not having wanted to outstay my welcome and the fact there were no new properties to view, and both Freya and Ben had to work, I'd reserved a seat on the nine o'clock train home the following morning. I had at least secured somewhere to stay for the short term, and if fate intervened, something would surely present itself very soon. But for now, Ben and I were adamant we were going to enjoy the sunshine while it lasted. So, inspired by last night, we packed a picnic to carry down to the beach with what food we could find in the kitchen, still having to pinch myself, realising it would all soon become a way of life. My life!

Ben remarked, again, on Freya's resemblance to how he remembered me, everything from her long auburn hair and freckles to her choice of footwear. Not that I'd worn riding boots last night! But, I still hadn't managed to dress for dinner. Realising, it wasn't only my life that was about to change. Though I supposed, the fact I'd not had to buy anything new to wear, spoke for itself. Working from home meant I could stay in my pyjamas till lunch if I chose, some of my greatest achievements having been accomplished whilst in the comfort of my tropically inspired lounge trousers and Henley top! Not that the recipients need know that! The only other requirement was a pot of coffee and warm croissants -preferably chocolate!

I began explaining to Ben, on our descent to the beach, other similarities between Freya and myself; our free-spirited nature and love of the outdoors and how Beth was almost the opposite, having always been predictable, conforming to what was deemed socially acceptable. Failing to mention her resemblance to Adam, especially his same eyes and beautiful hair. Avoiding, what I assumed to be a sensitive subject, still unable to fully comprehend the loss and magnitude of what he'd begun to describe.

The time arrived for me to pack and kiss goodbye on an immensely pleasurable weekend, Ben having to remind me that it was only for a few short weeks, his kiss lingering on my lips as the train took me home to pack away the final fragments of a life I was soon to leave behind. Beth would undoubtably always remain there, so it wasn't that I'd never return, and despite our differences, I would miss her and the distance between us.

Beth had insisted on collecting me from the station, for which I was very grateful, especially after such a long journey. Though, what I hadn't expected, was another lecture when I'd informed her of my plans. This time, accusing me of sofa hopping! Again, I'd tried explaining my decision to wait for the ideal property, and that not everyone aspired to living on Hawthorn Drive.

I really didn't have the patience to argue at such a late hour and wasn't prepared for her to destroy my happiness, informing her I was tired and that we'd talk in the morning.

I'd had every intention of waking early, never needing to set an alarm, waking at six-fifty most mornings, whether I liked it or not; I assumed, instilled from when Beth was younger, having always insisted on setting her own alarm, five minutes before needing to! Even then, a stickler for precision. So, I was quite surprised to realise it was already eight. Realising what I'd still yet to achieve and only having quickly checked my emails over the weekend, I wandered downstairs to put on the oven and make a coffee, having remembered to defrost a couple of croissants last night.

Before I'd got chance to open my emails, I received a message from Ben, missing me already! Shortly followed by a call from Beth, before she left for work, which I supposed was to be expected, but still too early in the day to have to contend with reiterating what I'd already said. But as ever, my words fell on stoney ground. Yet again, unable to convince her of my plan.

Of course, I hadn't enjoyed my croissants, and my heart just wasn't in the mood to respond to requests of a romantic nature. So instead, I turned my attention to packing up a tea set, only to drop the tiny milk jug, ruining the set! It wasn't as though I was asking for her blessing, just her acceptance of my wishes and possibly even a little support.

I'd somehow muddled through the rest of the day, having allowed myself some time out to reacquaint myself with Charlie, who was always pleased to see me. I'd also posted more samples to recently betrothed couples, 'save the date' cards to another couple, who, although only getting married next summer, had wanted to give their friends and relations every opportunity to be able to celebrate with them.

Adam called, providing a sympathetic ear, perhaps understanding our daughter more than I could; recalling a very similar conversation we'd had with her as a child. Then asking about his "little girl", as he often referred to Freya, considering his daughters to be like chalk and cheese. Perhaps more like us than we chose to imagine! Before going home to his own perfect life in Beech Tree Avenue.

Then last, but not least, Ben concluded the day, calling to wish me goodnight before he went to sleep himself.

Chapter 8

Memories to Treasure

The days soon turned into weeks, and the house became what Beth had feared, no longer resembling a home, and before long it was the eve of my departure. As the day had grown nearer it had felt more like a mourning than a celebration, though I had raised several glasses with close friends and even shed the odd tear. But ultimately, it was just the end of another chapter in life. I no longer belonged here without the love and laughter that had once resonated between the walls when we were a family living here together. It was time for a new family, at the beginning of their adventure, to enjoy making their own memories and breathe new life into the tired foundations.

Beth and I, had agreed to disagree, avoiding the subject that had caused so much distress. Hoping, in time, she would realise my plight and learn from it, just as Adam had appeared to have done, failing to have come over one last time to familiarise himself with what had once been his home; instead, proposing to Laura, accepting that life moves on for us all.

Beth had called last night on her way home from work, she'd cried when I'd given her a bowl of berries I'd picked earlier from the garden, and a jar of Rose petals, just as she had collected for me all those years ago. I'd already given her the blanket we'd crotched together that had lain at the bottom of her bed since she'd left home to start married life; not that she wouldn't have somewhere to sleep, when I eventually found somewhere to call home, but some things now belonged with her, just like the little box of special childhood memories and treasures I'd found stashed under her bed. The old, framed photographs displaying family memories, had already been distributed between Adam, Freya and Beth when Adam had left. We were after all, both still their parents.

I took one last walk around the garden, remembering how much fun we'd had as a family, celebrating birthdays outside in the warmer months, chasing butterflies and picking juicy red strawberries. Then, as autumn had descended, we'd pick the apples and sweep up the leaves before Jack Frost arrived with his own magic. Even in winter we'd venture out to feed the birds, and if we'd been lucky, the snow would fall for us to build snowmen who we'd watch melt away in the warmth of the sun. It was then I was reminded of Adam, who'd always wanted a son to play football with rather than join in our daughters' tea parties with their dolls, and then I remembered Ben.

The grass had never recovered from where Beth and then Freya had scraped their feet under the swing and the hole in the hedge at the bottom of the garden still remained where Beth's rabbit had finally won his bid for freedom. All that remained now for me, was to close the door and turn the key one last time.

Chapter 9

Behind Closed Doors

I arrived rather wearily, pulling onto Stella's driveway with the few essentials I'd envisaged needing, including my riding attire and of course work material - which in total, had filled the entire car. Though, I had never managed to travel light, even when going away for the odd night or going into hospital to deliver Beth and Freya, packing for every eventuality - boy or girl, large or small. Imagining it had all begun when I had first gone away on Guide camp, where my best friend at the time was experiencing her first period, remembering ever since, to always be prepared. It had been harder than I'd imagined leaving my old house behind, especially as all I wanted right now was the comfort it had provided. I just had to remind myself; it was the first step in the right direction. At least everything was ready and waiting, and I didn't have to start unpacking to make a cup of tea.

Stella had been very thorough, leaving written instructions on the kitchen island along with a few welcome essentials. No doubt, assuming it would be my first port of call after the cloakroom. However, my first concern was to check on Leo, who seemed as pleased to see me as I was him, rubbing around my ankles, which I assumed to be more cupboard love, than instant appeal! I bent to stroke him, reminding him that he would have to wait a few more hours as Stella had instructed, and that no amount of affection would change my mind. I resisted the temptation to message everyone as to my arrival - Ben included, needing a little time to myself, to relax, away from the stresses of the last few days and the long journey down here. I decided to reacquaint myself with what was to be home for the foreseeable future, not yet able to anticipate what lay ahead or where it might lead. I opened the windows upstairs, letting fresh warm air circulate, before the evening descended, then finished emptying my car before fixing a cold drink and joining Leo outside, finding a very comfortable sun lounger to relax on, positioned perfectly for the late afternoon sun.

It wasn't long, or so I assumed, that I was woken by Ben standing over me.

'You do realise you've left all the windows open, anyone could have broken in. I thought you were invited to take care of the property, not host an open house!'

'I must have dropped off!' I apologised, realising my mistake.

'Remind me never to ask you to house sit my property!' Dam! I thought, getting to my feet, feeling not only physically and emotionally drained, but now humiliated and guilty of negligence, especially when I noticed I'd left the door into the house wide open!

Fortunately, everything inside seemed as it should, and Leo was still dozing under the bush by the door.

'Let me take you out,' Ben suggested, after we'd kissed and reacquainted. 'I don't suppose you've been shopping yet?'

I didn't need persuading, accepting his offer immediately, remembering of course to first shut all the windows and check behind doors that there was in indeed no one hiding, waiting to make an escape or fill a van around the corner. Not forgetting to redeem myself and feed Leo his supper before locking the doors and following Ben out to his car, deciding on route that an evening in at his seemed far more appealing than dining out in the company of strangers. So, whilst Ben rustled up some dinner, I messaged my nearest and dearest, and of course Stella, informing them that all was well.

Of course, Ben had spun his culinary magic over a few simple ingredients and produced a veritable feast, along with a glass or two of a very drinkable red wine. It finally felt good to be back as we relaxed together in his bed.

I awoke to Ben's warm kiss, realising what else I'd been missing, living alone.

Ben dropped me off at my temporary abode a couple of hours later, before having to go into the office, promising to call on his way home. Of course, my short walk of shame didn't go unnoticed, as the woman next door was out pruning her front hedge.

Leo had survived, but nevertheless hungry for his fish breakfast, wondering if he really did prefer fish for breakfast, rather than supper, but nevertheless, did as I'd been instructed. Although, the speed he finished it, perhaps said more about the fact he had somewhere else to be, than his preference for what he ate. Surely, Stella had the occasional lie in!

Once I'd made sure Leo hadn't choked in his hurry to demolish his breakfast, I went upstairs to unpack my case and shower. Then, like Goldilocks, explored the rest of the house, so at least I wouldn't wonder where I was in the middle of the night. Not, that I had a tendency to walk in my sleep, but with all that had happened and the different bedrooms I'd encountered waking up in recently, I wouldn't be at all surprised if I had no recollection of where I was when I woke. Unless it was beside Ben!

Despite the short notice, Stella had left the house in remarkable order. Or at least I thought, until I entered the guest bedroom, where it had been decided I stay and opened the wardrobe door, which housed, what I assumed to be the overflow from both their wardrobes, leaving barely enough room for what I considered an acceptable amount of attire to see me through till next week, let alone the summer! I supposed there was always Ben's, which was devoid of any stray, surplus or other random garments - female or otherwise. Everything I imagined, in its rightful place. Stella's own room and her daughter's looked as though they could return at any moment, ready and waiting for when they did. Ruby's told a story of a schoolgirl embarking on womanhood, who clearly adored her mother, displaying a beautiful picture of them both when they were younger and several of Stella in her own adolescent years, that I still recognised. There was also a beautiful personalised framed embroidery above her bed, depicting her name and personality entwined in trailing red Roses.

Stella's own room was just as untamed, as though she had just left for work, ready and waiting for her return. She too had two beautiful pictures of her daughter displayed on a chest of drawers - one as a newborn baby, another a few years older. On her dressing table lay a gold locket, which I couldn't resist opening, revealing yet another picture, of who I assumed to be Ruby. On the opposite side, was a picture of a guy, I assumed to be special. I returned to my room to dry my hair, only to discover I'd forgotten to pack my dryer, returning to Stella's room, assuming there'd be one there. Without thinking, I opened the larger of her dressing table drawers, hoping she'd stashed it away - at the same time, realising she would have probably taken it with her. But something else caught my eye - a beautifully decorated box, tied up with a thin strand of pink ribbon. Realising I shouldn't have been in her room, let alone snooping in her drawers, I left it where it was, undisturbed. My hair would just have to dry untamed.

I next set about unpacking my work. The study, bright, but rather more compact than I was used to, realising I would just have to be more methodical. Though, I had already decided the ideal place to work would be at the kitchen island. Only today, I had decided to invite Ben over, not only to appease his appetite, but satisfy his curiosity, which of course was the easy part; trying to peel carrots with a knife was proving a little more difficult!

I'd found everything I'd needed, either in the local supermarket or Stella's kitchen – somewhere else that could do with organising! Though at least it was clean and seemed well equipped. My mind occasionally wandered as I chopped the vegetables to add to the tagine - a fail-safe recipe I loved preparing as much as eating, wondering what Stella had hidden inside the box in her dressing table. Once the vegetables were all prepared, I began preparing the lemon soufflé, realising Stella obviously enjoyed baking, having all the utensils you could possibly require - apart from a peeler! Despite which, I'd still managed to prepare the vegetables.

Having anticipated a romantic dinner, I'd purchased some candles before leaving home which I'd dotted strategically around the house, not forgetting to update my lingerie drawer.

Ben arrived early evening, having been home first to shower and change, adding a fresh splash of whatever he sprinkled over his body to seduce me!

As requested, Ben had brought chilled beers rather than wine to compliment the meal, which was now bubbling away and warming the house with its appetising aroma, allowing me time to quell Ben's curiosity and show him around the house - inviting him first into the kitchen: now clean and sparkling and smelling divine, to pour us each a beer.

'I bet you've been dying to see upstairs,' I said, leading the way to the top. 'The master suite is quite spectacular,' I began, entering Stella's room, 'having an impressive floor to ceiling, glazed gable, overlooking the back garden. The room being complimented by an en suite,' I continued, enticing him away. 'Unfortunately, the only glazing in here comes courtesy of the rather immaculate shower screen!'

'Then, across the landing is what is now known as, my room,' I said, rather flirtatiously. 'Though, not being the mistress of the house, I have to use the bathroom on the landing!' We lingered briefly, before returning to the kitchen to satisfy our appetites, if not our lust!

'So, how was your day?' I asked Ben, over dinner. 'Did you sell anything?'

'No, but we did have a couple of holiday makers call in to enquire about a couple of cottages with a view to buying a second home here. And then Emma was late back to the office this afternoon.'

'Where'd she been?'

'Showing a couple around a very expensive furnished holiday home, not too dissimilar to the one I showed you.'

'Did she manage to sell it?'

'It's unlikely,' Ben explained. 'She left them to look around themselves. It's often advisable, so the clients can get a feel for a place, imagine themselves living there. Especially if it's unlived in. Only, sometimes they're gone for some time!'

'Really!'

'The problem being, you never quite know exactly what they're getting up to, or exactly how long to leave them.'

'So, what did Emma do?' I asked, dying to know.

'She just sat it out in the garden. Fortunately, it was a nice day!'

'Gosh!'

'You have to just hope, they leave it as they found it.'

I was actually speechless, trying to obliterate any notion of anything of that nature having occurred upstairs in my own house, before remembering I no longer owned anywhere to call home.

'I do hope you're hungry?' I asked, clearing the plates, before proudly presenting a perfect lemon soufflé.

'You do realise the neighbours 'll be talking,' I declared, as Ben was preparing to leave after lingering in bed a little longer than anticipated.

'I didn't see a neighbourhood watch sign on my way here last night, so they're probably all pretty discreet. Besides, who knows what they all get up to behind closed doors. Stella isn't going to chuck you out on the street, who'd pander to Leo?'

'Speaking of which, I haven't seen him since you arrived! I do hope he's alright.'

'What is it with you and cats!'

As soon as Ben had left, I wandered out into the back garden, whispering Leo's name, hoping cats had sensitive hearing, so as not to raise alarm amongst the other inhabitants of Pengelly Crescent, I had barely met.

It seemed Leo had perhaps also been out enjoying himself last night, returning unscathed, once I'd poured myself another coffee to tide me through the morning. He'd obviously worked up an appetite, wherever he'd been!

Chapter 10

A Box of Broken Hearts

The days continued and Leo and I established a routine, were he'd arrive in the kitchen or be sat waiting on the front doorstep as I arrived home from staying over at Ben's; albeit a little later this morning, having remembered to call at the shop and get a hairdryer and a few other essentials for this evening. Leo of course, was well provided for, with enough boxes of prepared food to cater for his discerning taste and to possibly last him through until Christmas!
The island in the kitchen had proved to be the ideal place to work and capture the morning sun, with the added advantage of being in striking distance of the coffee maker. Today's task being to complete an order for a Christmas wedding, although a romantic notion, I still found tartan and gold bizarre for such an occasion! To me, it was like writing Christmas cards in July! Though looking at my emails, December was becoming more and more popular, already having two new requests for 'save the date' cards for the end of next year. Then something I liked best of all – a thank you. Tonight, it was my turn to cater, not only for Ben, but Freya and Clether, who'd accepted my invitation, having considered they could afford an evening off, having taken advantage of the good weather and finished cleaning the stonework that remained on their barn. The missing stones had been sourced from a local farmer who'd apparently had enough to complete the build and was happy to sell what he had. I'd even bought candles to decorate outside and sewn a

pretty cloth to cover the picnic table on the patio, trying to emulate the evening we'd enjoyed together at theirs. All that remained was to roast the chicken and vegetables; the summer pudding already doing its magic in the fridge. As I placed the last of the invitations in the box my thoughts returned to this evening, suddenly remembering I'd forgotten to buy more matches to replace the box I'd finished the other night. Surely, Stella would have a box somewhere - she seemed to have everything else, though not always where you'd expect to find them! I'd eventually found the tin opener in a drawer with the tea towels and the foil in the pan cupboard! Fortunately, Leo's meals came in sachets. I'd always considered Stella to have been a bit scatter-brained, often forgetting or losing books and other paraphernalia at school, even ingredients for baking. Despite which, she'd still managed to achieve the best rise on her Victoria sponge! But I just couldn't imagine where else to look for the matches. Then I recalled having seen some candles in her bedroom and beside her bath.

Although the candles had been burnt, either Stella or Ruby had moved the matches for whatever reason; I honestly couldn't understand their reasoning. I had even packed birthday cake candles with the cake tins, ready for the next celebration. But then again, my own large box of matches that had once lived in the drawer of my bedside cabinet, ready for romance, had more recently resided in the hall cupboard, along with the odd glove and spare keys, ready for the next pumpkin or Christmas lantern.

Before I knew it, I'd become distracted and was opening the lid on the box from inside Stella's dressing table drawer, by which time it was all too late to try and remember what it was I'd been looking for. Not that I recognised the picture of the rather attractive guy that lay on top of the pile of photographs inside the box, but he was obviously special to Stella. However, rather baffled as to why he was hidden inside a box rather than behind a glass frame. And perhaps, more to the point, how long he'd been there?

Unlike Stella, I had always been meticulous at school, always prepared and well organised for lessons, but had had a reputation for prying. Even now, I was unable to resist eaves dropping on conversations - whether sat in a restaurant or on a train, listening to the woman behind talking about her date the other night. Or simply lingering a little longer down an isle in the supermarket, pretending to read the ingredients on a jar, whilst engrossed in the contents of someone else's gossip. I just couldn't seem to help myself! I had of course gained my observational skills award in the Girl Guides, who appeared to have an awful lot to answer for!

Underneath the photographs was what looked to be a journal, beginning with a blossoming romance, which when reading between the lines, resulted in a pregnancy, and then what had appeared to have been an awful tragedy, involving, I imagined, the guy in the photo. Stella, I assumed the person who had begun describing a roller coaster of emotions:

"Unable to sleep, so excited to tell you. My heart's singing with joy and I'm dancing on air at discovering our baby is still alive and kicking inside me. By some miracle she has survived!"

Then, on the next page she'd written:

"If only I could have told you when I'd found out. What a difference a day makes. Instead, I heard of your accident on the grapevine, having realised something was wrong when you didn't show to collect Stephanie from dance class, each careless whisper adding to my agony. How I managed to remain calm and conduct the last class, I'll never know!"

Then other entries: her guilt at not telling him sooner, him having died not knowing, believing Stella had miscarried their baby. The only thing that had seemingly kept her going, was their baby growing inside her. Then, out of all her grief and sadness, came a beautiful new life.

Now I felt as bad as Eve in the garden of Eden, unable to resist temptation. Some things, nobody need ever know, perhaps even her own daughter. What had I actually gained? apart from satisfying my own curiosity? How would I ever be able to look Stella in the eye again, having betrayed her trust and violated her privacy. Perhaps this time, I'd finally learn my lesson.

Ben had brought some matches as requested, only reminding me of my guilt. No doubt, every time I smelt a burning candle, I'd be reminded of Stella's sadness. Perhaps, if I was lucky, it'd stop me ever doing something as unforgivable again.

Freya and Clether were ravenous, and between them, managed to devour everything, including the fruit pudding, leaving no leftovers for tomorrow's lunch!

'It suits you here,' Freya commented, once we'd retired inside and to the comfort of the living room. 'It's not as though there's any evidence of who actually owns it, unless you've stashed it all away.'

'I noticed that too,' Ben commented. 'Absolutely nothing. Not even a photo in a frame.'

'It's exactly as I found it,' I assured them, reminded again of my misdemeanour.

'So, what's she like?' Freya asked.

'Who Stella? As far as I know she just lives here with her daughter,' I informed them. I could hardly tell them all what I'd just discovered. So, I continued to explain her current set of circumstances, including her profession, feeling like I was betraying her trust, with every word I uttered.

'My sister teaches ballet, not here, she lives in London,' Clether informed us.

'I can't wait to personalise our home,' Freya said, leaning into Clether.

'It even smells of you!' Freya commented, reaching across to retrieve her glass from the table between us, where I'd placed a blackberry and sandalwood candle that I'd brought with me from home. 'And I do like her choice of colours!' she continued. 'Can I have a peek upstairs? Purely for research!'

'I'll come with you,' Clether decided, 'I need the bathroom,' he said, following her out of the room, stopping to admire a picture on the wall that couldn't fail to catch your attention as you left the room.

'Wow, my father painted this!' he informed everyone. 'I often wondered where they'd eventually end up, but it's almost as if it was made just for here.'

'I didn't know your dad was an artist,' Freya commented, now intrigued.

'Yes, I haven't got any of his work myself, but I remember he always loved to scribble down ideas, even when we were little. There's no date on this, but look, he's signed it,' he indicated to Freya. 'I expect it must have been bought at a local exhibition.'

'It's a shame we can't ask your mother if she's got any we could have for the barn,' Freya commented.

'I very much doubt she'll have kept anything of his, least of all his paintings. Unless of course they were valuable. In which case she'd have sold them by now,' he explained, giving the impression she hadn't been an admirer of his work; which, on closer inspection was rather good for an amateur.

'Just no looking in cupboards or drawers,' I reminded Freya, as they left the room.

'As if we would! I'm just curious as to how the rest of the house is furnished really. She's obviously got good taste!' Freya replied, as she followed Clether out of the room.

Ben snuggled closer once they'd left the room, complimenting me on dinner and questioning my apparent change of mood, having noticed I'd seemed a little distant all evening.

'Perhaps they'll leave early, and we can have an early night,' he said, optimistically.

'That'd be nice, they must be exhausted!' I commented, considering how busy they'd both been. 'I do hope they're not trying out the beds up there!'

'Speaking of which, do you remember me telling you about that couple who went to view that rather ostentatious property with Emma?'

'The one where they disappeared for rather too long?' I questioned, trying to hide my concern as to Freya following in my footsteps.

'Well, they've booked another appointment.'

'So, you were wrong in your assumption?'

'We'll see, I'd be surprised if they put an offer in. I bet she just lost an earring!'

'I suppose you've got to assume they're interested, or you could potentially lose a sale.'

'Yeah, though they weren't very flexible on time, adamant it had to be tomorrow. So, we agreed, but stressed we were fitting them in between appointments, and if they wanted longer, to arrange another time.'

'I suppose she could need her earring for a party! Or they just want to check if their vehicles 'll fit in the garage. If I was spending that much money, I'd at least want a second look.'

'I think anyone who could afford that property wouldn't want to hide their vehicles away.'

'I suppose they could even be adding more photos to their holiday album before returning home,' I considered, beginning to question people's motives, whilst still unable to comprehend my own actions.

'Did you get lost?' I asked, as Freya and Clether returned.

'We were actually watching the sunset from the balcony. Though we did have a peek at your room.'

At which I felt even more guilty, having considered my daughter could behave in the same manner as myself.

'I must admit, I do find this house rather intriguing,' Clether responded. 'As though I've been here before somehow.'

'What deja vu?' Freya asked.

'Something like that. Perhaps it's just seeing something my father created, out of context.'

'I could take you to look at a barn that's approaching completion over in Maudley, if you'd be interested in taking a look; they've included some lovely features,' Ben suggested, enthusiastically.

'Really, that'd be great, thanks,' Freya said, sharing his enthusiasm. 'I've just started creating a mood board, so I'd really appreciate it.'

'Awesome!' Clether agreed. I'd definitely be interested.' Unfortunately, I couldn't get excited about turning stables and cowsheds into luxury living accommodation, so got up and left to fill the dishwasher and feed Leo, leaving the three of them to talk. Leo, it seemed, had also taken advantage of the glorious weather we'd been experiencing, as he still wasn't home yet.

Freya and Clether stayed for another hour or so, before they both started to yawn. Perhaps allowing themselves to relax had finally induced sleep!

'I'm a little worried about Leo,' I told Ben. 'I haven't seen him since this morning.' Though Ben was quick to remind me it wasn't the first time, and that it was probably only natural for him to stay out occasionally.

Unsurprisingly, I'd had a bad night reflecting on not only what I'd done, but on what Stella had obviously had to endure. Realising, I too would have to keep her secret.

Unfortunately, Ben had had to leave for the office once we'd enjoyed a leisurely breakfast; although, being Sunday, not quite as early. But, perhaps not early enough to escape the glare of the avid occupants of Pengelly Crescent, who appeared to always have an excuse to be lingering outside when Ben decided to leave! Perhaps that was why Leo hadn't returned – waiting to evade their scrutiny.

Sure enough, half an hour later, Leo appeared through the cat flap!

Chapter 11

Lessons in Love

It appeared the housing market had not only gone quiet, but had possibly gone into hibernation, at least in this quiet corner of suburbia, apart from the inhabitants of Pengelly Crescent, who perhaps had all once been either intrepid Girl Guides or Boy Scouts and just couldn't help what had been instilled in them from a young age. I assumed Ben had perhaps missed out on these valuable life skills, having been completely wrong in his assumption about the couple's intent when viewing the property yesterday, as they'd only gone and put an offer in this morning!

I had cleared my work and was now on my way over to the stables to meet up with Freya who was going to introduce me to Bella, who she imagined would be an ideal match for me. she was usually busy with the pony club up until about four, when normality would resume. Though, it invariably meant longer hours into the evening - not that she'd normally mind, but it meant work on the barn had to take a back seat as there were only so many hours of daylight, even at this time of year.

As soon as I walked into the yard, I realised just how much I'd missed it all, now eager to get back in the saddle.

Freya greeted me, walking back from the field. Bella, I assumed, in tow.

'Do you want to tack her up, whilst I get Trixie ready? I'll show you where everything is. They'll both be keen to get out for some exercise, they must be feeling a little neglected just recently,' she explained, as we entered the stables where all the ponies where now tucked up, enjoying a well-earned rest after the day's activities.

'I see you've been doing a bit of plaiting,' I commented, admiring the well-groomed ponies, remembering how Freya had loved to prepare her pony for the Gymkhana.

'Though I don't think Star here would win anything, she looks like she's had a bucket of dirty water thrown over her, and I'm not sure what's happened to her tail! I think we need a few more lessons!' Freya laughed. 'Bella, I suppose, is more of a beach babe and has rather an expressive trot,' she continued informing me of her nature. 'You'll soon see what I mean.'

'We had a boy join us this year for the first time, or at least as far as I can remember,' she started telling me, until a young girl returned to collect her lunch box. 'She's a complete scatter brain, but once she's in the saddle, shows potential for a great horse woman. She actually lives next door to Grandma's old place.'

Bella, it seemed, was indeed as happy to be out as I was, displaying her elegance as Freya had described. Freya rode beside me on Trixie, filling me in on the barn that Ben had taken her and Clether to see, full of admiration and inspiration for what they might hope to achieve themselves. Not that they needed any spurring on in their determination to finish what they'd started.

'I'm going to ache tomorrow!' I realised, as I dismounted.

'You'll just have to come again,' Freya enthused, no doubt hoping I'd agree. Not that I needed any persuasion.

Everyone but me it seemed, was progressing with their dreams, Freya and Clether had now started what appeared to be an endless task, pointing the outside walls of the barn, and Ben had sold two properties in as many days! I'd kept myself busy, hoping something would present itself before time ran out and Stella returned, but it was becoming clear I would have to compromise, at least for the short term.

Ben, it seemed had picked up on my mood and had invited me out for dinner tonight, somewhere rather more discerning and a little further afield than I would have chosen myself, but nevertheless, felt deserved a little more preparation and attention to detail, choosing a dress I seldom wore, and a necklace that hadn't seen the light of day for more years than I cared to remember. I was already looking forward to our evening of indulgence, not least, being able to pamper myself in readiness and alleviate all other concerns, at least for a while. But for now, I had to clear my desk and dash to the post office before I could truly relax, but more importantly, before they closed.

Having ridden Bella again this morning, I'd allowed time in my busy schedule to soak in Stella's lavish bath, something I was definitely going to miss when the time came to leave, realising I would actually miss her house and the place I'd come to call home.

Ben arrived, punctual as ever; I supposed, a trait of his job, whereas I had learnt to be more disciplined, although I would have to admit, there was still room for improvement! However, I did pride myself on my achievements and the quality of life I had made for myself.

Ben complimented me on my appearance, before kissing my recently applied lip gloss and ruffling my hair, which as always, he seemed unable to resist! Not that I complained!

The restaurant was as beautiful as I'd imagined and well worth the effort I'd made. We sank into the sumptuous sofa to first peruse the extensive drinks menu, choosing a blackberry prosecco to toast the evening and whilst we scrutinised the chef's selection of produce he'd chosen to combine; something I was always eager to consider and experiment replicating myself.

Realising Ben was on my case and would inform me the moment something suitable came to the market, I avoided the subject and instead told him of my day, enthusing about my morning excursion across the beach with Bella, who was an absolute dream to ride, whether along the beach or bridleway.

The food was exquisite, but at the same time, left me wondering if I could possibly emulate what the chef had achieved. Each to their own, I supposed, reminded of the card I'd received this morning - thanking me for the beautiful wedding stationary I'd supplied. Astonished, that anyone would acknowledge my work, let alone compliment. I had, however, recently achieved a surprisingly, remarkable fish pie, though I had followed every step of the recipe after discovering it in a book; without which, I'd have had no idea how to season the sauce, let alone known what fish to include. How anyone could possibly survive the technical challenge on 'Bake Off', was remarkable! I still hadn't got used to Stella's oven and failed to understand how the same temperature could vary from one oven to another! Just something else I was going to have to get used to, again! It seemed, no matter what I did, I just couldn't get away from the elephant in the room.

Ben, it appeared, was becoming quite apt at reading my mind.

'Do you remember saying you wish you could try before you buy?'

'It'd help if there was anything to consider!' I said, picking up my wine glass, assuming he was referring to an earlier conversation regarding properties.

'Well, I think I might just have the answer,' he said, before picking up his own glass.

'You obviously know something I don't,' I said, lacking his enthusiasm.

'Move in with me.'

'Seriously?' I asked, quite shocked, having never considered the possibility myself.

'Surely, it makes sense. I know it's still early days, but I think it could work.'

'Well, I suppose there's only one way to find out, and it beats sleeping under the stars!'

'Splendid!'

We declined another bottle of wine after being alerted to the fact we'd almost consumed an entire bottle, before we'd even considered a dessert.

'We could always have a dessert wine,' Ben suggested. 'Or we could see if they've got a room, they look stunning online. After all, it is weekend and I'm not in the office again until Monday!'

'Remember, we said we'd do Sunday lunch for Freya and Clether,' I reminded him.

'I wasn't suggesting we stay all weekend! Although, we're not actually that far from theirs, we could call in on them in the morning.'

'I haven't come prepared for either, really,' I considered. Especially the remains of a farmyard!

'Live dangerously!' Ben continued his persuasion.

Ben had got his wish, and we'd extended our evening of indulgence, opting for a leisurely breakfast in bed rather than appear in the dining room in the same clothes we'd left in, the previous evening.

'Did you mean what you said last night?' I asked, needing confirmation, before I got carried away with the idea.

'Why, are you having second thoughts?'

'No, but we'd both had rather a lot to drink.'

'I've been thinking about it for a while, I just wasn't sure what you'd think,' he explained.

'I'm over the moon!' I said, placing my cup on its saucer before losing myself in his warm embrace.

Leo was nowhere to be seen when we arrived at Stella's house, though I suspected he wasn't far away, just waiting for Ben to leave. I'd eventually come to the conclusion, that he just didn't like male visitors to the house, as he would always reappear, once either Ben or Clether had left.

Ben, it appeared, had obviously given a lot of thought to what he'd said, suggesting I move in sooner rather than later. Not that I had a lot to move from where I was, and what I decided to do with the rest of my stuff in storage, could wait for now. Of course, I would still have to care for Leo, but I could easily manage that.

'So where are we hosting Sunday lunch?' I questioned, as I gathered a few belongings.

'Ours of course!'

'I like the sound of that,' I smiled.

Chapter 12

Seeds of Dreams

Freya had been as excited as me when I'd explained the change of address for lunch, sharing in my happiness. I was still on cloud nine myself, giddy with excitement and Ben hadn't stopped smiling all weekend!

'So, where is this house of Ben's?' Clether asked, as he and Freya prepared to leave.

'Mum refers to it as, "the house on top of the hill", sitting very proudly above the little village of Tresgilly.'

'You've got to be kidding!' Clether said, stopping in his tracks, suddenly turning pale.

'No. Why?'

'Because that's where I lived.'

Freya remained silent, aware of everything Clether had shared with her about his family home, that his mother had been willing to sell to the highest bidder, immediately after his father's death. The person who'd snapped it up had been a developer, eager to realise its full potential, being situated on a very large plot and in a very desirable location, quickly reducing their family home and everything his father had strived for, to rubble. Clether, still struggled accepting what had happened; not only had he lost his father, but the foundation of his family and everything it had stood for. Building his own home for his future family had been paramount in what she imagined to be the grieving process. It had been so much more than bricks and mortar to Clether, it had been the only home he had ever known, felt safe and loved, and where his earliest memories had been forged. That was fifteen years ago now, and although it wasn't as raw, it still hurt.

'Would you prefer we didn't go?' Freya asked, realising how traumatic it might be for him. Although she understood Clether's history, he'd never actually revealed exactly where his home had stood.

'No, it's important we go, and we can't avoid it forever.'

'But we don't have to go today,' she explained. 'We can go at a later date, when you've had time to get used to the idea.'

'You know, I still have my key,' Clether informed her.

'How about I call my mum and explain or make an excuse, I'm sure she'd understand,' Freya suggested, realising just how upsetting it would be.

'No, I know how much you've been looking forward to this. I insist.' So, Freya reluctantly picked up her bag and followed Clether out to the car.

'At least I know the way,' he laughed.

The journey there was quiet, and all too soon, they'd reached the top of the hill.

'Just say if you want to leave,' Freya stressed, as they pulled into the designated parking area beside Ben's and her mother's vehicles, appreciating the architect's clever use of the elevated position, whilst realising what Clether must be thinking, keeping her thoughts to herself.

'Let's do it!' Clether said, holding her hand and ringing the bell.

The formalities over, Freya and Clether followed Ben through to the kitchen, where I'd just taken the meat out of the oven to rest.

'It smells delicious!' Freya enthused, 'Can I do anything to help?'

'No, it's all under control. Did you find us Okay?'

'It's precisely where you said, "on top of the hill",' Freya answered, before Clether had time to think of a suitable response.

'I forgot,' I remarked, 'you once lived in the village yourself, Clether.'

'Yes, on top of this very same hill.'

'What a coincidence,' Ben remarked. 'It must have been the original property.'

'Yes, that's right. My father actually built it, pretty much.'

'Really, that's remarkable,' Ben said, totally unaware of the circumstances. 'So, what's the story. Had it been sold with planning permission?'

'No, my mother just stuck it on the market and accepted the asking price the very same day.'

'Clether's father had recently died,' Freya tried explaining.

'It doesn't take long, when there's scope to develop, I imagine someone must have seen the potential.'

'To destroy everything,' Clether continued. 'I don't blame them; I can understand why they would. It's just my mother, I can't understand.'

'Greif can manifest itself in strange ways,' Ben continued, excusing her behaviour.

'You didn't know my mother,' Clether explained. 'I doubt she's ever looked back.'

'Though still, I expect it was the right decision in the end,' Ben concluded.

'For her maybe,' Clether retorted, now unable to think of anything else.

'What would everyone like to drink?' I asked, understanding the sensitivity of the subject.

'Oh, now we're talking!' Freya gleamed enthusiastically. 'I'm actually driving, but I know Clether 'll have a beer, won't you?'

'You two go through to the other room, I'll bring them through to you,' I said, hoping to get Ben on his own, so I could fill him in on what I already knew. But Ben followed them through into the living room.

'So, how's the pointing going on the barn?' Ben began, changing the subject, whilst sharing their same enthusiasm for transforming a former residence for farm animals.

'It seems we've made little progress,' Clether explained. 'Though I must admit, I'm guilty of getting distracted yesterday and going in the sea. A guy I'd made a board for came to collect it and was eager to give it a go. So, as Freya was still at the stables and he'd travelled some distance, I couldn't resist joining him.'

'If you ever need a hand with anything and I'm free, I'd always be willing to help,' Ben told him.

'Thanks, I might take you up on that.'

'Seriously, I quite envy you. I tried showing your mother a project,' he addressed Freya, 'but she just couldn't see the potential.'

'So, what input did you have in the construction of this?' Clether asked Ben.

'I only bought it off plan, once the site had been cleared and the necessary planning had been obtained. I could already see the potential, but didn't have anything to do with the construction, just the fitting out.'

'I must say, it's well designed. Nothing like the home I knew.'

'So, where does your mother live now?' Ben enquired, as we all sat down to eat.

'Over in Port Ida, as far as I'm aware.'

'Gravy anyone?' I asked, trying to change the subject again.

'So, not that far away,' Ben continued, accepting the jug.

'She could be halfway around the world for all I care,' Clether said.

'What you have to understand,' Freya began, in Clether's defence, 'is Clether's father died, rather suddenly, in a tragic accident, and he feels he didn't have the time he needed to grieve before his mother sold the family home.'

'I'm so sorry Clether, I can only imagine how difficult this is,' I offered, unable to avoid the subject any longer.

'No, you have a right to understand. This is a beautiful house, and in a way, it's perhaps a good thing it doesn't resemble my old home, that would be odd somehow, don't you think? Though, I might take a look outside after, see what's left.'

'It's got a marvellous view across the valley,' Ben told him.

The rest of the meal was enjoyed discussing the advantages of a wood fired boiler, reconstituting the scraps of wood and shavings that would otherwise be swept up, not only in the construction of the internal fitting out of the barn, but from Clether's workshop. Clether accepted another beer, taking full advantage of Freya offering to drive - not that she blamed him.

Then, whilst Clether and Freya surveyed the grounds, I filled Ben in on what little I appeared to know regarding Clether's unfortunate set of circumstances.

'But, like he said,' I recalled, it's perhaps better this way. Can you imagine being invited inside your old family home and it not resembling what you held dear?' I said, considering the notion for a moment.

'I suppose I'm still fortunate to still have that connection,' Ben considered, 'I've just always taken it for granted, everything where it always has been, more or less. Imagine losing all of that and your father, all in one go.'

'Poor kid!' It's then, that I suddenly remembered the entries in Stella's journal about a tragic accident, fifteen years ago. But before I could make any connection, Freya and Clether arrived back inside with smiles on their faces.

'I'm glad to see you smiling again,' I commented, catching Clether's eye.

'I suppose I'll get used to it,' he said. 'And it's nice to see the tree and the seat around it have been retained.'

'I love that,' I said, 'I never actually considered whether it'd always been there.'

'Yeah, the house was actually named out of respect for the tree. So my father once told me.'

I wanted to tell him he'd make so many new memories here now, but refrained from opening my mouth, realising it perhaps wasn't quite what he needed to hear right now, whilst realising he'd always have his own memories.

Chapter 13

Tides of Change

I'd gone along with Ben's suggestion, still not entirely convinced it was the right thing to be doing. Although, like he'd said, I was already sleeping there most nights. But also reminded that I had started this process to make a new start on my own, not jump into bed with someone else. I suppose it was all just going to take a bit of time to get used to the idea. Not that it appeared I had much choice in the matter at this late stage.

Today, I was returning to Stella's, not only to feed Leo, but to also pack a few remaining things and tidy and clean for her return. The long summer holidays had, as always, almost run their course and the beaches and lanes would soon empty. Then, as the sun dwindled, nature would deliver a final, dazzling display of colour before autumn descended, and we took solace in the comfort of our homes.

Freya and Clether had now nearly completed the walls, in order for them to begin work on the roof before the onset of winter, which according to Clether, was paramount to protect the structure from the harsh winter storms and to enable them to progress internally. Once the roof was on, I was informed, the windows and doors would then be installed, and then the former cowshed would, at least from the outside, resemble a home.

Only once I'd picked up the post from behind Stella's door, included in which, the usual literature to inspire a makeover and a ballet magazine addressed to Ruby, was I reminded of what had struck me yesterday, when Clether had revealed the nature of his father's death. Though, with everything else happening, it was hardly surprising it'd taken so long for me to make the connection. So, before I forgot and whilst I still had the chance, I dashed upstairs and opened the drawer. Then, without a second thought, opened the box that would hopefully solve the riddle. Sure enough, the evidence was as I'd thought; Clether's and Ruby's father, had to be the same person! So, as to understand the whole story I took the box downstairs to peruse over a coffee, just once I'd fed Leo.

As I'd already suspected, I had indeed been correct in my assumption. But, what I had previously missed, was that Stella, as had already been explained, had still miscarried a baby. But, unbeknown to her and Ruby's father at the time, she had been carrying twins and only one had survived. Her joy and excitement at which were evident in her entry, prior to receiving the devastating news of his tragic accident. Perhaps, if Clether's father hadn't fallen, he may still have lost his home, or I suppose, there was the option that Stella could have moved in there. Who knows what the outcome would have been. Still, what good was it knowing any of this. Either way, Clether now had to get his head around visiting what would probably become my home, and perhaps in time, introducing his children to the place he'd once called home himself. I continued reading Stella's entries, sharing in her sorrow at losing someone she had obviously loved so dearly and had planned to spend the rest of her life with, and how quickly all that had changed. Wondering, if she ever opened the box herself these days, or if the memory was just too painful. I expect, like Clether, she's been building a future without him. Though, I imagine his memory lives on in both their hearts.

I'd replaced the box carefully, leaving it as I'd found it, then loading my car with the last of my belongings before driving back to Ben's, realising I still had to address the far larger issue of what to do with all my other possessions still in storage.

As I turned the corner into Church Street, I noticed a new 'For Sale' board outside the property tucked in the corner at the end of the lane. Typical! I thought. Isn't it always the way! I suppose it wouldn't do any harm to just take a look, at least online. Knowing my luck, it was probably going to be out of my price range anyway. The outside was far prettier than I could have ever imagined, with a beautifully tended cottage garden and a pristine thatched roof to top it off.

Once I'd unloaded the car and found room to hang my garments, I couldn't help opening my laptop to see if my suspicions were indeed correct and the property was unsuitable. But, as luck would have it, both the price and floorplan were indeed favourable. Instead of arranging an appointment to view at my earliest convenience, I began completing a stationary order, something I could do whilst pondering the possibility of living somewhere so beautiful, still unsure of exactly what to think. After all, I'd only been seeing Ben for a few months, and he'd only offered to put me up because of my current predicament. This way, we could still continue seeing each other and Clether would then at least have time to get used to the idea. But, then again, if Ben and I continued seeing each other, we would ultimately move in together. I'd refrained from calling Ben, hoping I'd have reached a solution, one way or another, before he arrived home, and he could then express his thoughts on the matter. No doubt, using his powers of seduction to persuade me otherwise. He may actually be right, but I liked to feel I was in control of my own destiny and not feel pressured into making a decision without first considering all the options. The property had looked to be everything I'd dreamed of finding, a home of my very own that reflected my personality, that I could fill with my own treasured possessions rather than adopt someone else's. This was Ben's home, filled with his things. Not that it wasn't comfortable or attractive, just they were his choices, not mine or even ours. Ben would surely be able to understand this. If only it had gone on the market two months ago!

Whilst packing the order I'd been working on, my mind continued to wander, considering as to where my things would even fit into Ben's house and that it could never really work. I just wanted my own home, somewhere to unpack all my treasured belongings that meant so much to me and that I missed.

Of course, when Ben did arrive home, I was no nearer a decision on what to think, but I had had an otherwise productive afternoon. Not only had I completed two very different orders - One, for a traditional wedding ceremony with ninety-six guests. The other, on a relatively smaller scale, where the guests had been informed to leave their vehicles parked on the church car park and carry with them, either stout footwear or possibly wellies, depending on the weather - which would be needed after the ceremony, to walk the short distance across the fields to a marque on the bride's parents lawn, where the reception was to be held. Which I assumed, was at Foxglove Farm, where all correspondence regarding the wedding was to be collated. I only hope the weather is clement next July, and that the guests consider this in their choice of outfit, as well as footwear! Something, it appeared, I would have to consider myself, when Freya marries. I suppose, if the weather was inclement, there was always the possibility of transport from the church to the farm. Unlike the depths of a forest, where I imagine Freya to be saying her vows. Although these ideas all seem very romantic, in my experience, the reality, can be very different! Only last year, an acquaintance of mine had planned her own second wedding to be conducted in the summer to coincide with a meticulously planned honeymoon in Florida. Only the reality was a completely different scenario they had never anticipated, leaving them fleeing for their safety as the hurricanes hit and nature took its course.

Though, I suppose, if we were all as diligent as I'd once considered myself to be, then life just wouldn't be quite as much fun, and from my own experience, you can never plan for unforeseen circumstances. For example, my own wedding had been meticulously planned, everything from the carriage to the cake, or so I'd thought. The fact it had rained hadn't mattered to either of us, as according to my mother, it signified good luck. However, what we hadn't envisaged, was the registrar striking and refusing to conduct Saturday wedding ceremonies, meaning all our plans were scuppered! But, as with most things, we'd found a solution to suit everyone, signing the register a day earlier. Then, when I had arrived at the church the following day, all my dreams had come true. So, can perhaps understand why Freya wants what she does.

I suppose it isn't just the guests who have to consider their outfits, the photographer too, having to consider the opportunities the weather might present for shots, along with his own attire. And then, at the other end of the spectrum - a funeral, often beside a muddy graveside, the weather unpredictable, often miserable to match the mood, not that a photographer would be involved in a ceremony of this nature!

Freya had explained, after I'd enquired after Clether, that visiting the site of his old home had come as rather a shock at the time, reminding him of things he'd have perhaps much rather forgotten. But, on reflection, he'd come to realise it was perhaps easier in some ways that the house had been redeveloped rather than maintaining its original state with someone else living in it. At least this way - once inside, he was in an entirely different house, rather than the old four walls. Assuring me he would come again - for my roast, if nothing else!

Ben was also very appreciative of my culinary skills and a meal already prepared on his return each day, if only in the oven for later. I still wasn't entirely sure as to what to think about the property in the village having come on to the market, despite thinking of little else all afternoon. Realising, I did love the thought of Ben returning home at the end of the day.

'You'll never guess what sold today,' Ben said, as we tucked into our lasagne.

'The renovation project?' I hazarded a guess.

'No, Church Cottage!'

'Really!' I said, as surprised as Ben. 'So, who's bought it?'

'Ah, that's confidential.'

'Seriously?'

'Absolutely!'

'So, at least tell me if it's someone I know,' I started quizzing him. 'It's not you, is it?' I asked, alarmed.

'It isn't me,' Ben declared. 'I can tell you that much.'

'Whilst we're on the subject of houses,' I began, 'did you know there's a cottage come up in the village? I was thinking I might take a look.'

'Why?' Ben looked up. 'I thought you were happy here. I meant what I said when I invited you to stay. I hoped you'd call here home.'

'I am happy, really. I suppose it's just all happened so quickly,' I tried explaining.

'I realise that, but why change what works?'

'I suppose.'

'Then, no more looking. Unless you're having second thoughts?' Ben considered. 'Or there's not enough room!'

'It's absolutely perfect,' I determined.

Chapter 14

Comfort and Joy

Following Ben's suggestion, I'd accepted delivery of my boxed belongings, reacquainting myself with the contents and a few favourite things that I'd stashed away for safe keeping. It still felt strange when I stopped to think how things had worked out, when I'd anticipated a completely different scenario occurring. But ultimately, I knew this was the right decision. Obviously, much of what I'd packed was now redundant, who needed two toasters, or another set of cutlery, not to mention spare beds. There were of course, certain pieces I did want to include, even replicate and have in the kitchen. Like my own teapot and favourite cookery books. Only this morning, I'd discovered a soap dish that had adorned my bathroom sink. It's amazing what you forget you even have, when they're no longer visible. The rest of course, would go back in the boxes, until Freya and Clether would undoubtedly be able to put them to good use.

Today, was the last week of the school summer holidays, evoking memories of my childhood days and holidays spent here with the girls; the taste of freedom, away from the constraints of suburban life. Of course, all good things must come to an end and life moves on for us all, with or without us onboard. Reminding me once again of how much my own life had changed so significantly, in such a short space of time and since I'd first met Ben and then Stella. Unearthing her connection to Clether, and then to the property I now call home. Freya and Clether, hadn't as yet returned to visit, purely due to time constraints and not the address, as I'd first envisaged. I'd met with Freya a couple of times at the stables, either early in the morning or later in the day, once pony club was over. It was nice to be able to spend more time together, rather than having to rely on snatched video calls at her convenience; now realising, just how much I had actually missed. Not that I wasn't now missing Beth.

The more I saw Freya, the more it became apparent just how much Clether's mother's actions, after his father's death had affected him and how, even now, all these years later, it still hurt. Obviously, recent events had opened up old wounds and he had naturally shared his feelings with Freya, who in turn had needed to share it all with me. Not that she wanted advice, she was always keen to form her own opinion rather than accept someone else's ideas. Just, we all need somebody sometimes to share the load. She had of course disclosed little things over the years whilst formulating her own opinion, despite having only met his mother on the odd occasion herself: a family wedding or christening or having heard Clether's siblings own accounts, subsequently sharing in Clether's own contempt. Of course, if Freya knew what, or more to the point, how I'd discovered what I now knew, she might not have been as willing to confide in me. Anyway, Freya had disclosed that recent events had disrupted their sleep. Although she was aware of a certain amount of animosity between Clether and his mother, she had never actually asked too many questions, having learnt to avoid the subject and the hurt associated with it. Clether, had fortunately appeared to have learnt how to manage his grief, putting all his energy into creating a forever home for his own future family and very rarely looked back these days. So, recent events had understandably been difficult. Apparently, according to Freya, it had made him relive the harrowing experience of all those years ago, when his mother hadn't appeared to have given a second thought for Clether and his older siblings, selling their home from under them, so soon after the sudden death of their father - almost as though she'd been waiting for an opportunity. As far as I was aware, Clether was completely unaware of his father's relationship with Stella, though the more I learnt, the more I imagined he would perhaps understand if he was ever to find out. In his eyes, his mother was heartless and more interested in her husband's wealth than his wellbeing, claiming she hadn't the time to go out to work herself, lessening the load on his father's shoulders and adding to the family's income, too busy spending his hard-earned money on frivolous things. Even his father's funeral had appeared to have been an excuse to go to town on a new designer outfit and heels, that Clether had half expected her to have subsequently worn to dance on top of his grave. Despite Freya knowing the destruction his mother had already caused, it had upset her to hear Clether say some of the things he had. But in his defence, found it incredulous, how anyone, especially a mother could behave in such a manner. By all accounts, she was now living, as he had explained to Ben, not that far away, having in his words, "hooked up with a suitably ostentatious sucker, who could keep her in the manner she'd become accustomed"! Imagining her name wouldn't be appearing on their wedding invitation list any time soon!

I had also been upset, having previously read Stella's own personal account of how she'd actually stayed away from Rob's funeral. Realising, although she could have explained her presence, she wouldn't have been able to hide her deep sorrow, that wouldn't have gone unnoticed. Instead, she'd spent time where they'd first kissed, reflecting on happier times and what might have been, returning home to the bed that still smelt of him.

Listening to Freya however, had made me consider Beth's attachment and reluctance to accept the sale of what she had known as her family home, although the circumstances were different, I could perhaps now appreciate her feelings. Not that I would have changed my decision, still believing it had been the right thing to do at the time. Something I expect she will come to realise for herself one day. She had of course, already criticised the new owners of our old house for changing the window dressings and their choice of vehicle they parked on the driveway, which in her opinion, spoiled what had once held her fondest memories.

Though, I very much doubt anything in her eyes would have ever been acceptable. On the other hand, their own new neighbours had recently invited them in for drinks in their newly erected orangery, which I imagine, she and Lucas have subsequently investigated as a possible extension to their own home. She had naturally seemed quite surprised when I had explained my new living arrangements with Ben, considering I hadn't mentioned him before. Though, got the feeling Freya may have already enlightened her. However, I imagined, once she'd had time to digest the update, she would undoubtably pass comment!

I had informed Stella of my recent change of address, assuring her of course, that Leo was still being cared for and in good health. Unlike Beth, she hadn't seemed as surprised to hear of my recent union with Ben, excited to hear all about it over lunch on her return. I'd given a lot of thought to what I'd found hidden away and what had emerged since, deciding of course, not to mention my indiscretion. Instead, I'd decided to drop Freya into the conversation and her involvement with Clether and then his connection to Ben's house, realising Stella would then perhaps realise who Clether was for herself, and if nothing else, it might offer some comfort, imagining Rob to have spoken fondly about his children to her. What she told their daughter was entirely up to her. But, possibly one day, she might understand for herself.

Despite it having been the summer holidays, it hadn't stopped the influx of requests from brides to be, arranging their nuptials for next year, although one request was for January, which despite the short notice, I had agreed to do, as it was only a relatively small gathering and their request nominal. Speaking of which, I would have to mention to Freya to advise me of her plans, so I could set the wheels in motion. Despite their informal approach to conformity, I was sure they'd still require some regimented order to the ceremony. And even without Clether's mother, he still had two other siblings, who were both married themselves, with children in tow. Not forgetting Adam and Laura and her two sons, whom Freya would obviously want in attendance.

Adam had informed me himself of the date of his own forthcoming wedding, not that he'd require my services, but it did feel slightly odd to consider him even contemplating marrying someone else. I would no doubt hear all about it after the event from Freya and Beth, who wouldn't be able to resist sharing in his happiness. Not that I'd want to be there myself, but wished him well on the next chapter in his life.

I was more than comfortable sat working in what I still considered and referred to as Ben's house, realising I still hadn't quite accepted it being what I should now consider my home. I was, however, quite happy to ignore yet another property that had only this morning come onto the market, resisting the temptation to view, either online or otherwise. I suppose, it was only natural to feel a little unsettled somewhere new, especially surrounded by someone else's things. I began wondering, as I stood in the kitchen pouring a coffee, how Ben's home might change and look over time, with the addition of my own family photographs alongside his and whether he'd ever grow to love my daughters like I did, or how he might perceive them. I suppose, it would all happen naturally, in its own time. As I finished compiling orders, I happened to look up - each day something different catching my eye, that I'd somehow failed to notice before. I stood to study the photo that had caught my attention of Ben at his graduation amongst a happy throng of other graduates in their caps and gowns, suddenly realising I must have an earlier school photograph amongst all my own treasures, depicting the two of us with our classmates. Seizing the moment and easily distracted, I set about trying to find one, which remarkably, turned out to be easier than I'd imagined!

Once I'd managed to find what I was searching for, I stood it proudly on a bookshelf, awaiting Ben's approval, before affixing it to a wall.

The weekend arrived, but as usual, Ben had had to work most of the day. But it also allowed me to crack on with my own work, already collecting ideas in my head for Freya's big day, something she appeared to have put on a back burner whilst addressing more important issues involving their home. Having already experienced Beth's wedding, I was well aware of just how much time was actually involved in planning such a special event, in order to incorporate everything you'd ever dreamed of, whether or not you conformed to tradition. More couples these days, thinking outside the box. Only last week, I'd had a couple planning a seaside themed wedding next summer, only a month earlier than Freya's. I would perhaps get chance to talk to her this evening, after agreeing to meet up in town after Ben had finished work to celebrate his birthday. Something Ben was particularly looking forward to. Not only enjoying Clether's company but hearing all about the progress they had made on the barn. Perhaps I could get to talk to Freya about wedding plans whilst they discussed the benefits of using wool to insulate the walls. I wouldn't mind so much, but Freya was usually as enthusiastic as they were!

I so wanted her wedding to be an enjoyable experience and memorable day, realising from experience, the importance of meticulous planning and just how much thought goes into something that is over much too soon. Something Adam will no doubt be realising for himself, and although he would be contributing financially to his daughter's wedding, I imagined that would be the extent of his support. Freya, it seemed, as well as Beth, surprisingly accepting of Laura and her two sons. Though, they had had several years now to get used to the idea. Not that Freya got to spend too much time with her father or his new family, living so far away. But Beth always seemed more than happy to include them all in her weekend plans, even babysitting for them occasionally.

I sometimes wondered if she had more in common with Laura than myself and imagined she would be on hand to offer any advice she might need with her wedding plans. Freya, had of course informed Beth of her plans, which I imagined Beth to be still trying to comprehend, envisaging what she might be asked to wear to such an unconventional occasion, especially as she'd been asked to be Freya's maid of honour, escorting Clether's two little nieces through the woodland. The more I imagined it, the more I considered its magical appeal and now having Ben to share it with, made it even more special. Beth remained unusually quiet, no doubt trying to make sense of my recent revelation, that I imagined must have come as quite a shock to her. Though, at least now I had a home, albeit with someone she had not yet met.

All of which would be rectified next weekend as she'd invited herself and Lucas down to meet Ben for herself. Personally, I would have preferred a little more time to get my own head around the situation myself, before inviting them into my new life. But, like she had pointed out, Freya and Clether had already been invited, and of course, Ben was as eager to put names to faces. So, I was left with little option.

Despite all the distractions going around in my head I'd made reasonable progress on satisfying and answering my customers' needs before Ben had arrived home, especially as I hadn't had to prepare dinner. I'd even had a request from a previous bride, asking if I could produce some invitations for a baby shower- something I would address later, realising it could be quite a lucrative path to take. Considering, I could then offer birth announcements and christening invitations when the need arose. Not that I was short of work, but it would make a nice change to work on some new material.

Ben and I arrived together at the restaurant and had already sat down and ordered our drinks before Freya and Clether joined us.

'You look happy,' I commented, as they approached.

'We've been looking for sanitary ware,' Freya explained, approaching the table, attracting the attention of everyone else in earshot! Astounded at her revelation, I remained silent, not knowing quite what to say in response. Ben spluttering, having just put his glass back on the table.

'I didn't realise how much choice there was on offer,' Freya continued enthusiastically, producing brochures from her bag.

'As in bathrooms!' I now realised.

'What did you think I meant?'

'I think it's time I took you shopping,' I suggested, considering her excitement at something I can't say I'd ever paid too much attention to, just as long as it was clean. But suppose, compared to what they currently had, it must be quite exciting! 'How about we go dress shopping next weekend when Beth's here?' I suggested.

'What would I want with a dress?' Freya laughed.

'Your wedding!' I reminded her. 'If it hadn't slipped your mind, you're getting married next year.'

'But that's ages off!' Freya exclaimed, returning to their earlier shopping spree and the decisions to be made.

As we enjoyed our meal the conversation changed, Freya enquiring as to whether I'd started to unpack yet, something she couldn't envisage doing herself for a long time. Much of her own stuff remaining packed away in storage along with mine, until she's able to reveal the true potential of the former barn and realise her dreams for the future.

'No, she hasn't,' Ben answered, although sympathetic to my situation.

'It takes time,' I began explaining. 'I first have to adapt to my new surroundings.'

'I don't know how you'd have gone on moving into an empty property,' Freya said.

Realising Freya may have a clearer vision, having worked with an architect to incorporate their every need, as far as possible, rather than the other way around.

'We could always make a new start together,' Ben suggested, having begun to understand my dilemma. 'There's plenty to choose from.'

'Don't say that!' Freya said, glancing across at Clether, assuming he'd be mortified if he had to lose it all again. 'Your house is beautiful.'

'Thank you,' Ben said. 'I'm sure it'll soon feel like home.'

'Clether's sister is actually moving back,' Freya explained. 'You'll almost be neighbours.'

'Not quite,' Clether interrupted. 'Though, I imagine you'll be able to see her property from a certain angle.'

'Really, where's that then?' I questioned.

'Church Cottage,' Clether informed us. 'She's just put an offer in, so she should be in in time for Christmas.'

'Doesn't she live on Dartmoor?' I asked, trying to place her, then reminded of who she was.

'Yes, but her heart has always been here, and her daughter is starting school next year. She's had her eye on it for a long time I believe.'

'So does she not mind its proximity to the church,' I asked, curious as to how anyone could find it appealing.

'No,' Clether said, 'she's always had a strong connection to the church. Well, fond memories I suppose. She used to belong to the bell ringing group and practised there every week. She helped ring them every Sunday morning.'

'A campanologist, I believe,' Ben offered.

'That's right,' Clether agreed. 'I can never remember that!'

'I can't wait!' Freya smiled. 'All we need to do now is relocate Ted and Tilly.'

'So where does your other brother live?' I asked, realising how much their roots obviously meant to them all. Wondering if Ben and I where to relocate, whether one of them may actually be interested in his house.

'He lives and works in London. I doubt they'll ever consider moving back.'

'Maybe not yet, but possibly sometime in the future.' Freya shared her considered opinion, continuing to enlighten us on her thought process. Albeit, a pipe dream of her own making.

Today I was out again, meeting Stella for lunch, who apparently wanted to thank me for enabling her to attend her residential summer course and naturally keen to catch up on the home front.
We'd chosen 'Tiggie's' to eat, a cosy little gem, tucked down a narrow street that was only known to the locals as a gastronomic delight. The day trippers more inclined to choose somewhere along the high street rather than off the beaten track.

'So, tell me,' Stella began, 'I've been wondering if Ben was perhaps the reason for your return?'

'No, it was pure coincidence that he was the estate agent I first met when I started looking. Though I must admit, it was an extraordinary twist of fate! And if the property he'd shown me had been right, I imagine it could have been an entirely different story.'

'I bet you'd still have got together; you were always destined to be together.'

Stella filled me in on her own summer away, the people she'd met and how energised she felt as a result, whilst we munched our way, first through a delicious salad, garnished with pumpkin seeds and pomegranate fruit, followed by a deep bowl of shellfish, entwined in linguine and an exquisite sauce - accompanied with an obligatory glass of the house white wine.

'This is fun,' Stella said, squeezing my hand. 'It reminds me of school dinners. Well, eating together, not the cuisine!'

'The good old days,' I added.

'My mum always told me they were the happiest days of my life,' Stella recalled. 'And I've now found myself telling Ruby exactly the same.'

'So how old is she now?' I asked.

'Nearly sixteen. Though she seems to have changed so much over the summer.'

'Adolescence!' I said, hazarding a guess, remembering it well. 'Trust me, you're in for the ride of your life!' I told her. 'But it won't last long and then you'll have a friend for life.'

'I remember when she was little, always asking "why?" Only now she wants to know more. Up until now she seemed to accept what I was prepared to share with her about her father. I suppose, she never missed what she'd never had, accepting her father had died before she'd even been born. But now she wants me to fill in all the gaps.'

'I suppose it's only natural.'

'Only, it's so long ago,' Stella began explaining. 'Not that I've forgotten,' she explained. 'But I've kept it to myself all these years.'

'I suppose it's a bit like Clether, Freya's boyfriend,' I said, reminded of his situation, forgetting for a moment their own connection, whilst continuing to explain to Stella his connection to Ben's house and the difficulties it had posed.

'That's sad,' Stella sympathised, 'I'm sorry to hear that. I suppose Ruby is fortunate in that respect.'

'Every cloud...'

'But you say, they're building their own home?'

'Yes, Freya describes it as a good thing, almost therapy in a way, for Clether,' I tried explaining, hoping she might realise that talking to Ruby might actually help. Though, at the same time, realised that time itself, was a great healer.

'I've never told anyone this,' Stella began, whilst I felt a pang of guilt at what I imagined she might be about to divulge. 'But Ruby's father was married. I've never told Ruby and I don't want to spoil the picture she's already built, or taint his memory.'

'I imagine you still loved each other, regardless.'

'Dearly, it was only a matter of time before we'd be together. But he died before we got the chance. We'd so many plans for the future,' she continued, her voice

quivering and tears welling up in her eyes. 'I'm sorry,' she said, dabbing her eyes. 'Like I said, I've never told anyone this before.'
Wondering how she'd managed to contain her emotions for so long with no one to share her sorrow.

'I used to tell Ruby all about him when she was little, but of course she couldn't understand then, she was too young. Then, as she grew, I was careful not to upset her and doctored what I told her, careful how I answered any questions she asked. It was only fair she knew how wonderful her father was, which he was; I'd planned to spend the rest of my life with him, raise our child together. The sad thing is, he never knew about Ruby, not that it would have changed the outcome.'

'I'm so sorry,' I offered, my own heart breaking, hearing Stella say it out loud, realising just how much they had loved one another and the impact his death had had on his loved ones. Considering Ruby was perhaps the lucky one in some ways; like Stella had said, "you never miss what you never had". Then I remembered the anguish Ben had endured, never cradling his new born son or daughter. I suppose, we all have our own cross to bear in life, we just have to learn how best to deal with it.

Chapter 15

Memories are Made of This

Ben had been adamant that Beth and Lucas were to stay with us, not that Beth had any other intentions herself, least of all pitching a tent in Freya's back yard. Though, I expect she would be suitably surprised to see the progress they'd already managed to make. But doubt she'd truly appreciate the potential until it was finally completed and she could see the space and design features for herself. Though doubted she would ever appreciate their way of life and proximity to nature.

Freya had agreed to take the opportunity to go dress shopping whilst Beth was staying, especially as her visits were few and far between. Who knew when we'd see her again, once she'd satisfied her curiosity and met Ben for herself.

So, this morning, I'd dealt with any work issues before downing tools to begin preparing the guest room for their arrival. Then after lunch, shopped for a few ingredients to accompany a chicken that could take care of itself in the oven, not forgetting a couple of bottles of white wine and a selection of beers for Ben and Lucas, remembering how much Lucas liked his beer. It still felt odd planning to entertain in Ben's house, especially as it hadn't been that long since I'd been a guest myself. Though, I was at least familiar with the oven now and knew where to find everything.

Now the date for Freya's wedding had been confirmed, she had, as I'd suggested, already begun a mood board and informed two, very excited little girls that they were to be bridesmaids. Even Freya, I noted, seemed more onboard herself, asking my opinion on her choice of footwear and flowers and whether or not a veil would be at all practical, given she'd be walking through a forest of trees. But as autumn was fast approaching it was easy to imagine the rich burgundy and orange colours she seemed to favour. As to what dress she had in mind, was yet to be seen. And of course, once she'd chosen her colours, Beth and I could plan our own outfits to compliment hers. Beth had chosen a traditional white gown and a diamond encrusted tiara to adorn her hair and attach her long veil for her own wedding and procession down the aisle. Her bridesmaids, including Freya, had worn pale pink. Her flowers had been a beautiful cascade of soft pink and almost sorbet-coloured peonies mixed with creamy white roses. Considering I should perhaps try and find a photo to remind them both; or better still, find the framed photo to display.

Despite Beth and Lucas having taken the day off so they could travel down during the day, they actually hadn't arrived until late afternoon. They had though, arrived before Ben, who I had hoped would have been here to welcome them. It felt rather odd standing at his door welcoming guests inside without him, but welcomed them in all the same. The smile on Beth's face showed her approval, just as I remembered feeling myself when I'd first set eyes on here, together with the added joy of finally reaching their destination.

Ben of course won both their hearts as soon as he'd arrived home, delighted as them to finally meet, having heard so much about each other. The meal was a triumph and devoured in no time, taking our drinks to enjoy and relax in Ben's sumptuous lounge.

Beth, it appeared, was more excited than Freya as we left Lucas and Ben, whilst we checked out a local bridal boutique with Freya; the assistant having to be corrected in her assumption as to who the bride in question was! Although Freya had had to be persuaded to take a look, she seemed to have a very clear idea as to what she liked and disliked, much to Beth's disapproval, dismissing several of her sister's suggestions. Though I'm sure Beth still hadn't quite got her head around Freya walking through a forest, rather than down an aisle. Despite Adam agreeing to pay for her dress, Freya was appalled at the price tags, comparing them to the entire cost of the barn roof! And whilst appreciating the intricate detail, she couldn't quite understand how anyone would be willing to pay such an astronomical price to only wear something once, appalled at how many would then be relegated to a box in the loft for the remainder of their married life. Needless to say, we came away empty handed and demoralised. I'm sure Freya will, in time, choose something perfect for the occasion, but probably on her own and in her own good time. Considering Beth and I should probably go shopping for our outfits without Freya. Beth and I may not see eye to eye on everything, but we've always shared the same passion for shopping for clothes, appreciating each other's opinion, if not the price tags!

Freya returned to the comfort of the stables for the remainder of the day, or at least until dusk, when she would join us with Clether for dinner. Meanwhile, Beth and I headed out for a leisurely lunch with Ben and Lucas, before taking advantage of the beautiful weather to explore and rediscover some of the favourite places I'd shared with her when she was younger. Then back home to prepare a veritable feast for this evening's supper.

Ben as ever, was the perfect host making us all very comfortable in his home, not that he didn't allow me full reign in his kitchen whilst he relaxed outside in the garden getting to know Beth and Lucas a little more. Despite not having children of his own, he seemed more than accepting of mine; I suppose, just as I've been of Lucas and Clether, the more I get to know them, the more I consider them to be part of the family. I suppose in a way, the more time we spend here together, the more memories we'll make and the more it'll begin to feel like home.

Chapter 16

All Good Things

The weekend over, the house returned to its former tranquil space to work, especially now Ben and I had transformed an unused bedroom into my new work station, reinstating my own work surfaces and chair under the window, overlooking the front of the house - not as appealing or inspiring as the back view, but not without its own attraction of being able to watch the coming and goings of the local residents and whoever Mr Thomas's new acquaintance was!
I'd even discovered the box containing framed photographs to dot around, and with my favourite mug filled with coffee, it was already beginning to feel like home, at least up here anyway. Yesterday, I'd had a request for invitations for a thirtieth birthday party, which I'd just agreed to, understanding exactly what the client wanted depicting. Especially as the birthday girl in question was beginning to become a valued customer of mine, opening my eyes to all manner of options I could add to my repertoire, having already supplied invitations for a baby shower and her parents pearl wedding anniversary; the list it appeared was endless, if I ever ran out of brides and grooms.
The children that had enjoyed the pony club had now all returned to a more sedentary life in the classroom for another year, or at least until Saturday, when the yard would fill with young enthusiastic equestrians, keen to reacquaint themselves with their beloved ponies and enjoy the outdoors.

It also gave me more time during the week to exercise between the constraints of work and whilst Ben was out at work. In fact, anyone whose life revolved around the school holidays had returned to their normal routine; for many, far away from the dramatic cliffs and breaking waves of the ocean.

Ruby's adventures had also ceased, at least for now, reacquainting herself with her old timetable and life as she knew it, allowing Stella and myself some time to enjoy together.

'So, how's Ruby?' I enquired, as we enjoyed lunch out together.

'Settling back into her old routine. And spreading her wings.'

'How do you mean?'

'She's got a part time job at the stables,' she continued to inform me. 'Just mucking out really, but she gets to ride as well, so that's a bonus.'

'What, where Freya works?' I enquired.

'Yes, though she's obviously only there over the weekends, and she's still dancing on Saturday mornings,' she explained. 'Though, I'm not sure which she'd choose if she had to make a choice.'

'A busy girl then!' I surmised. 'So have you spoken to her yet about what you mentioned last time?'

'If only I knew how,' Stella explained. 'Fortunately, she's been too busy addressing other issues. Whereas, I haven't been able to think of much else. How do I begin to explain that her father already had three other children and that he was about to walk out on his wife to start a new life with me? They're all grown up now obviously and had all flown the nest, so to speak, at the time. But as far as I'm aware, have no idea about Ruby or myself. I shouldn't imagine his wife would care, but I worry about his children finding out, and the repercussions, especially all these years later.'

'Maybe it'll be easier to accept now than it would have been back then.'

'But look at Clether, Freya's boyfriend,' Stella began, 'if he was to find out something like this. It seems he still hasn't got over his father's death. Who knows what affect finding out something like this would have on him or how he'd feel towards Ruby?'

'It's a little more complicated than that,' I explained. 'He lost everything he held dear at a crucial time. He'd only just lost his father,' I paused, fortifying myself with another large glug of wine. 'Clether's dealing with his grief and you're not talking about losing someone.'

'Other than their respect for their father. Not to mention memories,' she considered, joining me in a drink. 'I feel responsible for potentially destroying everyone's future happiness.'

It's then, that I considered the enormity of Stella's dilemma, and the implications of her actions. Not only for Stella and the dreams she'd had, but for her daughter and Rob's other children.

'You know,' I began, 'I was quite surprised how Beth and Freya accepted the demise of my marriage to Adam. They've even accepted Laura and her sons and consider them family. You have to realise they are all adults now. I know Ruby is still young, but she needs to know. The fact she's asking, must mean she's ready to find out more and fill in the gaps. You have to tell her before she finds out for herself,' I told her, reminded of the association now between Freya and Ruby. Considering it to be only a matter of time before the connection was made.

'I know, I just never envisaged having to do it on my own,' she explained. 'It's times like this I miss him even more and contemplate on what might have been. Not that I'm not reminded of him every day in Ruby.'

'It'll be fine,' I assured her. 'You just wait and see. You've probably all got more to gain than you have to lose.'

'Let's hope you're right,' Stella said, picking up the dessert menu.

Freya and Clether were making good progress on the barn with everything on schedule, the roof trusses already up, offering some semblance to a home. Meaning it was on track to be watertight before the onset of winter, when they could concentrate on work inside. The weather, as predicted had remained warm, in fact positively balmy, appreciated all the more at this time of year. It was Saturday, and as Ben was in the office, I took the opportunity to start work on some thank you cards that had been requested to accompany and compliment an order of wedding stationary. Understandably, something many couples fail to include in their order, which I can totally appreciate, when the event itself has yet to take place. But it kept me occupied and allowed me more time with Ben, later in the week. The good weather also meant we could continue as planned and join Freya and Clether this evening, for what might be a final feast outside before we were forced inside, and after some considerable persuasion I'd agreed to stay over and camp. Ben had been delighted to have received another invitation, having enjoyed the last experience so much and had been checking the weather all week, afraid it would break and spoil his fun. His excitement reminded me of a child waiting for Christmas!

Once I'd completed the order, I began preparing the dessert for this evening, having chosen a trifle again, realising it was a favourite dish for us all. I packed what I imagined we'd require for our little excursion into the wild, not forgetting a warm duvet, pillows and an air bed, I'd insisted we buy before agreeing to what I considered a mad idea. Still unsure as to whether I was doing the right thing!

Despite wanting to catch a glimpse of Ruby, I had learnt to avoid the stables at weekend when the children would descend, preferring to enjoy the escape it provided during the week.

Everything it seemed was falling into place, I even recognised where I was when I opened my eyes each morning, though still had to pinch myself. There were still boxes that lay unpacked, realising the remainder of the contents had either served their purpose or had belonged to a previous life without Ben. However, I had retrieved a few special photographs and objects, placing them around the house, looking forward to filling it with our things, as and when we chose.

Ben, had as expected, managed to leave the office a little earlier, allowing us more time to enjoy the evening. So, with his car loaded with the necessary essentials, not forgetting our woollies for later, we set off in pursuit of Ben's dream. It appeared, Clether had also been out doing what he loved best, taking advantage of the good weather on offer. His wetsuit hanging from a tree, still dripping beside his board. Despite which, he had obviously allowed time to prepare supper, the pot bubbling away over the fire pit, the aromas, as welcoming as the smiles on their faces.

'Ah, good man!' Clether declared, accepting a crate of beer from Ben.

'So, what's on the menu tonight?' I asked, whilst considering what to drink.

'A sausage casserole,' Freya enlightened us. 'We've got some local cider from the farm down the valley, if you'd like.'

'I'll give it a go,' I volunteered, a little unsure. 'It's a long time since I've actually had a cider.'

'Then you have to try it,' Clether said, pouring me a glass from a barrel.

'This gets better all the time,' Ben said. 'You know, I rather envy you and your lifestyle.'

'It's hardly glamourous,' Freya enlightened us, squashing next to me on an old wrought iron bench. 'And I'm not sure mum would agree.'

'It's not that I don't appreciate what you're striving to achieve,' I tried explaining. 'And I can almost visualise what it'll all be like one day. But if I'm honest, I'm a creature of comfort.'

'I have to remind myself sometimes of what we're striving to achieve,' Freya said, a little wearily.

'It'll all be worth it babe,' Clether reminded her.

'I know, I'm just knackered!'

'We don't have to stay,' I offered, keeping my head low, so as not to catch the disappointment in Ben's eyes.

'Don't be silly, we wouldn't hear of it,' Freya said. 'It might be the last chance you get for a while. I'll be fine when I've had something to eat.'

'Here, have a drink,' Clether said, passing her a glass of the golden liquid. 'How's that new girl got on today?'

'Ruby, she's great, not afraid of hard work and uses her own initiative rather than having to be told what to do all the time. She hasn't been riding that long, but you'd never guess, she's quite competent, and so elegant in the saddle.'

'I imagine it'll be her ballet training; I suppose deportment becomes second nature.' I deduced.

'You're probably right,' Freya agreed. 'She's probably had it instilled from a young age. she could definitely teach some of the newer ones a lesson or two.'

I considered Stella for a moment, realising how proud she'd be of her daughter if she could hear Freya singing her praises. And then recall her sadness at not having Rob to share her pride with.

'You liked it then?' Clether noted, observing my empty glass.

'Umm, it was rather good!' I determined.

'Well, before you get too comfortable,' Clether said, 'I suggest you pitch your tent.'

Ben of course, didn't need much persuasion, leaping to his feet, reinforcing what I'd already suspected, and that he'd possibly had a very sheltered upbringing and been deprived of these experiences as a child. Then not having children himself, had never experienced the delights that were about to unfold.

'Right, this looks ready,' Clether instructed us, as we rejoined them both beside the fire, each accepting a large bowl of the hearty stew.

Suitably refreshed and not having to worry about driving home or upsetting the neighbours, we'd wrapped ourselves up and enjoyed another glass of cider around the fire as the light faded and the owl began to hoot, before retiring to our bed for the night.
We were awoken by the dawn chorus, snug and surprisingly warm; no wonder Freya got so much done when her life was dictated by nature. Early to bed, early to rise. Sure enough, Freya and Clether were up and about when Ben and I surfaced, greeting us with a bowl of porridge and a cup of coffee beside the open fire.

'Did you sleep well?' Freya asked, as we emerged into the sunshine.

'Surprisingly well!' I considered.

'It was the best night's sleep I've had in a long time,' Ben deemed. 'We should do it more often.'

'We'll see,' I said, still not entirely convinced.

'Are you sure you'll be able to cope being cooped up again once it's finished?' Ben asked,

'I'm sure we'll get used to it!' Clether said.

'We've got winter to contend with yet.' Freya reminded us. 'The thing I'm most looking forward to, is being able to have a soak in a warm bath again.'

'And we'll still have all this,' Clether said.

'But I bet you'll think twice before coming outside to cook.' I considered.

'I suspect we'll just appreciate everything all the more,' Freya considered.

'You've certainly a lot to be grateful for,' Ben said, appreciating their way of life.

'This is delicious,' I said, tasting my porridge, resisting the urge to tell them just how much I was enjoying eating it whilst sat around the open fire it'd been cooked on. Realising, how such simple pleasures can bring so much joy.

'I thought we'd wander down to the beach after this,' Freya said, 'if you're not in a hurry to get back?'

'Bring it on!' Ben smiled.

'As long as we're not stopping you from working,' I added.

'It's not all work and no play,' Clether explained. 'And I think we've earned some playtime. We're actually ahead of schedule.'

'But we also realise we've still a long way to go,' Freya explained. Never one to rest on her laurels. 'I expect we'll encounter a few setbacks before we finish.'

'Ever the optimist!' Clether said, squeezing her leg.

'I am an optimist!' she said in her own defence. 'You can stay and help point the walls after, if you like.'

'Try and stop me!' Ben answered, without consulting me.

Not wanting to miss an opportunity, Clether donned his wetsuit whilst continuing to chat to Ben. No doubt introducing him to the thrills of more uncharted territory.

The beach was deserted, not that I remembered it ever being that busy. Not many prepared to make the descent down, especially with all the paraphernalia one deems necessary, given the opportunities on offer once down here. Only the intrepid amongst us able to appreciate its full potential.

Ben had remembered his camera he'd left on the back seat of the car, having decided to record the progress of the barn for posterity. Something I imagine Freya hadn't even considered, more interested in getting the work done and enjoying the fruits of her labour than document the journey.

'So, tell me, what's wrong?' I asked Freya, once we'd found a rock to sit on whilst Ben followed Clether towards the sea.

'Oh nothing, I'm just tired.'

'Come on, you can't fool me,' I reminded her, eager to find out and put an end to whatever was troubling her.

'Oh, just something Beth said got me thinking.'

'What was that?'

'Dad getting married,' she explained. 'It just seems odd to think he's got another family. I just have to get used to the idea, that's all.'

'How about you come back with us, let us make you something to eat, and you can have a nice long soak in the bath,' I offered, aware of her fragility, when normally she's able to take everything in her stride.

'It does sound tempting, but we had a night off last night. I'll be fine, it's just messing with my head a bit. What was it you used to say? "Count your blessings".'

'And you've got plenty!' I reminded her, making a mental note to talk to Adam.

'I know, I just have to remind myself sometimes.'

Chapter 17

Outside the Box

Freya's concerns all became clear when Adam had called to announce he was going to be a father again; his joy apparent, as I imagined was my shock at hearing his news. Not long after, Beth had also called, delivering her own news, that she and Lucas were also expecting a baby, both babies due, simultaneously it seemed, next March. No wonder, Freya had been struggling! I was having a little wobble myself!
Ben had also been surprised to hear the news, though it had taken him a little while to realise I'd be a grandma! Imagining him to be considering how fortunate Adam was to be able to conceive multiple times, with two different women. And then my thoughts automatically turned to Stella's dilemma, and how Clether would react if he ever found out about her and Ruby.
Freya had still seemed a little subdued when I saw her at the stables this morning, even when I'd explained that I had heard the news.

'Beth seems happy,' I said.

'I can understand Beth having a baby, just not my dad! Both their babies will be growing up together. How mad is that!'

'Beth doesn't seem worried,' I told her, wondering if Adam and Laura had even considered the effect it would have on their other children. I hadn't really had time to absorb the news myself yet, so hadn't mentioned Freya's reaction to Adam. And we did still have another six months to get used to the idea.

'Come here,' I said, wrapping my arms around her and giving her a cuddle.

'At least I know you won't be springing any surprises on me!' Freya smiled.

'Life's full of surprises!' I told her.

As each day passed, the more zest, it seemed, I acquired for life. Ben and I establishing our own little routine as the days bumbled along. Inevitably, the days were becoming cooler, especially as evening drew to a close. Not that I minded our cosy nights in together. It also meant we could talk freely, without worrying who else might be in their garden or out and about, and able to caves drop on our conversations. Ben, often reluctant to share any interesting snippets he'd acquired whilst out and about, always promising to share them with me later. Only, when 'later' arrived, the day's events faded into insignificance and his whispers more intimate.

Tonight though, he began airing his frustration, unable to comprehend some people's behaviour, continuing to explain about a couple he had just met - surprisingly for the first time, as they had now viewed, a staggering fifteen properties. All of which, including today's offering, were unsuitable! Continuing to explain how they just couldn't see past the decor and realise the potential on offer.

'Surely, they'd seen the photographs before arranging to view the property?' I said, whilst considering Ben's aptitude in that department.

'No, it's only just gone on the market,' Ben explained. 'I don't think it'll be on long though.'

'Maybe they'd be more suited to a new house?' I suggested. 'A blank canvas.'

'I don't doubt you're right, but they come at a premium. Sometimes you've just got to think outside the box.'

'So, is that what you told them?'

'Something along those lines. Though, like I said, someone else will soon see the potential, the location alone will sell it. We had someone else today, viewing a property for the fourth time,'

'Really?' I questioned. 'That's thorough.'

'Oh, they're definitely that. We'd always recommend a second viewing; you're always going to miss things the first time round. But at this rate they're going to be on their Christmas card list! Speaking of which, the couple next door have invited us over for a drink at the weekend.'

'What's the occasion?'

'I guess they're just being neighbourly.'

'So, is it just us?'

'They didn't say. We'll just have to wait and find out.'

'Maybe they're just missing our little rendezvous outside in an evening,' I considered. Though, I'd never heard them!

I continued to fill Ben in on my day and my conversation with Beth, who now seemed more enamoured with the new owners of our old house, who had recently gone up in her estimation, having reportedly purchased a new vehicle to adorn the driveway, observing the lady of the house retrieving a Waitrose bag from the boot of the car! Not only that, but she'd also managed to deduce that their son appeared to attend the highly regarded public school in the neighbouring town, having seen him arrive home in his school blazer. All of which seemed to help compensate for what she still held dear, or at least help her in what appeared to be a difficult period of adjustment.

'Correct me if I'm wrong, but it's beginning to sound a bit like stalking!' Ben said.

'Not really, she has to drive past there every time she leaves the village,' I corrected him, remembering what Adam had said when I'd told him I was leaving. Considering she'd soon have more important things to occupy her.

Our conversation dwindled as the evening wore on, the need for anything to be said, becoming pillow talk. We were after all, enjoying our honeymoon period!

A new day dawned, and for a while, all was well with the world, Ben reminding me just how much I was loved before leaving for work. I continued in my own endeavour to create a little romance in the lives of my customers and their friends and families, imagining the joy at receiving an invitation to share in such a special occasion. Then I was reminded of Beth, and how upset I'd been to hear her say that she was going shopping with Laura at the weekend for some maternity clothes and that she was feeling more tired than usual, but that Laura had said it was perfectly natural and nothing to worry about. Wasn't that supposed to be my role as her mother? Imagining they'd be going shopping for baby clothes and prams next. I couldn't even begin to work out what relationship they'll all be to each other. No wonder Freya was distracted!

I decided to avoid the subject and enjoy the sunshine on offer and relax with a glass of white wine whilst Stella filled me in on Leo's recent escapades and her pride in her own daughter, realising her own situation to be not too dissimilar, although she had no other children of her own to consider, and as yet, everyone else seemed oblivious. As ever, she was keen to hear all about Freya and Clether, and their progress on the barn, almost with as much enthusiasm as Ben!

After lunch I couldn't help wandering by to say hello to Ben, but not before stopping to peruse the ever changing and attractive display of photographs in the window. Not that I could be tempted. It might still be early days, but it seemed Ben had been right to persuade me to move in, as I couldn't be happier. Whilst Ben was on a call, I chatted to Emma, who it seemed was yet another bride to be, in need of some inspiration for wedding stationary, answering her plea and promising to send some samples in with Ben tomorrow.

Ben decided now would be the ideal time to grab some lunch, having satisfied a customer's request to view a property in the town, suggesting we take a walk along the headland – just once he'd nipped inside the café for a crab sandwich to satisfy his hunger. Making a mental note to pack him some lunch in future. I really loved this time of year, when the weather was still warm and the majority of tourists having packed up and gone home to more familiar territory, leaving the beaches relatively quiet and undisturbed, apart from natures intervention. Even the streets and harbour were quieter, compared to only a few weeks ago, when I wouldn't have even contemplated eating out at lunch time. This is what I had missed, not that I could ever have imagined sharing it all with Ben.

After leaving Ben, I allowed my mind to wander, and instead of returning to my desk, I changed into my jodhpurs and riding boots, craving a little more freedom before returning to work. There were definitely advantages to working from home, especially when I was responsible for managing my own time. And now my workspace was up and functioning, it was all made that little bit easier. Ben had advised me that he might be a little late this evening, his last appointment for a viewing having to be at five O'clock. So, with that in mind, and the fact he was having to work Saturday, I felt I could justify a couple more hours of unadulterated relaxation time. For me, that meant saddling up and being out amongst nature. After all, all work and no play, can lead to a very dull life!

As ever, all the fresh air and exercise had left me rejuvenated, ready to embrace the rest of the day, regardless of what it threw at me, wondering if my happiness would be portrayed in the batch of order of service booklets I was assembling. Though judging by the hymns and music selected, I doubt there'll be a dry eye on the day. Before I forgot, I gathered a few of my favourite pieces of stationary to send to Emma as requested, already guessing which design she'd favour, having listened to her explain her ideas and theme for her wedding. I attached a little message of love and a little wooden heart before tying the bundle together with string, slipping it inside a beautifully labelled box, as if ready to send in the post.

Then, as I was returning to my desk, an email popped up from one of my brides, asking for a change of date, having managed to rearrange everything else so that it didn't clash with the birth of their daughter, who when all of this had been planned, had been nothing more than a twinkle in their eye. I quickly replied, offering first my congratulations, followed by my assurance that I could recreate something suitable to inform their guests as to their change of plan, now happening two months later, having secured a cancellation. Which at this late stage is always unfortunate, but I suppose inevitable.

Freya it seemed, was also beginning to have doubts about the month they'd chosen for their wedding, now still over a year away and summer already drawing to a close; especially after all the progress they had recently made on the barn. Not that I didn't admire their optimism, but even I could see they had a long way to go yet, and they still had the winter to contend with. Of course, the normal considerations a bride might have, were all a long way off as far as Freya was concerned, the positioning of the soil pipes being paramount before she could even begin to contemplate celebrating her love for Clether, let alone the order of service or what she might wear! Having learnt from experience, I encouraged my brides to be, to send their guests a 'save the date' card as soon as they'd set the date, that way avoiding disappointment. Even then there were always going to be some, who for whatever reason, couldn't attend.

Fortunately, having all the materials I needed, I quickly made a start on recreating the change of date, incorporating the initial essence and design features, just rewording the original text, the majority of which remained the same. Deciding I would finish the rest in the morning, realising there was nothing I could actually do to get them to her any quicker. I didn't have a set finish time as such, but I had already worked later than I would normally, having been out most the day and with Ben working late. Ben may have had a late lunch, but I was beginning to feel a bit peckish, and Ben would surely be expecting a meal on his return. So, I shut the door for today and headed downstairs to apply a little bit of science to a few ingredients. My mind already returning to Beth and Laura, still unable to fully comprehend the implications of them both having babies at the same time. And upset she seemed to be sharing what I imagined to be a special time between mother and daughter, with my ex-husband's fiancée! I realised I was at a disadvantage, being so far away now, but I had hoped she would have consulted me when it came to advice, rather than Laura being her first port of call. Imagining Laura and Adam to be the first to know when her baby is born.

'Well, that was a complete waste of time!' Ben announced, as he walked in.

'Never mind,' I commiserated. 'It's perfect timing as far as I'm concerned,' I told him, opening the oven door.

'So, what was wrong this time?' I asked.

'Oh, it was a beautiful mid-terraced property, only both sides were obviously home by the sounds of things!'

'Oh dear!' I said, returning his kiss. Continuing to fill him in on what I'd achieved since our little catch up earlier and sharing my concerns about Freya's change of heart and Beth's apparent bond with Laura.

'Laura's more of a friend,' Ben explained. 'It could be anyone; it just happens to be her father's partner. I bet she'd tell you exactly the same. It's better they get along than the other way.'

'I just miss her.'

'Well, we can easily remedy that,' Ben said, offering a simple but obvious solution. Ben had always been a logical person; I think that had been part of the attraction. Believing his calm, rational approach to solving problems, complimented my somewhat irrational nature. Apart from, having failed to consider an alternative explanation to what had led to our first demise. Though, I suppose it's always easier when the problem isn't one close to your own heart. After we'd put the world to rights, we took ourselves to bed, our own safe haven at the end of each day.

Chapter 18

To the Moon and Stars and Back Down to the Sea

Today was Saturday, and despite work beckoning, we lingered in bed a little longer, as customary to a long-held tradition of mine I was in favour of maintaining. Obviously one that Ben had learnt to respect and was keen to adopt, whilst reserving the right to adapt the rules.

'Don't forget we're off out next door this evening,' Ben reminded me, picking up his lunch box and the samples for Emma.

'I shan't,' I replied, before another long lingering kiss - exactly what I needed to kick start my day.

I quickly set about addressing any enquiries, including another from a couple who seemed completely out of their depth when planning their wedding, having asked for my advice on anything and everything regarding what might or might not be appropriate when wording correspondence. Today they wanted my opinion on how long to wait before chasing up the remaining guests who had failed to reply. Honestly, I'll be glad when these two have finally tied the knot!

Unperturbed, I continued with my task of finishing the change of dates I'd started yesterday, only to be disturbed by the letterbox shutting - one of the many things I am unable to ignore, even when it means going downstairs. Obviously, I am often disappointed in my quest, but today I was rewarded for my perseverance in the shape of one of my own creations, adorned with a photograph of a recently betrothed couple celebrating their wedding day, thanking me for my contribution. It's days like this that make me stop and appreciate the extent of what I've actually achieved and the part I play in creating such a special day, that will last in the hearts of many for years to come, and for the lucky ones a lifetime.

Once I'd finished the alterations to update sixty-eight guests to the unforeseen predicament one couple had found themselves in, I turned my attention to this evening, leaving them to dry before parcelling them up to send on Monday morning. I was still unsure as to what to wear tonight, especially as I'd never met John and Esther before. Reminded of my old neighbours, Jenny and Joe, who'd lived beside us through life's trials and tribulations and managed to ride their mid-life crisis, to survive the storm and age graciously together. Unable to ever imagine them apart. Though, I suppose that's what they had perhaps once said about Adam and me. But life has a way of changing us all, for better or worse. Reminded for a moment of my grandmother, who'd have said it was meant to be, or even written in the stars, whereas I preferred to believe we were masters of our own destiny, choosing to decide our own fate. And, although Ben and I met up when we did, it was surely inevitable that our paths would have crossed before too long and that the initial attraction we'd once felt would always resurface. It was more a question of the right moment in life for us to be together and rekindle our love. Though, I had always been more of a dreamer, believing life can be just as romantic as stories.

I eventually decided on my trusted jeans and heels, opting for a pretty, if rather conservative top to wear for the after-dinner soiree, realising how little I actually knew about either of them, having only seen them from the confines of the car. But I supposed more would be revealed this evening.

Ben arrived home as happy as he'd left the house this morning, having finally agreed a sale on the house I'd first looked at; the couple seemingly unconcerned about what went on over the garden wall. He was also full of compliments, expressing Emma's delight in my beautiful creations.

As ever, Ben was ravenous. Despite which, I suggested we omit the dessert course, unsure of what might be on the menu later - our hosts, not having specified exactly what sort of liquid refreshment was on offer.

'I hope it involves alcohol,' I said, as I followed Ben out of the house, not forgetting to pick up the chocolates I'd bought as a gift.

'I imagine it will,' he replied, just as John opened the door.

We were led through the hall into a similar sized living area to Ben's, although the furnishings and decor were rather more traditional than contemporary. Perhaps, not having been updated since their arrival. Then, I spotted photographs, of who I assumed to be their children, depicted through the decades. Imagining for a moment, being in Ben's shoes, trying to estimate a value on something we hold so dear. Wondering if he was already realising its worth. Not that I imagined he'll be replicating their choices.

Esther introduced herself, expressing her pleasure in meeting me, before John offered us something "warm and full bodied"! Assuming he meant wine, I accepted.

Sitting down on the rather sumptuous sofa, the reason for our presence soon became apparent, as Esther began her interrogation, still under the impression I worked at the stables, assuming Ben having perhaps mentioned this to her previously. Accepting my rather large glass of red wine from John, I corrected Esther on my change of profession, explaining the benefits of working from home. Something, it appeared, she had never considered. Whilst realising that not every profession could afford this luxury. However, I'd yet to discover what either of them, actually did.

'Oh, I nearly forgot,' Esther exclaimed, excusing herself and disappearing, shortly returning with a selection of savoury hors d'oeuvres. If I'm honest, I think I'd have preferred one of the chocolates I'd brought. Of course, Ben was happy to accept anything on offer!

No sooner had we finished the first bottle of wine, than another was being presented.

'A rather more, complex Cabernet', John explained, sticking his nose in his glass after swirling it around.

Not my favoured tipple in an evening; not that I was complaining! Wondering, if perhaps they'd just signed up for some wine club.

'You certainly seem to know your wines,' I commented, after taking a sip, whilst Ben cast me a frown.

'Did I not mention?' Ben said, 'John's a sommelier.'

'Well, that explains it!' I replied, taking another large sip.

'So, what is it you do?' I asked Esther, so as not to make any further blunders.

'I'm a dance teacher,' she informed us. I say, us, but expect Ben already knew. I really must do my homework in future. Hoping I hadn't brought an inferior wine to the table! Assuming Esther had meant a ballet teacher, I prattled on about the coincidence. Until she enlightened me, explaining she knew nothing at all about ballet, having only ever taught ballroom. Something else that was a complete mystery to me.

John continued to update me on how their relationship had begun aboard a ship thirty years ago; himself a sommelier in the Queens Grill restaurant and Esther performing in cabaret shows in an evening and teaching lessons during the day, their time together limited, until they left for pastures green. Even then, it appeared they were like ships that crossed in the night, the very nature of their professions dictating their time together. Only now, were they beginning to realise their dream and not have to coordinate their work schedules to fit in with family life.

After we'd exhausted every country they'd visited whilst at sea and as much local history and gossip they'd managed to accumulate, we expressed our gratitude for their hospitality and wandered the short distance home, careful not to disturb the other neighbours.

'Well, that was fun!' I said, as we closed the door.

'I'm glad you enjoyed it; I thought you may have felt a little awkward.'

'Whatever gave you that idea?' I said, a little sarcastically.

'Well, you know as much as I do now,' Ben said, wrapping his arms around me. 'How about we have an early night?' he suggested.

'Or I could always tell you what I already know about the Williams Family across the road?'

Finally, Ben had a day off and the sun was shining. So, after a leisurely breakfast we set off hand in hand towards the beach. I had always loved this time of year, appreciating the warmth and solitude as the seasons changed. The honeysuckle that straddled the hedgerows was still fragrant as we made our descent along the rugged path, stopping occasionally to gorge on the ripe, plump blackberries, glistening in the sun. We stopped as we turned the corner, just as we always did to appreciate the view below and the sun glinting on the gentle waves. Reminded of why I'd made the decision to return and call here home, and how lucky I was to have Ben to share it all with.

Most people associate the beach with the sun, and as much as I love to feel its warmth, the most magical time for me is after sunset, when I feel in complete harmony with nature. I've always loved the moon, even as a child I'd leave my bedroom curtains open, believing its energy would seep into my skin and recharge me whilst I slept. I've even been known to talk to the moon!

Though today, the sun seemed to be working its magic on Ben, who couldn't wait to kick of his shoes and run towards the sea. Lifting me up, I wrapped my legs around his waist, kissing him as the waves gently lapped around his legs as he carried me into the sea.

Back on dry land we lay together, all these years later, immersed in a love so strong. Perhaps my grandmother had been right after all and fate had finally intervened, and just like the different phases of the moon, our own two worlds had finally collided and become one.

Chapter 19

The Wonder of Love

After much deliberation, Freya had decided to bring their wedding date forward, confident that they would deliver on the work required to make the barn habitable by then. Deciding to marry in August, under the lush green trees, rather than the falling leaves in autumn. At least this way, they'd stand a better chance of being warm, even if the sun failed to shine; an important consideration, I suppose, when getting married outside. And she did want to continue the celebrations outside as much as possible. So, the race was now on to make the barn completely watertight so they could then begin the work inside, especially now that the nights were drawing in. Although, there was still no electric, but doubt that would stop them!

Thinking her wedding was to have been in autumn, I'd formulated a few ideas to depict the season in all its glory, reminded of the beautiful array of colours she'd imagined I could portray that she might also have chosen to use in her bouquet and hair. Realising just how colourful the season actually is and why it had resonated with Freya. I would just have to reinvent my plan somehow and try and incorporate as much as possible to evoke a summers day.

Today though, my task was to supply a suitable verse to include with a batch of invitations, informing the guests of the couple's request for a donation of money rather than a material gift, having already accumulated everything they needed to furnish their home, having lived together for the last few years. Fortunately, it wasn't the first request I'd had of this nature and had already formulated a few polite ways of asking for money without seeming rude. Remembering my own extensive list of wedding gifts that had circulated family and friends, crossing things off to literally furnish each room and kitchen cupboard in the house. Whilst very grateful and having tried to explain our colour scheme and preferences, it had still ultimately been their choice as to what we ate from or slept under! Personally, I thought the best solution was a store list, that way the guest doesn't have the dilemma as to what is acceptable, and you can relax in the sun without feeling guilty. Hopefully, Freya's home will be nearing completion by the time she sends out her invitations, or she might well consider setting up an online account at the local builders' merchants!

As ever, it wasn't long before my creative juices were flowing, my mind awash with ideas to incorporate into Freya's wedding stationary. Amazed at the rainbow of colours often overlooked beneath the canopy of trees in summer. Not only pretty petals, but vibrant berries, delicate butterflies and sweet-smelling herbs; not forgetting the birds and the bees. All I had to do now was to transfer my thoughts onto paper before submitting them to Freya. Perhaps I could even use my embroidery skills; it would mean a lot of work, but they had to be special. And maybe when Freya could actually see a template, she might be inspired to explore more ideas.

Beth had accepted Freya's change of plan, realising she would still have time to get her figure back after giving birth, but had expressed her concern about any dress fittings now that she was changing shape, frustrated with her sister's lack of enthusiasm for such a special occasion. Finding myself reminding her, that this was her sister she was talking about, and that she was never going to get too excited about dresses. As a child Freya had been far more at home in a pair of dungarees and sneakers, running wild outside, often exploring in the stream at the bottom of the garden or making dens. Whereas Beth had been happiest dressing up or shopping for new outfits. Freya had always been the more practical, even then helping her father build a tree house in the sprawling old oak tree at the bottom of the garden. Beth unimpressed, preferring a teddy bears picnic on a blanket on the lawn, to the dizzy heights of some old, gnarled tree. Making a mental note to remind Freya of this, wondering perhaps if that early experience had inspired her to create her own home. Although Adam had always been quite practical, I remained confident he would never attempt to build his own house, preferring the luxuries of a modern detached in suburbia alongside other likeminded people, to the quiet wilderness his daughter had chosen, imagining his garden to be relatively small and manageable. His lawn, neatly mown and tended and a garden shed, full of tools and potions to curtail any unruly behaviour. When Beth and Freya had been growing up, the lawn was more a meadow, often bejewelled with dandelions, buttercups and daises as nature intended. Freya would often thread daisy chains to adorn her hair or pick them to place in a tiny egg cup on her bedroom windowsill. Then as she grew, she would lie amongst them, watching the clouds drift by whilst revising for her exams. Beth on the other hand had found the outside to have too many distractions for her to study and preferred the relative quiet of her bedroom. Both, I have to say, achieving their expected grades.

Ben's own artistic flair had also continued into the garden, which blended seamlessly into the surrounding countryside that bordered the perimeter. All evidence of Clether and his siblings having once used it as a playground, eradicated. It was now a place to relax and nourish the soul, without being too demanding. Somewhere, I imagined Ben having spent many an hour contemplating life's irregularities, whilst reaffirmed of its beauty, in the solitude of his own safe haven. Not that he tended to dwell on things, but it's always nice to have somewhere that gives you peace of mind and comfort. Thinking about it, I quite missed our chilled evenings outdoors, although I did enjoy the intimacy that our four walls have to offer.

The house itself now felt more like home, especially now the remaining cardboard boxes had been relegated to the garage and I didn't have to encounter them every time I entered a room. It seemed odd to think of all the things I'd accumulated, that now seem irrelevant, as though they belonged to a different chapter of my life. I suppose, like when I'd married and moved out of my family home, I'd left the posters on my bedroom wall, the books I'd read on the bookcase and my old school uniform hung in the wardrobe. I was now starting a new life with someone else, making new memories together. Not that I'll ever forget the memories I'd already made, it's what made me who I am. I suppose that's why Clether, who according to Freya, seemed all the more focused on completing their home to start married life together and hopefully one day, start a family of their own. In doing so, able to begin a new chapter, and hopefully eradicate some of the painful memories. Again, I'm reminded of Ben for a moment, the dreams he and his wife must have had when they'd started married life together and how our expectations don't always materialise, changing the way we feel and altering our lives forever.

Then, I'm reminded of Stella, who'd eventually found the courage to sit down and talk to her daughter, having told me of how it had taken every bit of strength she could summon to begin explaining about Rob. Of course, Ruby being the innocent one in all of this, having never known or loved him. But she did love her mother, so for now, had accepted what Stella had been able to divulge. Whilst I'm left wondering how Clether will respond when the truth eventually comes out.

Once I'd sent a couple of options for Melissa to consider, regarding her request for money as opposed to any other wedding gift, I began concentrating on a very traditional order of service to be conducted on the anniversary of the day the couple in question first met, four years ago. Once I'd finished these I could address the seating plan, making it at least look attractive, even if your back was to be to the bride and you'd been relegated to table four with great aunt Celia who you'd never actually met and not Uncle Dick who appeared to have got a ringside seat! Reminded of the strict protocol that often was expected to be adhered to, whilst trying not to upset anyone. If my memory served me correctly, it appeared everyone had accepted their invitations, quite an achievement when planning something of this scale; though I suppose it is always going to be easier gathering everyone together once summer is over and before all the Christmas merriment begins. Especially, when the initial date was released a year in advance! As much as I'm a firm advocate of planning ahead, a lot can actually happen in a year. Only recently having had to change a table plan to substitute one partner and sit someone else in the grooms recently departed Grandmother's place. Wondering what might happen if a guest was to have a baby, especially if children weren't invited! Imagining for a moment Beth, cradling her own baby at Freya's wedding, until I realised that Laura would also be there with Adam's baby! Something I hadn't actually considered, until now, realising the inevitable consequences. At least I'd have Ben by my side. Then I'm reminded again of Ruby and her situation and whether she would ever be considered family amongst Clether and his siblings. Understanding Stella's predicament, something she could never have envisaged when she fell in love. Unable to imagine how I would feel in any of their shoes or react to such news. It will undoubtably come as a great shock after all these years to learn the truth. I can understand Ruby's need to satisfy her curiosity, but wonder if she was still perhaps too young to understand the heartache she could inevitably cause, when armed with this information. But my heart goes out to Stella, who has undoubtably suffered the most in all of this.

My mind was still wandering when Ben arrived home; I have always been a notorious day dreamer, my thoughts often distracted, a lot of my inspiration gleamed from the solitude my lifestyle offers, often losing all track of time, in a little world of my own. Ben reminding me of this when he ran upstairs to greet me, admiring the work I had managed to achieve, suggesting I finish off what I was doing whilst he started preparing the ingredients for dinner.

'My mum has invited us round for tea on Sunday,' Ben told me, as we sat down to eat, after he'd informed me about a house he'd gone to value this afternoon that had its very own bar at the bottom of the garden, unsure if it would prove to be a selling feature – though I suppose it had to be better than the other side of the garden wall!

I had never actually met Ben's parents; I knew who they were, though probably wouldn't recognise them now. When Ben and I had previously been dating we had never actually got to that stage, preferring to take advantage of the house whilst they were out, making the most of the limited time we had alone together, rather than being scrutinised as to our suitability. We had wanted to enjoy the process of getting to know each other ourselves first, before asking for their blessing. I can however still remember meeting Adam's parents, thinking I was impressing his father with my knowledge of horses, until I realised, he was far more interested in the probability stakes associated with such a barbaric activity than the welfare of the animal.

My mother had been the first to tell me about Freya's association with Clether, describing him as "dishevelled, in an attractive sort of way"! Comparing him to a younger Mick Hucknell, though I still can't see the resemblance myself, but was nevertheless reminded of, each time I saw him. Wondering if he'd inherited his looks from his father and if that's what had attracted Stella.

Lucas had been the perfect gentleman when Beth had first brought him home to meet Adam and myself, bringing me flowers and complimenting Adam on his new car parked on the driveway. They had both been seventeen at the time and studying together at college, sharing the same aspirations in life as each other, confident this would sustain them through married life. I suppose, none of us can ever be really sure, especially at such a young age.

Chapter 20

A New Light

Freya had been delighted to inform me that progress had finally been made on the barn roof, with the slates being laid as we spoke; even the windows were arriving tomorrow, giving them the protection they so desperately needed to make progress inside. Clether, had eventually lost his battle to adorn the barn in reeds, a material his father had so loved to work with, having to accept what the planning committee had deemed suitable for such a building. If I'm perfectly honest, I would tend to agree; despite the fact it had probably stored something similar in a previous life.

The clocks had changed, along with the weather and nature had begun its ever unwelcome transition towards winter; as ever, it meant less time to enjoy outdoors and more time behind a desk. Though, with every cloud, a silver lining always seems to follow, particularly as the weather was consistently inclement; Freya and Clether often accepting the comfort and warmth on offer, not to mention a hot meal prepared at the end of a very arduous day. Not that they could ever be accused of not putting the hours in; their recent progress was testimony to that. But tonight was to be a special occasion, to celebrate Freya's birthday, something I had missed being able to share with her in recent years. Freya had been more than happy to accept our invitation to dinner in the comfort of our home, as it seemed Clether had; though I imagine he would agree to anything to please his sweetheart on her birthday.

I had got up early, sneaking out of bed before Ben woke, making a start on work so that I could spend some time with Freya at the stables and still have enough time to bake a cake and prepare dinner. Fortunately, Ben always set his alarm to wake him, as I had completely lost all track of time, lost in someone else's romantic fairy tale. It was only when I smelt coffee wafting up the stairs that I realised the time.

Once Ben had left with a packed lunch, that would hopefully sustain him through until this evening, I set off towards the stables to see Freya. It still felt strangely odd celebrating her birthday without Adam, recalling the morning of Freya's birth and our hurried journey together to the hospital after having had to leave Beth with a friend. Something he would soon have to experience all over again.

I almost envied Freya, especially on such a glorious morning, just the smell of the stables was enough to evoke memories of the life I'd left behind and one in which I was definitely a lot fitter. Though, riding certainly helped curb the pounds I accumulated sat at a desk in the comfort of a warm home.

Once home and revitalised, I began preparing a cake for this evening; something else I had been unable to do for Freya over the last few years. However, I hadn't forgotten her favourite recipe and had remembered to get the cherries out of the freezer to sandwich it together later with a large dollop of Chantilly cream.

Despite not having to get dressed up to go out, Freya had arrived ahead of Clether after finishing at the stables, allowing herself time to have a bath and change, appreciating the rare opportunity she did have to pamper herself - after all it was her special day.

'The kettle's just boiled,' I said, as Freya found me in the kitchen, preparing the vegetables.

'You read my mind! But where's he keep the tea?'

'Oh, here,' I said, opening the cupboard door above the kettle. 'He insists on keeping it behind closed doors!'

'Why?'

'I don't ask, I just leave things how I find them.'

'It seems a bit fastidious for a man, don't you think?' Freya commented. 'I'm only saying,' she finished, catching my expression.

'It's probably attributed to his profession,' I explained, trying to defend the man I'd fallen in love with, despite the odd peculiarities he displayed.

'So, what other idiosyncrasies does he have?'

'You don't get any less cheeky with age, do you!'

'That reminds me, I got a card and some money from Gran. She said to treat myself and not to spend it on building materials!'

'So, how did Ben being tidy, remind you of Gran?' I asked, unable to comprehend Freya's thought process.

'No, it was just what you said.' she recalled. 'Don't you remember; she would always ask how it felt to be another year older?'

'Now you come to mention it. So, how does it feel?'

'Don't they say we all turn into our mothers? You'll have me quoting you next!'

'Perhaps one day,' I considered. 'Only time will tell.' realising it's often only when we become mothers ourselves that we remember the advice our own mothers bestowed upon us.

'So, what are you going to treat yourself to?' I asked, just as Ben arrived home.

'Happy birthday Freya,' he greeted, with a kiss on the cheek for the birthday girl.

'You did tell Clether dinner would be ready at six thirty?' I asked Freya, putting the vegetables in the oven to roast.

'He'll be here!' she said, ever the optimist! Reminding me of the same words my mother had uttered on my wedding day, thirty-three years ago to the day; often overshadowed whilst Freya had been growing up, but never forgotten, as I imagine Ben must remember his own; some things you can never just simply forget.

'What did I just say?' she announced, as the door chimed, allowing Ben and I a brief interlude to reacquaint. Dinner had been another resounding success, as always. Though how Freya could eat so quickly still astounded me!

'You're getting soft in your old age!' Clether had teased. When to my surprise, Freya had accepted our invitation to stay.

'We're already here, that's all. Are you sure you don't mind?'

'Not at all,' Ben assured her. 'Another drink anyone?'

'I think we'll retire,' Freya announced, yawning. 'We're usually tucked up and fast asleep by now.'
Ben and I, both astounded by her revelation, though it would account for their boundless energy!

'We could always follow in their footsteps?' Ben concluded, as we finished tidying the kitchen after they had climbed the wooden hill.

Chapter 21

A Christmas Carol

The days grew greyer and less green, even the leaves that lay fallen were now soggy rather than crispy underfoot; but the hedgerows still sparkled with brightly coloured rosehips and fragrant gorse. There were even tiny clusters of blackberries that the frost would surely nip if the birds didn't find them first, though even they seemed to have flown to warmer climates, only the hungry robins daring to brave the cold, unafraid to show their faces.

Freya and Clether were also becoming more frequent visitors through our door, surrendering to the long cold nights when a welcome meal and warm bed beckoned less than a mile away.

Fortunately, I had Ben to brighten my days, loving nothing better than to feel his warm embrace at the end of each day as we shut the curtains on the world outside.

Tonight, it was just the two of us and the delights of the property world and the mysteries of the local inhabitants of the village in which we dwelled; after all, I had a lot of catching up to do!

'I hear old Mr Bartholomew has died,' I informed Ben of what I had learnt. 'I imagine his funeral will be well attended, given he was such an esteemed figure in the local community.'

'Who told you that?'

'Esther, next door. Why, hasn't he?' I asked, surprised.

'Rumour had it Mrs Applemore had died not so long ago, turned out she hadn't! It was only when a neighbour went to offer her sympathy to her husband, that she was informed to the contrary! It appeared someone had misunderstood what they'd heard!'

'That's dreadful!'

'But if you're right, it means his property will be destined for the market. It's been in the same family for a long time.'

'So, what's its history?' I asked, only aware of him having ever lived there.

'You remember Harold, don't you?' Ben asked.

'Now you come to mention it. Though he was older than us, wasn't he?'

'Yes, but an only child, as Roger, his father was. He inherited the whole estate when his parents died. I believe he was already well off. Or so the story goes! I expect it'll fetch upwards of a million, though I wouldn't like to be the one to estimate its value. It's not as though it's your average dwelling.'

'No, but very desirable.'

'In your dreams!'

'I'd love to take a look inside.'

'Did you ever sneak behind the outbuildings as a child, and go scrumping?'

'I can remember a little more recently than that!' I admitted, blushing.

After an early morning ride and another productive morning's work, I'd accepted Stella's invitation to lunch. It had been as much an impulsive decision as it had impromptu invitation, leaving me wondering as to her summons. But I was never going to turn away a free lunch or a friend in need. Driving towards Stella's house already brought back happy memories of returning from Ben's house after spending the night there, even Leo was there to greet me, before Stella opened the door with her open arms to embrace me.

It transpired that Stella had started to unfold more to Ruby about her father and therefore felt compelled to enlighten me, especially given my connection to Clether. Ruby, had apparently taken the news remarkably well, imagining it to come as more of a shock to Clether and his siblings - if and when they were to ever find out, which of course was the dilemma Stella was now facing, given her daughter's curiosity. Of course, all this would have an impact on Freya, but at least she was now prepared. I don't suppose any of us really know how we'd react to hearing such news; it wasn't that long ago that Freya struggled to accept her own father's news. But, I think even she might struggle fifteen years later! Only time would tell.

Work inevitably became quiet this time of year, Christmas taking precedence, as it appeared, the same could be said for the housing market. So, for a change I began the morning with what I deemed the daunting, yet necessary task of writing Christmas cards and explaining my change of address; introducing Ben, could be explained at a later date, or I'd be here until next Christmas! Writing cards always took far longer than first anticipated, feeling compelled to send more than the obligatory love and festive greetings, especially as it may have been a whole year since I last wrote to the recipients, and in most cases I always received more than a few words back. On principle, I was never the first to write Christmas cards, not because I was someone who wouldn't send one unless I had first received one, but because I found it rather odd to be celebrating Christmas too early; even the kings didn't show up until twelve days later! Something I am quick to remind myself, when having forgotten someone's birthday. What I found even more absurd, was receiving greetings for the new year whist we still had several weeks left of the old – as though the remaining weeks were somehow irrelevant. As ever, my cards depicted the origin of the celebration, rather than Christmas jumpers or penguins or an overweight Santa Claus trying to squeeze down a chimney, or what I found truly bizarre, was a photo blazoned across the front of the card of the people having sent the card, celebrating their own child's arrival into the world!

After lunch and a quick catch up on emails, I decided to head out into the sunshine and post the cards and attempt to find something suitable to wear for Ben's Christmas office party. It had been quite some time since I had been invited to such an event, or come to think of it, any party, so had nothing remotely appropriate I could fall back on. Although working from home, as I do, can be advantageous and hugely rewarding, it does lack a certain amount of social interaction, and the only wardrobe requirement is comfort over style, and a toasty pair of slippers. Though these days, I consciously made more of an effort; Ben need never know I'd worked in my pyjamas up until lunchtime!

Of course, I was unfamiliar with the current independent shops; the majority having changed since I'd last lived here or were completely out of my price range or suitability. Though judging by the window displays, some things never changed, apart from perhaps our modesty!

Unable to resist a bit of glamour, I opted for a sleek black dress, bejewelled with just the right amount of sparkle to justify sophistication, yet allowed for an element of fun. After all, it was to be an evening of merriment, and I wanted to give the right impression to everyone – including Ben!

Whilst out shopping I'd been unable to resist buying Ben the obligatory bodywash to make him smell divine. Then after straying into another shop, and despite having enough homeware to furnish a hotel, I had been unable to resist a wool throw, something I knew Ben would appreciate strewn over his sofa and to warm his cold toes in an evening. Then, having recently discovered several old school photos, I had been unable to resist buying a frame for our very first, class photo I'd managed to find and so it could be displayed on a wall, the very beginning of our story together. Freya would be proud of me beginning to furnish our home. The only problem being they were new additions! Apart from the photo, which had been hiding away in a box for nearly fifty years!

With the sun now low in the sky I headed home to hide my purchase, which I didn't intend to reveal until the night in question, hoping of course for the desired reaction.

I had remained quiet about Stella's revelation, realising it would all probably come out in the future in its own good time and probably when least expected.

Freya, had been quite excited about Clether's sister's arrival at Church Cottage; I suppose the more the merrier, especially at this time of year. And I suppose she must miss having her own sister for company. So, it was no surprise that she was on her way to see her before visiting me this morning.

'See that girl over there,' Stephanie pointed to Freya, from her kitchen window.

'That looks like Ruby,' Freya explained. 'she's just started working at the stables.'

'But why is she leaving flowers on my father's grave?'

'Oh, I don't know!'

'She was there the other day as well.'

'I suppose there's only one way to find out.'

'You stay here, I'll go and have a word with her,' Stephanie said.

'Can I ask how you knew my father?' Stephanie began, approaching Ruby.

'Your father?' Ruby replied.

'Yes, this is my father's grave.'

'Well, that must mean you're my sister.'

'I think you must be mistaken; you see I'm his only daughter; I don't have any sisters.'

'Let me introduce myself, I'm Ruby.'

'How about we go back to mine,' Stephanie suggested, unable to comprehend the confusion, whilst trying to remain sensitive at the same time. 'I'll make us a nice cup of tea, I only live just here,' she indicated towards the cottage.

Ruby followed Stephanie inside, only to find Freya waiting.

'Sit down, I'll just stick the kettle on,' Stephanie said.

'Are you all right Ruby?' Freya asked, unaware of what was exactly going on.

'I think she's just had a bit of a shock,' Stephanie started to explain.

'No, I haven't. My mother has already explained who my father was and that he died before I was born,' Ruby explained calmly.

Stephanie sat down, trying to comprehend the situation whilst Freya quickly attended to the tea.

'So, who is your mother?' Stephanie asked Ruby.

'Her name's Stella Harper, she teaches ballet.'

Stephanie remained quiet whilst her thoughts caught up with her, considering the possibility of what she'd just heard.

'Freya, can you pour me a glass of brandy please, there's a bottle I've just used for the Christmas cake over by the kettle.'

'I'd join you,' Freya said, wondering how on earth she was going to tell Clether, or how he'd even react. 'Only I'm driving.' Whilst realising she wouldn't be going anywhere, anytime soon.

Chapter 22

The Price of Love

It hadn't taken long for the discovery to unfold; the repercussions of which, still resonating, not only in Stella's abode, but in others across the country, not to mention our own, especially after Freya had expressed her concerns over Clether, who appeared to have lost all focus on transforming the barn and instead taken to the waves, whilst Ruby appeared oblivious to all the turmoil she'd created, smitten with the new vicar's son, who also shared a passion for riding.

'If only I'd told her earlier,' Stella said, preparing to leave for her end of term performance when I'd called to see how she was.

'There'd still have been repercussions,' I explained. 'At least now it's a different generation of people, no one's going to judge you on something that happened fifteen years ago,' I tried comforting her.

'Sixteen, it's her birthday next week,' she corrected me.

'Nobody 'll care,' I told her. 'They'll be too busy admiring their young prodigies to even consider anything else and come new year they'll 've all forgotten.'

'Let's hope so, I don't know how I'll manage otherwise.'

'It'll all have blown over by the time you next have to see them,' I explained. 'So how are you going to celebrate Ruby's birthday?' I asked, trying to change the subject.

'Quietly!' Stella announced.

Meanwhile, Freya continued in her quest to comfort Clether, trying to help him accept what had occurred when he had still been a child, the same sort of age that Ruby is now, his sister, a little older; at the time, completely unaware of how their lives were about to change and the unforetold consequences of their father's actions. I suppose it's only natural that there would always be repercussions, but hope they are all better able to cope with the inevitable emotions they are currently experiencing. Perhaps, as Adam had implied when he had left, Freya and Beth were better able to cope, both having left home themselves; left wondering how differently they would have viewed the situation a few years earlier. Of course, they were all innocent in all of this, including Ruby, who was perhaps the unfortunate one, having been deprived of a father. Though, like Stella had so often said, "she could never miss what she had never had", and she had obviously never been deprived of love. In my opinion, it was Stella who had suffered the most; her dreams shattered, and her heart broken. I expect in time, they'll come to realise this for themselves. But, at the moment, they still have to come to terms with the shock. I hardly think they'll be celebrating Ruby's birthday next week!

Despite the office being quiet, Ben had volunteered to work as everyone else seemed preoccupied with last minute shopping or visiting loved ones across the country. It did however, leave me time to prepare for my parent's arrival later in the week, which I found more daunting than exciting! I suppose it's only natural to always want your parent's approval, however old you are. Hopefully, we'd also find time to get together with Ben's parents over Christmas, as despite living near to them and them being aware of our relationship, the opportunity rarely presented itself. Perhaps it might even be a good idea to invite them round whilst my parents were over. I would have to suggest it to Ben later.

Today's post arrived – a couple of red envelopes addressed to Ben, and one I recognised the handwriting of straight away and knew the contents would depict a sparkly

Christmas scene. I liked that wedding planning got put on hold at this time of year as it meant I had plenty of time to enjoy the festivities.

I'd already baked the Christmas cake, so today I planned to decorate it and hide it back in its tin until Christmas eve. I loved having a full larder of deliciousness to enjoy and share at Christmas with friends and family, and this year with Ben. Freya had not let the news about Clether's father destroy her plans to celebrate Christmas with Stephanie and her family; she had been looking forward to it since she'd found out they were moving here and nothing was going to ruin it – not even chicken pox, which Stephanie's daughter Eliza, had managed to contract. Clether of course, was preoccupied with his day job and fulfilling Christmas wishes for bespoke boards; I suppose, anything to keep him busy and stop his mind wandering was good.

The weekend had been very productive, even Ben had managed a sale on an aptly named, 'Christmas Cottage', expressing his joy at selling it prior to Christmas, explaining how a house or road name can have such a significant effect on price or desirability. Not only that, but Harold, who had stirred my curiosity had already instructed Ben to market his father's property; only weeks since his poor father had sadly passed away! Though, I suppose at least now, I could swoon over the photos online.

This morning's offering of cards that had fallen on the doormat as I was preparing to leave the house to meet Stella included more glitter, humour, a candle burning brightly, six geese a laying and a nativity scene; something I realised, often got overlooked. Quickly remembering the fresh batch of mince pies that I'd had to hide from Ben, I grabbed my keys and headed out.

Stella, whose house was beautifully decorated both inside and out to mark the festive season, could not hide her sadness at what was clearly causing her heartache, not only now it was out there in the open, but as she began to explain, having to reacquaint herself with the events of all those years ago that had led to her silence, and in my opinion, remarkable valour in adversity. Though, whatever I said, wasn't going to change her current mood, so allowed her to persuade me into accepting a glass of Shiraz - how I got back home, I would just have to consider later.

As ever, Stella's main concern, was not for herself, or Clether and his siblings, but for her daughter Ruby, who she'd protected all these years, wondering how else she could have possibly managed the situation to avoid the current predicament. Though, by all accounts, Ruby seemed the least upset by the recent revelations. According to Freya, she was obviously besotted with the horses in her care; the only distraction, her recent infatuation for Luke, who she was out with as we spoke.

Of course, once Stella began to open up, I realised her sorrow was far deeper than it first appeared and began to regret having already nearly finished my drink. However, it was helping Stella to express her feelings, something she was obviously unable to do with anyone else or had ever been able to do. It also soon became apparent, that she was perhaps only revisiting the unfortunate events herself for the first time in all these years, trying to recall how she'd felt and the plans they'd both had before the tragic accident; something, I imagine everyone else would no doubt overlook, rather than considering the whole picture. Something I can only imagine Stella has had to put to the back of her mind whilst bringing up Ruby, rather than concentrating on what might have been. Only now, allowing herself to grieve whilst having to contemplate the consequences.

'Perhaps now though, all these years later and having accepted the loss of their father, Clether and his siblings will be more sympathetic towards you,' I said.

'I don't want their sympathy.'

'I mean understanding,' I explained, trying to console her.

'I don't actually want anything from them. I know they're his children, and of course I care about them. But I don't know them. I never got to know them. I never even got to imagine a future that included them. The difficulty is, he's Ruby's father too,' Stella explained. 'Anyway, let's eat,' Stella said, retrieving our lunch from the oven, instructing me to top up our glasses.

As we ate, I began considering how I could possibly help. After all, I was somehow in the middle of all of this. No doubt I would hear Clether's side soon enough, once he'd stopped burying his head in the sand. How Freya managed to put up with him sometimes, baffled me. Although, we have all been known to accept short falls in the name of love. Accompanying the bubbling macaroni cheese was a serving of leeks, which reminded me of my own vegetable garden where I'd previously lived and how at this time of year, I'd serve leeks with anything and everything. I so missed having such fresh vegetables on the table, all the hard work that was involved in preparing the plot was well worth the effort. Reminding me of a conversation I'd had with Ben the other night, about how even the vegetables from the local farm shop still weren't as fresh or tasted anything like the ones dug fresh from the ground and eaten the same day. Not only vegetables, but gooseberries and raspberries. My freezer would be heaving at this time of year. Ben, however, was of the same mindset as Beth - why go to all that effort when you can buy everything you want from the shop. Although Beth had been grateful for any produce that had come her way, she hadn't appreciated having to clean the soil from them. Though saying that, she had come a long way from being a little child when the only vegetable she would eat was carrots!

'Maybe it's time Ruby and I made a new start, somewhere new,' Stella said.

'Surely there's no need to do that. It doesn't have to change your lives, what's done is done now, you belong here as much as anyone.'

'It just might be better for all of us.'

'But surely in time it'll all settle down, you just have to give it time.'

'If only I hadn't told Ruby,' Stella continued, picking up her glass.

'She had a right to know.'

'Then so did his other children.'

'Just give them time,' I explained, 'they'll soon adapt. You never know, some good might actually come out of all of this.'

'But you moved, started again,' she reminded me.

'That was different, I'd outgrown the house, the girls had left home. This is where you and Ruby belong, your lives are here.'

'For now, I'm not sure for how much longer though.'

'Just wait and see what happens first, you might be surprised.'

Ben, who I'd alerted to my predicament, actually had an appointment in the village in the afternoon and offered to run me home once he'd finished. So, with a heavy heart I left Stella, who I made promise not to do anything she might regret later.

I quickly filled Ben in on what Stella had said, including her thoughts on moving.

'It would certainly sell easily,' he replied.

'Is that all you ever think about! Do you never consider the bigger picture – as to why these properties - people's homes come to the market?'

'That's not my problem,' Ben explained. 'It's not my job to be sentimental. I sell houses, not fairy stories. Those wedding invitations you make don't guarantee a happy ending.'

Of course, he was right, we could both vouch for that, and maybe Stella was right, and it was time to make a fresh start. Though after three glasses of wine, I really couldn't think straight, and I certainly didn't want an argument.

I soon realised that it perhaps wasn't the right time to ice the Christmas cake, but from past experience it couldn't be left much longer, or it just wouldn't set in time and would end up resembling an avalanche with Santa having slipped off with the snowman!

However, by the time Ben arrived home, the cake was safely encased in its decorative armour and dinner was in the oven. I'd even been inspired to add to Freya's mood board for her wedding, realising just how productive an afternoon I'd actually had before Ben arrived home, obviously having had a productive afternoon himself and our earlier conversation forgotten.

'Have I told you how happy you've made me?' Ben asked, returning to my side on the sofa after placing the cards he'd opened on top of a bookcase in the living room later in the evening.

'Remind me!'

Chapter 23

The Girl Next Door

Somehow the festivities didn't seem to be working their magic on Stella, who had reluctantly accepted my invitation to lunch prior to my parents' arrival tomorrow, after which I couldn't foresee another opportunity. I could hardly invite her over when Freya was here with Clether, especially if my mother was here as well!

'Another glass?' I offered Stella, after she'd eventually finished the one she was cradling.

'No, thank you, I must keep a clear head!' she laughed. 'I wish! All I can think of is the dreadful heartache I've caused for everyone and at what should have been a special time of year.'

'You aren't to blame,' I reminded her.

'I can't blame Ruby, can I?'

'No one's to blame,' I told her, trying to ease her pain. 'It's just an unfortunate set of circumstances that have led to where you are today.' I stopped myself from asking her to imagine where they'd find themselves today if the tragic events of all those years ago hadn't happened, realising how painful it might be to contemplate. Then, how we all have our own heartaches, including Ben. Though, I must admit, Stella's story is particularly distressing; one which I doubt Clether or his sister could ever begin to imagine or understand.

'Let's go through to the living room whilst the kettle boils,' I suggested.

'Ben has such a beautiful house,' Stella commented. Then before I got chance to remind her that it was now also my home, she stopped in her tracks as her attention was drawn to the outside and what had obviously been Rob's Garden.

'Are you all right?' I asked, obviously aware of what she was thinking.

'It's just as Rob described it! I never actually visited here, but he always told me how much he loved this view. Do you mind if I take a look outside?'

'Take your coat,' I suggested, 'and I'll bring the tea out.' I deliberately left Stella alone for a while with her own thoughts, pleased I could offer a little comfort.

'Here we are,' I eventually said, delivering a steaming hot cup of tea.

'Thank you. I could sit here all day!'

'Stay as long as you like, if it helps,' I told her, reminded of Clether's reaction when he'd noticed his father's painting in her house, realising it was probably one of the few things she had of Rob's, other than Ruby. And that Clether's father played a different role in his son's life and that they would each hold different memories, even regrets; but who I both knew loved him, with all their hearts.

'I'm glad you found Ben,' Stella began. 'I hope things work out for you.'

'Thank you,' I replied, unsure of what else I could say, other than, 'I suppose we all have to be grateful for whatever time we have together.' Realising none of us ever know how long that might be. Sometimes life surprises us and other times we simply have to learn to adapt, especially where love is concerned.

My parents arrived, a customary five minutes later than expected, but with open arms, as pleased to see me as I was them. Then, excited to come inside and share everything I had tried to portray to them about the place I now called home, before relaxing with a cup of tea and slice of Christmas cake.

Ben returned enthralling us with his various little anecdotes from his day to entertain us with over the dinner table, explaining how he had been asked to value a property being put on the market by the owner of a house who was only moving next door into an almost identical property, after falling in love with the girl next door!

'How romantic!' my mother offered. 'Who'd have thought an estates agent's life could be so romantic.'

'It can't all be happy ever after scenarios,' my father commented.

'Why ever not?' my mother asked. 'Look at Felicity, if she hadn't moved, she'd have never moved in here with Ben.'

My father failing to remind her that if my marriage hadn't failed, we wouldn't be sat here!

It's then I'm reminded of poor Clether, whose house had not only been sold, but demolished! Hopefully, by the time Freya and Clether arrived, the topic of conversation would have changed. Though, my mother has always had a way of wheedling information from even the most reluctant victims; I suppose it must have been a trait she'd learnt in her role as a journalist. It's only when I'm with her, that I'm conscious of my careless nature and am reminded to think before I speak – if I can ever get a word in!

Of course, Ben continued to be interrogated on his lifestyle choices by my mother, having only received a brief summary from myself. No doubt, by the end of her short visit, she will have acquired enough knowledge to sustain her curiosity; my only hope being, she doesn't upset anyone in the process.

Freya and Clether arrived an hour or so after we'd eaten, having been unavoidably delayed but still insistent on Freya seeing her grandparents and that I saved them something to eat, which as ever, was gratefully received.

'If this is going to become a habit, I'm going to have to seriously consider turning some of the garden over to growing vegetables,' I said, reminded again of my old plot that had sustained us.

'So, where have you been until now?' mother asked Freya.

'Work Gran, and then we had to call quickly and deliver something to Clether's sister, her daughters have both got chicken pox, so she can't get out.'

'Oh, where does she live?' mother asked.

'She's just moved into the village,' Freya informed her.

'Really, which property?'

'They've bought Church Cottage,' Freya continued.

My mother remained quiet for a few seconds, probably astounded as to why anyone would want to actually live there.

'She's your only sister, isn't she?' Mother asked Clether.

'Yes, and one brother,' Freya quickly interjected, before Clether had time to consider his response; well aware of the consequences.

Dad soon began to relax and closed his eyes, something he seemed unable to control, particularly in more recent years. I suppose age wearied him, not to mention my mother's incessant zest for life; not that he'd have her any other way! I only hope he can remain awake tomorrow evening when Ben's parents were over!

However, Freya, who appeared to have inherited her grandmother's genes, was more than enough company for my mother, realising it must be like old times for the two of them!

Of course, Ben and Clether also enjoyed each other's company, so I just took myself off to the kitchen and left them all to it.

Eventually, it was time to call it a night and show Freya and Clether the door and my father his bed. After all, I had to do all this again, tomorrow!

My mother had planned a full itinerary for her short stay, having organised coffee and lunch dates with old friends. So, after a good night's sleep and a leisurely breakfast she left with my father, leaving me some time to myself; more importantly, time to wrap up everyone's presents, which had somehow got neglected. Though, it seemed, no matter how hard I tried immersing myself in all things jolly, my thoughts kept returning to Stella, who having finished her teaching would obviously have more time to ponder on the situation she now found herself in, whilst Ruby seemed to have other things on her mind, and when not out with Luke, was required at the stables, leaving Stella alone to dwell on her unfortunate situation. Although, I imagined, it would give her the space she needed and time to think. I knew only too well how helpful distractions could be in maintaining equilibrium, at least until you've had chance to become accustomed to the situation. When I first learnt about Adam and Laura, my sanctuary had been the stables, immersing myself in riding. Charlie and I, had never been so fit!

I suppose like Clether, I had run away until I'd felt able to accept what I'd learnt. I suppose we all have different coping mechanisms, just as long as it works. It's just an unfortunate set of delicate circumstances that leaves me in an awkward position, especially now my mother had arrived. Hopefully, I would be able to find time tomorrow to call round with a card for Ruby's birthday, considering how unfortunate it was for this to have occurred at a time they should be celebrating. Though, I suppose there's never a good time for these things to happen, we just have to adapt the best we can in order to recover and pick up the pieces, which I have no doubt she will learn to do.

By the time my mother arrived back, I'd not only managed to wrap and place the presents under the tree that Ben and I had bought and decorated last weekend, but prepared dinner for six, which was now cooking in the oven. So, whilst mum and I caught up on each other's news over a cup of tea and a slice of Christmas cake, my father caught forty winks, hopefully enough to keep him suitably charged until bedtime!

Ben, as promised had left the office early for a change so he could be home to greet his parents, considering it might seem rather strange if they were to arrive and be greeted by my parents and me! Especially if Dad was still asleep in Ben's chair!

'Dad,' I said, a little louder than normal, but so as not to startle him. 'Ben's home,' I continued, once he'd reacted.

'I must have nodded off,' he said, sitting up. 'Good day at the office Ben?'

'Very productive,' he answered. 'We sold a house that only went on the market yesterday!'

'Wow, that's good,' I congratulated him, 'where is it?'

'It's actually just up the road from the office. You'll probably remember Carol Parker?' Ben paused, 'she lives next door.'

'I'd have thought people would have had enough to think about this close to Christmas,' My mother offered.

'I think it was just too good an opportunity to miss,' Ben continued. 'Anyway, she's buying it!'

'What to live in?' My mother enquired.

'No,' Ben began.

'I suppose, who doesn't want an extra bedroom or even bathroom?' I commented, trying to catch Ben's eye, imagining he was just being sarcastic!

'But who would want two kitchens?' my mother added.

'I suppose they might want to use it as a granny annex,' I added.

'I don't think her parents are alive, let alone grandparents!' mum stated.

'Seems ridiculous that they involved you,' mum continued. 'Surely they could have just cut out the middleman.'

'I suppose they weren't to know,' I said. 'Not everyone tells their neighbours all their business.'

'I'm still baffled as to why they wouldn't just buy a bigger house,' mother concluded.

'They're actually going to let it out as a holiday let,' Ben eventually informed us!

'I suppose that makes more sense,' I said, realising I'd jumped to too many conclusions! Whilst my mother was still trying to make sense of the whole situation! Hopefully once we'd all had a drink we perhaps might be on the same page; if not, it was going to be a long night!

Ben's parents, James and Sarah, arrived with a bottle of red, plus a bottle of something bubbly, which I accepted graciously, and which soon replaced the sparkling wine chilling in the fridge, which Ben opened and poured eloquently, whilst I handed round the canapé's I'd prepared earlier.

For a while, it appeared Ben and I were little more than the caterers to what seemed like a reunion. Although, it had to be said, it had been quite a while since they'd last seen each other; not that they had ever been close, but my mother for one, would never let an opportunity pass her by to attain gossip – she just couldn't help herself! As for my father, it made a nice change to see him engaging with someone other than my mother; perhaps it was just what he needed to prevent him from dozing – I suppose, we'd soon find out!

Ben followed me into the kitchen to help carry the dishes from the oven to the table and sneak a quick kiss along the way!

'Do you think they've even noticed me?' I asked, a little deflated after all the effort I'd gone to.

'You've not gone completely unnoticed,' he said, unable to resist ruffling my hair!

'Stop it!' I warned him. 'Or everyone will notice!'

'Dinner is served,' Ben announced, before I could compose myself and blushing ever so slightly when they emerged.

Of course, my praises were sung at the table, complimenting me on my roast and choice of vegetables, including my 'perfectly roasted' potatoes; not to mention gravy. I suppose, every mother hopes her son will find someone who can cook and be the perfect hostess – not that Ben had been looking for that. Besides, Ben was very proficient in both departments, and more besides!

I'm not sure if it was the second bottle of wine or my bread and butter pudding - my father's favourite, that ceased conversation, although tonight I had added a splash of brandy to the pudding and served it with a dollop of brandy butter – it was Christmas, after all!

So, Ben was at last allowed to delight us with his ever-popular dinner party conversation, including his professional insight into the romance associated with marketing property, that it appeared no one ever considered existed!

'Only yesterday, it seemed love blossomed enough for some guy to put his property on the market to move in with the girl next door!' My mother enlightened Sarah and James

'How romantic!' Sarah commented. 'I suppose they could always decide to let it out instead.'

'What a good idea,' my mother commented!

'Anyone for anymore pudding?' I asked, quickly changing the subject!

'You were lucky Felicity, bumping into Stella,' Ben's mother said.

'Right time, right place!' I replied.

'So,' my mother continued, 'how is she, and that daughter of hers?'

'Good,' I paused, thinking of something else I could add. 'Her daughter's got a part time job at the stables where Freya works.'

'So, how old is she now?' my mother asked.

'Sixteen, almost. In fact, it's her birthday tomorrow,' I explained.

'And Stella's still on her own?'

'Yes,' I answered, straight to the point,

'I suppose, we'll never know what happened and why she ended up on her own. I feel sorry for the child,' my mother added.

You should keep your noses out of other people's lives that don't concern you, I thought to myself.

Ben, conscious of the situation, changed the subject, telling us about another property, this time further along the coast that everyone seemed familiar with.

'Isn't that where Mark lives, who was at school with you?' Sarah, addressed Ben.

'That's right.'

'So, where's he moving?' she asked, suddenly interested.

'In with someone else,' Ben replied.

'That'll be Ellen,' Sarah deduced. I'm surprised it's taken him so long!'

'What, Ellen, Jim's daughter?' my mother asked.

'Yes, that's right,' Sarah confirmed.

'I never knew that,' my mother confessed, quietly reflecting for a moment.

It seemed Ben's mother was just as bad as my own! Suspecting, Ben and I had been the talk of the town not that long ago! Thankfully, Freya and Clether weren't here!

How about we retire into the other room,' I suggested, catching a glimpse of my father and alerting Ben as discreetly as possible; imagining the pudding was maybe just a step too far!

'Let me help you,' Ben offered his hand to my dad.

'Thanks son,' my dad replied, melting my heart and obliterating the previous idle gossip. He may be old and weary, but I loved him with all my heart.

Everyone it seemed, had still enough room for liqueurs and chocolates after their coffee, despite having refused a second helping of pudding! Though, I imagine if my father had succumbed, there would have been no rousing him!

Before too long, but more importantly, before my father finally surrendered to sleep, Ben's parents expressed their delight in having had a lovely evening, wishing my parents a safe journey home and a happy Christmas, before walking

the short distance to their house; no doubt, attracting some attention along the way!
Mum led dad up to bed, whilst Ben filled the dishwasher, and I cleared up.

'I'm exhausted!' I told him.

'Let's go to bed when we've done this.'

'I'm so looking forward to it being just the two of us,' I whispered, wrapping my arms around him.

'I'm counting the days!'

Chapter 24

It Came Upon a Midnight Clear

After my parents had left to catch their flight home, I decided to visit Stella, conscious of her turmoil and how upset she was.

'Is it just me or does time go quicker each year?' Stella sighed, handing me a welcome mug of coffee.

'I know what you mean,' I replied, 'sometimes, I feel there just aren't enough hours in a day or days in a week! Though, I don't think winter helps.'

'I suppose.'

'Roll on spring!'

'Now you're wishing it away!'

'So, where is she?' I asked.

'Out with Luke again. she's hardly home these days! I've even granted her wish to attend midnight mass this year, not that she's ever asked to go before! Thankfully, she's too young to go to the pub!'

'It's her birthday tomorrow, isn't it?' I asked.

'Yes, bittersweet in a way, it always is,' Stella explained. 'But especially this year, with everything going on. I just have to keep strong.'

'Just forget everyone else and concentrate on celebrating Ruby's birthday and Christmas. I'm sure that's what they'll all be doing,' I told her, whilst realising It would surely impact everyone's Christmas. 'And isn't that what Rob would want?'

'Yes, you're right.' Stella admitted. 'I'd never thought of that.'

'Let them worry about each other, I'm sure they won't be considering your feelings in all of this.'

'Have your parents left?' Stella enquired, changing the subject.

'Yes, they wanted to enjoy Christmas in Scilly.' It was only then that I considered that they may have felt a little uncomfortable in Ben's home when they'd never met him before. Until I remembered my father dozing in his chair!

'Perhaps you'll go there next Christmas.'

'If not before!' Failing to consider the events of next year, that would impact not only my life, but more importantly my daughters.

It was only later, when I was sat quietly with a cup of tea and a slice of Christmas cake that I allowed my mind to wander, considering all the changes in my own life over the last few years, even this time last year and how they'd impacted my daughters. Freya, I imagined, still coming to terms with her father's recent news, whilst Clether, dealing with his own emotions. Beth, on the other hand, appeared to have accepted the situation, and as a consequence, was enjoying her extended family. In particular, Laura, who if I was honest, I was still a little envious of. Not entirely - obviously! I didn't envy what she had with Adam and certainly wouldn't want to be pregnant again. But I did feel as though Laura was somehow performing what should be my role in my daughter's pregnancy. Though, like Ben had said, that Beth probably saw her as more of a friend rather than a mother. I suppose, in truth, I just missed my daughter, perhaps realising the implications of my own actions. But at least I was able to spend Christmas with Freya this year, something I had missed.

In no time at all Ben was arriving home for Christmas, the office now closed for a few days and a well-earned rest for Ben, awarding himself the remainder of next week off – as to what we chose to do, other than relax, had not yet been decided. We had however decided to join Freya and Clether and no doubt many more later for midnight mass at the village church. But for now, I'd cooked up a delicious feast to celebrate the eve of our very first Christmas together. Although not turkey, which in my opinion could only be served on the day itself, along with all the trimmings, I'd instead prepared a ham, smothered in a marmalade glaze – just like my mother had once shown me. My plan being, that the remainder could be served cold on sandwiches, or even in a stir fry or an omelette for breakfast. One thing was for sure; it would certainly be devoured over the next couple of days! Along with the ham, I'd roasted potatoes and sprouts, aware I'd be serving them tomorrow, but what could be better and more abundant at Christmas, and in my opinion, a hugely versatile and under rated vegetable.

'Something smells good!' Ben declared, hanging his coat in the hallway.

'I hope you're hungry!'

'Starving!'

'It'll be ready when you are,' I said, turning to welcome him home and eventually wishing him a happy Christmas.

Inspired by the marmalade, I'd baked a pineapple upside down pudding, oozing with syrup, which despite having been unable to resist a second helping of ham, Ben had enjoyed – accompanied by a glass of local cider, having sourced and replicated the exact vintage we'd enjoyed with Freya and Clether. Perhaps, even possibly, purchased enough to sustain us through till the next harvest! But I had always liked my larder and fridge full at this time of year.

'Thank you, that was delicious!' Ben declared. 'I can't wait for tomorrow!'

'You're surely, not still hungry?'

'No, I couldn't manage another bite. But, if tonight was anything to go by, the turkey will be amazing!'

'I'll try not to disappoint,' I replied, realising I'd set the bar high. Though turkey was pretty failsafe, in my experience.

Ben and I arrived at church with plenty of time to spare, having learnt from experience how popular the midnight service always was. Freya had asked us to save her and Clether seats - which was all going well, until Stella arrived with Ruby and Luke! And by the time Freya and Clether arrived, the only available seats were either at the front of the church, which everyone - no matter what the occasion, seemed to avoid, or directly behind us, perhaps only realising the implications of their choice, once they'd sat down. Though, as far as I was aware, Clether was still unaware as to the identity of his father's illicit affair and subsequent love child – for how much longer, only time would tell!
The front row seats, as was often the case, were inevitably occupied by party revellers, arriving as we had already stood to sing the first hymn and were now halfway through the first verse of "The First Nowel". No doubt they would sit this one out, having to first find the page in the book! Even I can't remember all the words, despite singing them every year. Then, to my amazement, one of the girls, around the same age as Beth, began singing with a beautiful, almost angelic voice! Ben, on the other hand, was mumbling beside me along with Clether behind me – not that Freya or I could sing, but each joined in. I tried placing the young ensemble at the front of the church, imagining them to have been at school with Beth, but failed. Perhaps if they had been sat with their parents, I may have stood a chance, but would first have to recognise them – which, truth be told, wasn't as difficult! Not that they hadn't aged in the years since I'd lived here, but they had retained their distinguishing features – I suppose, like Ben.
I suppose it was only natural in a way, that I was reminded of Beth and Adam and how they would soon be cradling their own new babies, and then of Stella, this time sixteen years

ago. It appeared, as I'd suspected, that Clether was oblivious to the identity of the people sat in front of him, for now at least.

The vicar, appeared both joyous and triumphant in his address, continuing to amuse us and prevent anyone from nodding off whilst he conducted his sermon. But, unlike the old vicar I remember when visiting my parents, kept it brief. I suppose, being new to the parish, would want to encourage parishioners rather than deter them and like everyone else would have to be up early. Though, doubt even the most religious of us would be sitting back here later this morning. Obviously, not everyone had to get up to prepare the turkey for the oven, suspecting Freya and Clether may even treat themselves to a lie in.

The service ended with a resounding chorus of "On Christmas night All Christians Sing", before we turned to leave.

'Happy Christmas,' Ruby exclaimed, turning to Freya.

'Happy Christmas,' Freya replied, keeping it short and sweet. No doubt, avoiding an unwanted confrontation.

Thankfully, Ruby followed Luke out of the pew, and we followed behind Stella, who realising the sensitivity of the situation, just smiled.

Then, just as we approached the door, Luke's father decided to stop and chat to Ruby and of course his son whilst introducing himself to Stella, who by this stage was immediately in front of us.

If Clether had made the connection, he had kept it hidden. Though, I suppose what other option did he have, considering where we were.

'See you tomorrow,' Ruby shouted back to Freya, once we'd finally stepped outside.

Clether looked questioningly towards Freya, who quickly reminded him it was Boxing day tomorrow. Still baffled, he accepted her explanation, at least for now – wondering, if like me, his thoughts would disturb his sleep. Then remembered, he was possibly too exhausted to have his sleep disturbed!

Ben and I embraced Freya and Clether, wishing them both a happy Christmas before walking up the hill and home to bed.

Having set the alarm, so that the turkey would be cooked for lunch, Ben and I returned to bed once it was in the oven, only surfacing once the aromas began to drift up the stairs, alerting us to the fact that we still hadn't eaten breakfast - or come to think of it, opened our presents.

We'd satisfied our appetites before taking our coffees back to bed to unwrap our gifts together – once we'd retrieved them from under the tree. Ben had bought me a pair of beautiful, diamond cluster earrings - my heart having skipped a beat when I'd opened the gift bag and seen the tiny box! Not that I was disappointed, more surprised. Ben had also loved my gift to him. The remainder of the gifts left undisturbed for now whilst we prepared the vegetables and everything else for our celebratory Christmas lunch before Freya and Clether were due to arrive.

As customary, I received calls from both Beth and my parents and exchanged greetings and thanks for the thoughtful gifts they'd left with us. Ben had already rung his parents who'd reminded him not to forget that we were invited round later this afternoon for tea, which I was quite looking forward to, letting someone else cater for a change, giving me a chance to relax.

But for now, I was busy enjoying my first Christmas with their son. At this precise moment, encased in his arms whilst dancing, ever so slowly to Bing Crosby's "White Christmas" between setting the table and chopping the vegetables so everything was prepared for when Freya and Clether arrived, and we could enjoy a drink of something sparkling together. As though on cue, Freya and Clether pulled up outside just as Ben had retrieved the champagne flutes from the cupboard where they had sat since the last celebration.

'That was good timing,' I told them, as I opened the door to let them in.

'I thought you said it wouldn't be ready until half past,' Freya remarked.

'No, we're just about to crack open a bottle,' I explained.

'In which case, we'll join you,' she advised, as I detected unrest between them, on today of all days! Then remembered last night and what might have occurred.

'Come through to the kitchen,' I instructed, dismissing their mood. I was determined to not let anyone spoil my day. If they wanted to dwell on something that happened sixteen years ago, they could do it later in their own time or when they visited Stephanie this afternoon, but certainly not this morning as guests in our home.

'Happy Christmas,' Ben smiled, handing a glass of bubbly to Freya and then Clether and myself.

We all raised our glasses, and the magic began.

Once we'd sat down to eat, the mood had lifted; Freya had always been impossible without a good meal inside her and as anticipated, everything had been devoured heartily along with a chosen bottle of Chardonnay. And perhaps like me, neither of them had wanted to spoil such a special occasion together and maybe, it might just go some way in eradicating what had obviously arisen as a result of last night.

For a brief moment, I was reminded of last Christmas, spent with Beth and my parents, returning home to an empty house, then realising just how different next year would be with the addition of Beth's baby and hopefully a completed barn to enjoy.

After Freya and Clether had left, along with their requested gift of a log basket to sit beside their new slate hearth and soon to be installed, wood burning stove, plus a little something more luxurious for each of them, Ben and I tackled the kitchen - by which time the turkey, or what was left of it, was now cool enough to go in the fridge. The rest of the day was ours, to do as we pleased – until Ben reminded me that we needed to be getting ready to visit his parents! Despite everything we'd achieved since we'd last slept and the memories made, we were in bed again; exhausted, of course – but very happy.

Having devoted yesterday to our loved ones and the fact the sun was beaming in through the window beckoning us outside, Ben and I had decided to pack a picnic from the vast array of choice already prepared in the fridge, along with a bottle of bubbly - whilst not forgetting two flutes. We knew the exact spot to head to, and despite it being Boxing day and the long-held tradition of a post-Christmas day walk, it was such a remote location that we were confident it would just be the two of us. Even in summer it was only usually the surfers, and intrepid ones at that, who frequented our chosen location.

It was so nice being outside after what seemed a long time, especially with Ben beside me and the thought of a whole week together without the distraction of work. I had briefly considered joining Freya today for the traditional annual hack, but quickly dismissed it, preferring to spend precious time with Ben. After all, we still had a lot of catching up to do and new memories to make of our own together.

The spot was perfect, catching the late morning sun, and although there was a breeze, it was sheltered enough to protect us as we unpacked our picnic.

The beach below, which was just visible below the cliff, appeared empty, despite the incoming prevailing breeze and tide, expecting even the surfers to be relaxing at home with their loved ones. Then, a moment later, who of all people, appeared from almost out of nowhere – but Clether, obviously having been hidden from view on his ascent from the beach below! looking as surprised as both Ben and me. Although, when I think about it, where else would he be!

Clether, declined my generous offer to share our lunch. I suppose, who would really want to invade what was obviously an intimate meal for two. So, with pleasantries kept to a minimum, and the fact he was still dripping wet, he left us alone and continued his ascent home. All Ben and I could do was giggle, at the likelihood of what had just occurred, happening.

Unbeknown to me, Ben had arranged a couple of nights away in a not so distant, but recently constructed, elite waterfront apartment complex. Despite it oozing everything Ben could hope for in terms of luxury and location, he confessed it hadn't been all his own idea and that the developer – a good friend of his, had suggested he experience it for himself, which in turn, might help to encourage sales as Ben and his team were marketing them, at what I considered to be an astronomical price. But, according to the sales brochure, what set these apart, were the uninterrupted ocean views stretching for miles and less than a hundred metres away. The private outdoor terrace spanned the entire width of the apartment, as did the floor to ceiling windows, all with magnificent views and doors allowing access from every living space – including the bathroom. But, as Ben explained, the architect had been designing similar spaces for almost thirty years and had learnt a thing or two and had even won awards for his innovative designs and features – including high performance acoustic matting to ensure privacy and quiet. Though being in the penthouse at the top of the cliffs with the doors open – all we could hear was the cry of the gulls as they battled the south westerly on the incoming tide!
Once we'd surveyed all the interior had to offer, we set about exploring the path down to the coast. The wind having eased as we walked hand in hand along the wide expanse of beach, imagining a life spent here with the beach right on the doorstep. We'd ambled into the local town to collect ingredients for tomorrow's breakfast before returning to the warmth and luxury of the apartment to prepare for an evening meal out.

Ben had obviously done his homework or perhaps simply read the details, as he knew exactly where to suggest for cocktails and an evening meal specialising in local seafood and the most knowledgeable waiter, suggesting the perfect wine to complement our dishes. Whoever was fortunate enough to be able to afford to purchase one of the apartments, would surely have plenty of opportunities and everything it seemed on their doorstep, whilst in one of the most beautiful locations. Though I realised, they would probably end up being sold as holiday rentals or second homes to the rich and famous.

'Or retirees,' Ben explained. Until I considered as to where they'd store everything they'd accumulated in life!

'You really must have a word with whoever is responsible for writing the details,' I informed Ben, as we relaxed behind the "energy efficient windows fitted with super fibre broadband!"

'I owe you one,' Ben declared. 'I know exactly who it is. She tries to romanticise with her descriptions, but does have a tendency to lose the plot!'

'I'd had to have word with Imogen the other week. She's started a photography course and was practising her recently acquired skills in marketing properties!'

'How do you mean?'

'Have a look at this,' Ben said, finding an example on his phone, depicting the design on a set of towels hung over a rail and another where the light caught a glass light shade, she'd captured. And then another of a reflection through a circular mirror depicting a shower head!

'It certainly leaves a lot to the imagination. Perhaps she has an assignment to complete,' I suggested, unable to comprehend why else she thought they might help sell the house.

'She took on board my comments and disapproval, so we'll see what happens.'

The days came and went as Ben and I enjoyed the luxury of a whole week together without the interruptions of work, although I did occasionally check my emails, sending a quick message to any enquiries I got, explaining I would be back in the office next week. I also realised from past experience, the number of proposals and betrothals that would have taken place before then – generating more work in the not too distant future, before the most romantic day of the year.

It seemed Freya and Clether had managed to talk through their difficulties as work on the barn had now resumed in earnest, and having had a wood burning stove installed yesterday, they could at least begin to warm the structure of the barn whilst they worked inside.

Beth had informed me that she had entered her third trimester of pregnancy and was already starting to feel uncomfortable, questioning what she'd feel like in another eleven weeks. With this in mind, they had taken Laura's advice and gone shopping for the pram and cradle whilst she still had the energy. Then, realising the amount of equipment required before the baby was even here, were now considering if they needed to move house! Both her and Lucas had enrolled on a course of antenatal classes along with Laura and surprisingly, Adam. Though, to be fair, it had been a long time since he last became a father! The thought of Adam holding another baby, still unsettled me – not least the fact I now knew they were expecting a daughter. I had of course, had the good sense to keep this and other details, including Beth's dilemmas to myself, conscious of the sensitivity, considering Ben's history.

Today had been spent preparing for the eve of a new year, full of exciting milestones for me to experience as a mother; maybe not as I'd envisaged a few years ago, but this time last year I could never have imagined my life changing the way it has and finding someone as special as Ben to share it all with.

I have never considered myself a pessimist, but have learnt from experience, never to take things for granted, as I expect

Ben and Stella have also learnt from bitter experiences of their own. So, although I was looking forward and planning for Freya's wedding and becoming a grandmother later in the year, none of us can actually be sure where we'll be this time next year. I suppose all we can do is enjoy the moment, which was exactly what I intended doing right now as I handed Ben the chilled bottle of wine to open for us to enjoy together.

The new year started on a relaxed note, quite simply, because we hadn't had to get up and could enjoy waking up beside each other, before Ben brought me up breakfast in bed, accompanied with a glass of Champagne from the bottle we'd omitted to open last night, in favour of an early night! The remainder, we could share with Freya and Clether who'd accepted our invitation to join us for lunch.

As customary, I'd wished my nearest and dearest a happy New Year, not forgetting Stella, promising to catch up next week when Ben was back in the office.

As ever, lunch was gratefully received and we'd even enjoyed the unprecedented, good weather, enjoying a walk in the afternoon before retiring, to relax in the intimacy of our own abodes; something I had grown very fond of over the last week and that I was definitely going to miss sharing and enjoying with Ben.

Chapter 25

Good Vibes

Ben had returned to the office and I had opened my laptop, answering enquiries and producing more invitations and place settings for spring weddings. And with Christmas now a distant memory, I had returned to the stables, only wishing I hadn't left it so long, reminded of the hot tub on the terrace of the apartment we'd stayed in.

I'd also managed to catch up with Stella before her new term began at the weekend. She had seemed a little apprehensive at the prospect, but realised it was probably now old news, apart from those it really concerned.

She opened a bottle of Sauvignon to accompany lunch as she began explaining what Ruby had recently shared with her and the questions being asked in the vicarage between Luke and his parents after their story had come to light and the implications it might have on them.

'I thought I was doing fine, I was always going to miss Rob, but I thought I'd learnt to accept what had happened. Only now, with everything that has happened recently, and now this, it's like it all happened yesterday.'

'It's bound to have stirred up memories,' I said, trying to sympathise with her. 'Here, have another glass of wine,' I said, filling her glass up, hoping it would help.

'I just feel like I'm having to process everything all over again, and I can't stop thinking of Rob.'

'Perhaps,' I said, 'it might help sharing your memories with Ruby.'

'Look where that got me!'

'At least it's all out in the open now, I'm sure things 'll settle down once everyone's had chance to absorb the news and then life 'll get back to normal,' I explained, not really knowing what might happen, but trying to offer some consolation. 'You said yourself, you learnt to accept what had happened. It'll just take time.'

As usual, Ruby was nowhere to be seen, no doubt seeking solace in the comfort of Luke's arms; I suppose as it should be, and something we should all be grateful for. As for Clether, he found his own solace sat in the middle of the ocean, waiting for the perfect wave to bring him back to shore. I suppose we all develop our own mechanisms to enable us to cope, and what works for one, doesn't necessarily work for everyone – otherwise, the ocean would be a very crowded place!

By the time Ben had arrived home, I'd quite forgotten about Stella's worries - until she called to ask for Freya's number as she was becoming a little worried as to why Ruby hadn't arrived home from the stables, assuming Freya would have dropped her home by now as they'd agreed, and Ruby wasn't answering her phone.

'Let me know if I can help,' I told her, before hanging up.

I filled Ben in on what Stella had explained earlier whilst we'd sat down to eat, debating their dilemma.

'I can see their point,' Ben said, understanding why Luke's parents were concerned.

'But surely, you'd expect them to be more compassionate than most,' I argued. 'They must hear about far worse things.'

'But that doesn't mean to say they are going to want their own son involved in such a sordid affair. It's not exactly practising what he preaches.'

Before I had time to correct Ben's terminology, Freya called, explaining she'd not only had Stella on the phone, but Luke's mother, as it appeared he was also absent without leave.

'I suppose, it's safe to say, they're probably together,' I concluded, wondering what else could be done.

The weather, as predicted, had turned nasty, with gales and wintery showers overnight; all of which would surely add to everyone's concern.

My first thought in the morning, having spoken to Freya, who'd returned to the stables last night to look for them - was for Stella. I had jumped in the car to be with her whilst Ben enjoyed a leisurely breakfast before a viewing at the Old Manor House.

Stella of course, was beside herself having been up all night as had Freya, having felt responsible somehow. She told me the police had been informed and that they were already making enquiries given the information she had supplied, including friends addresses and photos of both Ruby and Luke, that Ruby had kept in her bedroom.

'Here,' I said, having made us each a coffee and hot buttered toast. 'I know it won't bring her home, but you need to keep strong. I'm sure she'll be home soon; she's a sensible girl.'

'I don't even know Luke that well, nobody does. Who knows what he's capable of.'

'He'll be looking after Ruby, they love each other,' I reminded Stella. 'They'll soon realise they can work things out, without running away.'

'Will they? How can you be sure? They could be anywhere by now. The police have already said the first twenty-four hours are crucial. It's already been fifteen,' she said, looking at the screen on her phone. They could be getting on a ferry as we speak.'

'I think we can discount that. Have you seen the weather!' Regretting it as soon as I'd said it!

Wondering how long it'd be before Search and Rescue would get involved.

Meanwhile, Ben was arriving at the Old Manor House prior to showing a couple around, with a view to purchasing it. He'd arrived in plenty of time so as to familiarise himself with the layout and open a few windows to let some fresh air in, when he received a call from the office to inform him that the couple in question had been delayed but should be with him in about half an hour. As the property had already been completely emptied, there was nowhere for Ben to sit and relax, and as the wind had now dropped, he went outside to have a wander around the estate. A lot had changed over the years and much of the garden left to its own devices, most of which now entangled in ivy, other than the formal gardens to the front or the property. As he was nearing the outbuildings on his way back to the house, he noticed a tree had fallen, he presumed, probably in last night's storm, making a mental note to inform Harold. Only, as he was nearing to take a closer inspection, he heard what sounded like cries for help! Realising whoever was in there had been trapped, he ascertained they were uninjured and realising their identities rang the police to call off the search and arrange for their rescue, before informing me to pass on the good news.

Of course, Stella had been relieved and had wanted to get there as soon as possible to see her daughter. So, considering the state she was in and once we'd informed Luke's mother, I drove her over immediately.

Not having far to travel, we'd arrived ahead of the emergency services, shortly followed by Luke's parents. By which time, Ruby was sobbing; no doubt tears of relief, after what must have been a dreadful ordeal. Though, by the look on Luke's parents faces – one that would need some explaining!

Stella, on the other hand, was being really brave, offering reassurance that everything was going to be okay and that they'd soon be safely out – which considering no one as yet had turned up to even assess the situation, seemed somewhat optimistic, realising we could perhaps be here for some considerable time. But at least they were unharmed, grateful they had been found. Or so I thought, until the vicar's wife started giving Luke the third degree!

Finally, the police, paramedic and not for the first time, a fire engine arrived, almost simultaneously, just ahead of Mr and Mrs Roberts to view the house! So, whilst Ben began to give a statement, I took charge of the situation, leaving Stella with Luke's rather irate parents, whilst I assured a rather bemused Mr and Mrs Roberts that there was nothing to worry about as I led them into the house.

'I rather enjoyed looking round the Manor House this morning,' I said to Ben, as we cuddled on the sofa together, after an eventful day.

'You certainly didn't deter them,' Ben acknowledged.

'I suppose we should be grateful they had booked a viewing, or who knows how long Ruby and Luke would have been there?'

'You've got a point. Though I don't envy Luke. His parents didn't seem at all pleased to see him when he finally emerged. Whilst Stella on the other hand, was reluctant to let Ruby out of her arms.'

'Poor Stella, though at least she'll sleep well tonight knowing Ruby's safe,' I concluded, having decided to wait until morning to talk to her.

It seemed, despite all the obstacles and heartache, nothing could stop the course of true love, as my inbox was full of requests for wedding invitation samples – all of which would now have to wait until morning as I had my own love story to write.

Stella had been the one to call me later the following morning to explain the events that had led to Ruby and Luke's unfortunate set of circumstances. Describing how they had run to take shelter from the weather, when the tree must have fallen, trapping them inside. Luke's phone had been lost in the rubble and Ruby had had no signal. So, if it hadn't of been for Ben, who knows how long they'd have been there.

'At least they're both safe.'

'That's what I said. Though I think Luke might have a bit more explaining to do!'

It wasn't long before the local grapevine had started processing what had been seen and heard, suggesting the vicar's presence along with the paramedic, had been called to administer the last rights! Considering, that if the tree had fallen at a different angle or hadn't broken its fall, Ruby and Luke might well have been lucky to survive. But as Stella reminded me, she had never been good at understanding probability or angles and had learnt not to dwell too much on what might have been, instead settling for enjoying having her daughter back where she belonged.

The new year continued to pick up where the old one had ended, but with new hope and aspirations for the year ahead. Beth had started her maternity leave and was enjoying preparing her home for their daughter. Even the barn was beginning to resemble a home, and with internal walls and first fix electrics, Freya was now ready to turn her attention to wedding plans and had asked me to create a design for their big day in August. She had taken my advice and created a mood board to help visualise her dreams which she'd hung in what was to be the living room alongside an almost identical board depicting a photograph of the byre as it had once stood in its derelict state, a schedule of jobs to do and a photo of our evening together sat under the stars.

Ben had also been busy helping people achieve their dreams of owning a new home, including the couple I'd shown around the Manor House, who'd arranged another viewing, Ben explaining that period properties within that particular price bracket were actually few and far between and ones that came onto the market were often snatched up quite quickly. As well as attaining dreams, it also seemed that many dreams had been shattered over the course of the Christmas period and there had been, according to Ben, the customary influx of properties being marketed.

As for Stella, it appeared she'd had nothing to worry about regarding the future of her dance classes other than being oversubscribed and having to start a waiting list. Ruby, it seemed, still more interested in spending every opportunity at the stables rather than help her mother out. Though, according to Freya, she was somewhat of an asset, unafraid of hard work and wonderful with the little ones.

It had also transpired that Clether, had inadvertently met Ruby whilst waiting to give Freya a lift home from the stables the other evening whilst her car was in the garage being repaired. And by all accounts had given her a lift home! Freya explaining that she had been pleasantly surprised and although she realised there was still a long way to go, it was definitely a step in the right direction. It had even spurred him on to place the order for their kitchen appliances. Perhaps there was something to be said for sitting out in the middle of the ocean, after all!

Chapter 26

Bring me Sunshine

Christmas now seemed a distant memory as spring was in the air, at least the birds and the bulbs thought so. The snowdrops nodding their tiny heads as the daffodils began to emerge to portray the sunshine that was beginning to last a little longer each day. Love, was definitely in the air, as my inbox continued to fill each day, requesting samples from my range of wedding stationary to suit couples chosen themes. This morning was no exception, other than an exceptionally large order for a complete package, in what I considered the most romantic of all my creations, beginning with 'save the date' cards, which I couldn't wait to get started on – just once I'd finished some samples to give to Freya that I'd been working on over the weekend whilst Ben had been busy in the office between viewings. He had also left earlier this morning, having arranged a viewing a little further away, hoping to arrive before the couple in question turned up, as Emma who had instructed the sale and was familiar with the property in question, was currently taking a week's leave. Hopefully, it wouldn't be too long before Ben and I could enjoy a long weekend together again.

As well as catching up on work and designing Freya's wedding stationary, I'd also managed to catch up briefly with Stella yesterday, not our usual leisurely lunch, but instead, a coffee in town and a stroll along the beach to blow away the cobwebs – something it appeared, quite popular on a Sunday morning. No wonder Luke's father was questioning where all his congregation where, when we had all this to marvel in, wondering if people would be more inclined to attend if the service was perhaps later in the day when they were possibly more relaxed and receptive. Though, not being a regular – who was I to judge! But I had listened to Stella explain, that now Luke had been banned from seeing Ruby, she had devoted more time to her other passion – where Luke would inevitably join her later!

Despite the sunshine continuing into the afternoon, I'd resisted the urge to prolong my sit in the strategically placed chair, bathed in sunshine, imagining all the people, including Rob who'd enjoyed a similar view across the valley and towards the church and beyond and why he'd wanted to share it with Stella. Instead, returning upstairs to finish what I'd started, so that I could visit the stables, not only to deliver Freya's samples, but for some well-earned relaxation. And not having been for some time - much needed exercise!

I so enjoyed the solitude my work afforded me, plus the flexibility to arrange my hours to suit, even the ability to work evenings or weekends when Ben was working, so we had more time to enjoy together, and the fact that I loved what I did, made it easy.

The afternoon had flown by, and after sending more stationary requests to happy couples, I'd reacquainted myself with Bella and helped Freya stable the horses, not forgetting to give her the samples I'd created especially for her, which she'd been delighted with. By the time I'd wandered home, the light was beginning to fade, silhouetting the trees, still resting their weary limbs, whilst the daffodils underneath, couldn't wait to make an appearance, and the lambs that had been frolicking and bleating in the fields were now hushed, huddled up to their mothers.

Ben had arrived home, rather tired after a long and what appeared, fruitless day, especially as he had just had to inform the couple, who after viewing the Manor House for a second time, that the vendor was still awaiting probate to be granted, which was normally obtained before putting a property on the market to avoid any delay in the proceedings, apart from the obvious authority to grant the sale of the house! Whereas the couple had assumed it would be a quick sale as it was already empty – something Ben and I were not alone in thinking was both despicable and disrespectful behaviour, given it had only been weeks after his father's death that Harold had employed someone to not only put a value on his father's home and contents, but clear the house and destroy all trace of his father's existence. No doubt, now in some auction room or lining the shelves of an antique shop, the rest, probably in landfill. How sad, all that family history had been destroyed forever. It seemed, all Harold had wanted, was to get his hands on his father's money, no respect for his life lived or that of his ancestors who'd lived there - the remains of which having gone up in smoke on a bonfire which Harold had left burning after his departure, alerting a concerned onlooker to call the fire brigade!

'I hope he loses the sale,' I told Ben. 'It might even teach him a lesson! I still can't believe he's got rid of everything. Can you imagine all the history inside that house?'

'I agree, it's sacrilege! From what mum said, Violet is still slowly emptying her parents' house next door to where they live, and her father died last April.'

'You can't rush these things, surely. Once everything's gone there's no one left to tell you anything anymore.'

'That's exactly what mum said. Violet has found all sorts of things alluding to not only her parents, but her great grandparents, that she had no idea about.'

'It's surprising what you forget,' I said, recalling having sorted through many boxes that had come to light whilst packing to move - full of memories I'd almost forgotten about, that one day my daughters or their children might find interesting.

'Not that I've accumulated much myself – until you arrived!'

'Just the house itself, has a story,' I reminded him.

Freya had called having shown Clether the designs for their wedding stationary and after agreeing on their favourite, had asked me to make the 'save the date' cards – once they had confirmed their guest list! Their dream it seemed, was eventually falling into place. Even the barn was well on the way to being finished in time for Clether to carry Freya over the threshold, especially as they had now found the perfect reclaimed stone doorstep for the front door – imagining the stories it could tell!

Chapter 27

Birthdays in Abundance

Half term had arrived, not that there was much evidence at this time of year, other than the local children out and about with their parents or grandparents - apart from the more adventurous, who had decided to brave the weather, come what may. You could usually tell the locals from the tourists, not that I recognised many of them yet. But, like me, they were obviously out on a mission as opposed to the rather more relaxed demeanour of someone enjoying a break from the usual constraints of a working day. My own mission this morning, was to send perhaps the largest order I'd ever supplied, to a couple living in the Yorkshire Dales for their wedding in July. In summer, the post office sold buckets and spades, sun cream and ice creams. Today however, there was no evidence of those long summer days, other than a little boy choosing a postcard for his grandma. It wouldn't be until Easter that we'd see more holiday makers navigating our quaint narrow roads towards their destination, only the occasional one turning off the beaten track to enjoy one of the few holiday cottages on offer, and of course our lovely stretch of coast.

I'd also had an email from Ben's colleague Emma, confirming what Ben had alluded to, placing an order for forty-five 'save the date' cards and a further forty-five invitations of the same design for her forthcoming nuptials later in the year. Informing me, that once they'd decided on the order of service and met with the hotel wedding planner, she would request more stationary. Shortly after, she'd sent another email headed: 'Last, but by no means least' - having forgotten to mention additional invitations to their evening reception.

The school holidays meant Freya was busy with pony club again – always popular whatever the weather, even with Ruby, who seemed to be following in Freya's footsteps and was not only keen to learn but had a natural flair with the younger riders she'd been asked to help with. As a result, leading parents to recognise how their children responded to her ability to engage with them and achieve the desired outcomes – not least, mucking out the stables!

And when Saskia's mother had enquired if she could babysit one evening, she had accepted.

Stella was also busy, starting an adult ballet class whilst the younger students were having a break; not just for retired ballerinas, but anyone. Stella having explained the benefits to me over a cup of coffee the other day. Not that a glass of wine could have persuaded me differently, as my feet, like it appeared Ruby's, were far more comfortable in a pair of stirrups than ballet shoes. But if I ever felt the need to feel more graceful or improve my balance, I'd know where to go!

Ben arrived home, and as ever, or more often than not, ready to share his day; at least, once he'd greeted me and asked me about my own achievements. Today was no exception as he shared the properties he'd been to value – nothing on our doorstep or indeed intriguing, other than one that had the potential to be developed into a holiday let, set in a secluded spot and seemingly, not much bigger than a traditional miner's cottage, which had obviously been quite adequate when it was first built and had obviously sufficed the late occupant. But today, even a single person might struggle, especially if they were any taller than five foot five! Whereas nowadays, all that was considered quirky when it came to finding a characterful place to stay, away from the constraints of modern day living. The other property had been the complete opposite, and which had been in the same family for generations but was now destined for the market before it fell into a state of disrepair having been almost abandoned over the years.

Some days it seemed spring would never arrive, despite which, Freya's optimism and energy prevailed, only occasionally accepting a warm meal and bed for the night, whilst her dirty laundry was washed in the machine and tumbled dry. Both Freya and Clether had made remarkable progress on the barn, considering they were doing much of the work themselves. The bathroom suite had been chosen and was ready for delivery, just once they'd had the staircase installed!

Before we knew it, March had arrived, though spring was definitely not yet in the air this morning, unless of course you were thinking of selling your house, as Ben appeared inundated with work, just as it appeared I was, as I opened my inbox! Realising, the sooner I made a start, the sooner I could finish and visit Stella, whose birthday it was today. Fortunately, for her, it had fallen on a day she didn't work and had insisted on making lunch for the two of us, accepting my offer of preparing the obligatory birthday cake; which I'd finally managed to decorate this morning, just once Ben had left for work, conscious of the time I had previously spent in the kitchen last night, after he had already gone up to bed. By the time I had eventually joined him, he was fast asleep. In my defence, I had also baked a cake for Ben, which we could enjoy together later.

Not forgetting the cake, I picked up the flowers I'd bought for Stella along with my keys, suddenly remembering the bottle of sparkling wine chilling in the fridge! An early night was definitely on the cards this evening!

Stella welcomed me with open arms and a smile.

'Happy birthday,' I chimed, embracing her, before presenting her with her gifts.

'Come on in out of the cold,' Stella said, shutting the door behind me. 'Who, in their right mind would plan to have a baby in this weather?'

'Well Adam for one!' I reminded her.

'Oh, and Beth of course. How is she?'

'Just two more weeks to go,' I informed her.

'Two weeks can make all the difference at this time of year,' Stella offered, apologetically. 'Let's just hope she doesn't deliver early!'

I couldn't actually believe I'd mentioned Adam before considering Beth – whatever was I thinking. I really must have an early night!

'Right, let's get this party started,' Stella declared. 'I've been waiting all year for this! You have to remember; I don't get out much and find very little to celebrate these days. Ruby always seems to be having far more fun than I do.'

'Young love,' I reminded her. 'Or young and in love,' I corrected myself. Not that being in love at any age isn't fun – just different, I suppose.

'Their whole lives ahead of them,' I continued, trying to explain.

'However long that might be,' Stella added.

'But, better late than never,' I replied, attempting to console her.

'Exactly.' Stella agreed.

I got the impression, that if Freya hadn't informed me of Stella's birthday by carelessly sharing Ruby's plan, it would have gone unnoticed. Obviously, I had had to be very careful whilst hatching my own plan to celebrate today, suggesting to Stella, we go out for lunch as I would be pushed for time, having a lot on and a deadline to meet – which wasn't completely untrue, and my mother always said a white lie never hurt anyone, though I doubt the vicar would agree! Fortunately, Stella was adamant that I joined her, so here I was, having somehow pulled it off! Little did she know what was in store for her later.

'I hope you're hungry,' Stella asked, opening the oven door and retrieving our lunch. 'Not only did I go shopping on an empty stomach, but I was ravenous when I prepared it!'

'Blimey,' I exclaimed, when she presented the dish. 'It looks divine,' I continued, having resisted the urge to comment on their only being the two of us. Realising, just how proficient I was now becoming in avoiding saying the wrong thing.

As ever, our daughters were the main topic of conversation, wondering if we ever came up in their own conversations. Or if perhaps, they just led more interesting lives! Including a conversation Ruby had had with Luke during their night together at the Manor House, where he'd disclosed a conversation he'd overheard between his parents, claiming Harold's inheritance wasn't quiet as he'd expected, and that once the sale on the house completed, the church stood to gain a large chunk of money.'

'Really? I do hope he's right.' Realising it would have come just at the right time, as it had long been in need of some costly repairs. Just to replace the wooden steps to access the bell tower was estimated to cost ten thousand pounds, and better it goes there, than on his son, who had behaved the way he did.

Realising the time, I finished my drink and made my excuses, thanking Stella for a lovely lunch.

'See you later,' I blurted out, realising my mistake as soon as I'd said it. 'Listen to me, I sound more like Freya every day!'

Stella, simply laughed, as I breathed a sigh of relief - once I'd reversed out of her driveway.

Fortunately, the weather had improved and was set to continue for the next couple of days. So, as soon as I returned home, I began the plan of action, returning to the kitchen to finish the final preparations for this evening's celebration. Ben had already helped move and position the garden furniture as Freya had instructed; the only thing we couldn't orchestrate was the perfect light to match that in the picture that Rob had painted and Ruby had managed to stumble upon in the window of a second-hand shop. Apparently, the shop owner had been reluctant to sell the picture as it was part of her window display - until Ruby had explained its significance, letting her have the easel it was stood on as well!

The scene was set, and the fridge was laden with treats. I'd even found candles, not forgetting the matches for yet another birthday cake for everyone to share. How Ruby was going to persuade Stella to drive here and then get out of the car and come inside, was for her to figure out!

However, with Freya's astounding help in the meticulous planning that had gone into creating such a wonderful surprise: Luke, Clether, myself and even Ben, were poised with glasses filled to the brim with sparkling wine, waiting for Ruby to arrive with Stella. On cue, we heard their car pull up at the front of the house, shortly followed by them both appearing.

'Surprise!' we all cheered, as Stella stood looking at Ruby.

'Happy birthday mum,' Ruby said, embracing her mother.

'What, this is for me?' Stella asked, completely dumbfounded.

'And there's more,' Ruby explained, leading her over to the easel and unveiling her gift.

'Here, drink this,' I said, handing her a drink, realising she was more shocked than surprised.

'Thank you,' she said, accepting her glass and taking a sip. 'I don't know who arranged all this, but you kept it very quiet. All I can say, is thank you, very much. You've completely blown me away!'

By which time, Freya had emerged from the house with the birthday cake complete with candles as we all sang happy birthday.

'Make a wish mum,' Ruby said, as her mother blew out the candles and we raised our glasses once more.
I sort of knew what Stella might wish for; but as we all know, wishes are secret and can't be shared.

Stella's party had been magical, the only thing missing had been Rob; although, he had certainly been there in spirit. It had also been nice to see Clether talking to Stella, perhaps one day they'll become even closer and share memories, new and old.
Today especially, made me realise just how much can change in such a relatively short space of time.
Beth had called to tell me that Laura and Adam were now parents to a healthy baby girl, who'd arrived in the early hours of the morning. I'd listened as she filled me in on every detail, unable to contain her excitement. After our call had ended, I sat quietly for a few moments, trying to absorb the news. My first thought was to grab my keys and drive to the stables, not to share the news with Freya, but to saddle up Bella and clear my head; but resisted the urge, returning to the work in front of me; realising, it wasn't really my place to announce the arrival of her father's new 'little girl'.
It seemed Ben's Day had been almost as strange as mine, having been asked to value his old house that he'd shared with his wife.

'We're a right pair,' I confessed, after sharing my news.
'In other words,' Ben began, perfect for each other!'
Not having the restraints of children and our dinner already in the oven, we continued our admiration for one another upstairs, where we could forget life's troubles and fall deeper in love.

Spring had officially arrived, and with it, Megan Elizabeth, just one day later than predicted. Lucas had called to inform me of her safe arrival, assuring me of my own daughter's wellbeing and elation, whilst completely overwhelmed with everything that had just happened, unable to recall his daughter's weight, asking if I would inform Freya and promising to call later with Beth.

I had no hesitation in calling Freya, who remarkably, answered her phone immediately and was as delighted as me to hear the news, as of course was Ben, especially now he could call me grandma!

By the time Ben arrived home with a bunch of pink roses and a bottle of sparkling rose wine to celebrate another milestone in our lives together, I had called my mother, received several photos of my granddaughter and spoken to Beth, who had naturally seemed overjoyed to be cradling her daughter. Unable to contain my joy, I'd slipped a little note into the order I had just completed, sharing my happiness and wishing the betrothed couple as much joy as I had experienced myself today.

Chapter 28

Home is Where the Heart is

'She's adorable,' I agreed with Stella, showing her some photos I'd recently taken of Beth's baby daughter.
Freya and I had gone up on the train for a couple of days before the schools had finished for Easter and Freya was required for pony club; the barn, having been left in the very capable hands of Clether - who by all accounts was recrafting some old spindles he'd sourced for the stairway; all of which, had flown out of the window once Freya had cradled her sister's baby daughter for the first time.
We'd stayed in the newly refurbished pub, or to be more precise, the en suite rooms above – less than a hundred yards from where we'd once lived together as a family! But which already felt like a lifetime ago. Freya had naturally wanted to visit her father and his new baby daughter; both Freya and Beth's half-sister – something I couldn't quite contemplate and had absolutely no desire to become involved with. Sensing my reluctance to talk about her father, Freya had kept her feelings to herself, or perhaps shared them with Beth.

'What a pity she's so far away,' Stella commented.

'I suppose,' I replied. 'But we have to go where life takes us. Besides, I have Freya and Ben here. I know I made the right decision moving here, away from Adam.'

'So, no regrets?' Stella asked.

'None at all,' I confirmed. 'Home is where the heart is, and mine is definitely here.'

'I know what you mean.' Stella began, 'I know when I thought about moving, I had no idea where I would go or where to even start looking; we belong here.'

'I'm glad you decided to stay and that things are improving.'

'I'd have had a battle on my hands if I had tried to persuade Ruby, that's for sure!'

'I assume she's at the stables?'

'Yes, honestly, she's never at home these days, though you'll never guess where she is tonight.'

'In which case you'll have to tell me!'

'She's babysitting Stephanie's children.'

'What, Clether's sister?' I asked, trying to hide my astonishment.

'Precisely! Freya normally looks after them, but she's got something on tonight, so she suggested Ruby. She already knows the eldest one, Eliza. She's been going to pony club this week and appears to love her as much as the other kids do.'

'Well, that's a good start!'

'I just hope it works out for her. I suppose Ruby and Freya's situations are somewhat similar,' Stella said.

I considered for a moment what Stella had just said, unable to find any resemblance. For once, keeping my thoughts to myself. Surely, Freya would have more in common with Stephanie than Ruby. But, like Freya said, it was all very complicated.

It was only later when I was sat at my desk addressing a seating plan that I considered the consequences of Adam's betrayal, not least for his mother, who considering she only had one child, had become a grandmother and great grandmother in the space of a few short weeks and would be attending her son's second wedding just a few months before her granddaughter's! I suppose, we all just have to accept that things change, including us, and we have to somehow learn to adapt.

The sun was shining as I stepped outside and made my way towards the shops. Normally the streets would be quiet once the children were in school, but now they were off and the warmer weather had arrived it appeared so had the tourists, making their way to the coast for the day, oblivious to the beautiful stretch that ran closer to home. Though, I suppose there is only so much you can discover in the space of a week or two, not that we'd want them invading our beautiful stretch of shore.

Ben had left me in bed this morning, having been disturbed at around two o'clock this morning by the milkman, not only clattering next doors empty bottles, but talking on his phone! To whom, I have no idea! If I'd known we were out of milk, I could have asked him to leave us one. But at least this way, I could grab a fresh loaf and croissants and maybe even a vanilla slice for after lunch, unable to remember when I last treated myself to one, wondering which Ben would choose, whilst considering just how much I had still yet to learn about him.

It seemed, no sooner than I'd sent Emma's invitation order out that Ben and I received one, waiting for me on the doormat when I'd returned. Not for the actual ceremony, but one I had curated for their evening celebration to allow friends and work colleagues to celebrate with them on the dance floor.

Suitably recharged, I set about my work, opening my mail before printing out numerous invitations and menus for two different weddings, realising it wouldn't be long before Adam's big day, wondering what they'd planned and reminded of the aspirations we'd both shared before our own wedding day.

Now the clocks had changed, it made it far easier to fit in a ride at the end of my working day and after the pony club recruits had all gone home. Ruby of course, was still there when I arrived, whispering sweet nothings in the ear of one of the ponies, as she secured his hay basket.

    'Good day?' I called, as I approached.

'Hi Felicity,' Ruby replied, 'wonderful day. Lucy here,' she said, tickling the pony's chin, 'was superb, weren't you?' Freya appeared, so I left Ruby to continue her praises, whilst I followed Freya to go and retrieve Bella from the field. It was always nice to see her doing what she loved best, making a mental note to report back to Stella on her own daughter.

Having been busy all day with pony club, Freya decided to take the opportunity to join me, as keen to escape the confines of the yard as I was my desk. We headed westward, the sun still warm and with no intention of setting anytime soon. The hedges already adorned with Hawthorn blossom and green leaves slowly unfurling in the warmth of each new day.

The sun was still warm as I arrived home, feeling invigorated, and since Ben appeared to be home, considered the option of a drink together in the garden before contemplating what to create for dinner.

'How about we have a drink outside before we eat?' I asked, once we'd kissed.

'Are you sure? It's still only April?' Ben declared.

'But it's lovely outside, trust me,' I said, opening the fridge and realising the cake I hadn't eaten earlier was missing – No doubt, all evidence, inside the dishwasher.

'I see you've eaten the cake!' I said.

'It was divine, how did you know they were my favourite?'

Well, if I didn't, I certainly did now!

'I assume you couldn't resist eating yours earlier?'

'Hm!' I mean, what else was I meant to say! Realising, in future, I would just have to buy two!

'I've missed this,' I said, relaxing beside Ben, gazing into the distance. 'You're very quiet,' I commented, wondering what he was thinking.

'I was reminded only this morning about the importance of discretion,' Ben explained, recalling an earlier appointment he'd had with an elderly gentleman to value his semi-detached property.'

'It was rather disconcerting, is all I can say,' he explained.

'I'm intrigued,' I said, turning to see a puzzled look on his face.

'Remind me later,' was all he'd say.

'Oh look,' I said, noticing the buds on the apple tree beginning to burst into life. Reminded of my old garden, realising It'd soon be warm enough to transplant the seedlings growing inside on every available windowsill and sharing my thoughts with Ben.

'I was just thinking the exact same thing!' Ben declared. 'Speaking of which. What's for dinner?' Something, only Ben would say!

As I poured us each a glass of chilled white wine from an open bottle, left over from a previous evening, I asked Ben about his earlier comment about discretion.

'In all my days, I've never come across anybody quite like the guy I met this morning. After asking me to remove my shoes, he invited me to follow him upstairs.'
I continued listening, intrigued already.

'He led me into a bedroom and gestured to a chair, whilst he sat on the edge of the bed. By which time, I was beginning to feel uncomfortable, wondering if the guy was even in his right mind. Anyway, he then went on to explain, that, "walls have ears"! And surprise surprise, he wants a discreet sale.'
Leaving me completely baffled as to how anyone could keep moving house a secret! Wondering, what would have happened if Emma had gone instead of Ben.

'It gets worse,' Ben continued, 'I had another appointment, less than a hundred yards away at an elderly ladies house, which resembled,' Ben paused, 'I'm, actually at a loss at how best to describe her home. Cluttered, I suppose. Although that is somewhat of an understatement!'

'I suppose, a lifetime of memories,' I suggested.

'No, it was almost as if she'd set the scene for what she imagined to be attractive. But somehow, got carried away in the process. Literally, every surface was laden with either soft toys, dolls or ornaments. Not only that, but the floors and soft furnishings, and come to think of it - walls, were covered in patterned fabric. Even the garden was full of gnomes and other strange artifacts, and she had more pots than your average garden centre!'

'Not to everyone's taste then?'

'I did suggest she might like to start packing some of it away, so it wouldn't detract too much from the original features, explaining that most people struggle to imagine their own things in another house. In which case as empty as possible helps. Some people just fail to realise that not everyone who dreams of living in their property, shares their vision.'

'I'd perhaps avoid that neighbourhood in future!' I suggested.

'I certainly won't forget it in a hurry!'

Despite the sun penetrating through the curtains, Ben and I were reluctant to emerge from the warm confines of our bed and each other's embrace. It seemed so long since Ben had had a weekend off, allowing us time to relax in bed together.

'Come on lazy bones,' I eventually said. 'We've a vegetable patch to prepare if we're going to have anything to harvest.' Experience had taught me the benefits of preparing the ground and adding a wheelbarrow full of well-rotted horse manure before planting out the delicate little shoots, that would still have to wait another few weeks, in order to escape getting bitten by any frost.

'Just think, we'll soon be able to whizz everything up and have a healthy smoothie for breakfast,' I shared, filling the kettle.

'I think I'd still prefer a couple of eggs,' Ben said. Quickly adding, 'But don't go thinking I'm having hens out there!'

'That's not a bad idea!'

Once we'd enjoyed a hearty breakfast, we donned our wellies and woolly jumpers, collecting our spades from the shed. The garden had been mostly my domain when the girls had been growing up, sharing my passion and teaching them all I knew, that I'd learnt from my own parents. Although both my parents shared a passion for gardening, my father, had actually preferred attending to his perennials, until it came to mealtime! Whereas my mother knew exactly what to grow, attaining remarkable results that not only tasted delicious, but won prizes at local shows! Beth had never really enjoyed getting her hands dirty, even when it came to picking the fruit and harvesting the vegetables. Freya, on the other hand, would help herself to whatever was ready, leaving discarded pods and stalks in her trail! No doubt, a fruit and veg patch will be a must in her garden plan – just once the barn was finished!

'Are you sure it has to be this deep?' Ben groaned, straightening himself up.

'Unless you want wonky carrots. Besides, it's good for the soil. They'll be easier to dig up as well. And just think, next year it'll be easier still.'

'I'm beginning to wonder if it's really worth it,' Ben considered. 'It's a lot of effort when you can just nip to the shop and buy a bag.'

'Just you wait, you'll soon change your mind.'

'So, what else are we growing?'

'Sweetcorn, peas, beans, potatoes, and over here,' I pointed, 'I thought we'd have some fruit bushes, raspberries and gooseberries and maybe even blackcurrants.'

'What about blackberries? I love a blackberry and apple crumble,' Ben asked enthusiastically.

'We can pick those anywhere,' I explained. 'For free!'

'Oh, look at this,' I said, bending to retrieve what looked like a piece of broken tile.

'It looks like it's an old kitchen tile.'

'When did you last update your kitchen?'

'It's nothing to do with me,' Ben admitted.

'Then, I wonder if it was from Clether's old house,' I considered, putting it to one side.

'Quite possibly.'

'Oh look, there must be more!' Ben declared, hitting something with his spade. 'It looks like a toy car or something.'

'Let me see,' I asked. 'It's some sort of excavation vehicle,' I said, examining it, unable to remember its correct title.

'An excavator!' Ben informed me.

'That's what I just said! I assume it isn't yours?' Wondering what else we might find if we were to continue digging a little deeper. Making a mental note to clean anything we found and keep them to show Clether.

Chapter 29

Memories to Treasure

Pony club had been another resounding success by all accounts, the good weather making it possible to spend most of their time outdoors, improving on riding skills, instead of being confined to the stable yard, resulting in numerous rosettes being awarded and according to Stella, Stephanie's daughter Eliza, was delighted to have been awarded her first ever rosette. Not only that, but Ruby had also declared her desire to make her hobby her full time career, once she'd left school, and had asked Freya to look into the possibility of offering her an apprenticeship, explaining how Rob would have been so proud of them both. I suppose there are always going to be reminders for her and things she should have been able to share with him; just like I had taken for granted that Adam and I would have been attending Freya's wedding together and been delighted in our first grandchild, who was already nearly a month old. The reality is though, that none of us can ever predict what the future holds; we just have to enjoy the moment.

Stella had also tried again to persuade me to attend her new adult ballet class starting this morning, not that it wasn't already popular, just not my thing, so had declined gracefully. I suppose, each to their own, just as I'm sure Stella wouldn't consider ever mounting a horse. Apart from which, I didn't need any more constraints on my time, especially if it meant I would have to forfeit time with Bella; something I was already missing, having avoided the stables over the school holidays. But now the clocks had changed and being blessed with lighter nights, it wouldn't be long before I could enjoy an evening hack, realising what else I had missed and how much more I'd soon be able to achieve.

After a productive morning's work at my desk, I wandered downstairs to grab some lunch, not that I intended rushing it, and the fact it was already prepared made the proposition even more inviting. Though I had to agree with Ben, that now my vegetables had taken root, the kitchen was rather starting to resemble a greenhouse! But, as I'd explained to him, that despite living where we do, I was still concerned there might still be frost. Besides which, the moon was entering a waning period, so we'd just have to wait until next month now; believing the best time to plant was during a full moon when the seeds would naturally absorb the most water and light.
Clether had been delighted with what we had found whilst digging over the garden, or to be precise, the relatively small patch of earth, though was unable to shed any light on the odd horseshoes we had found. But to let him know if we ever decided to extend the plot so he could join the dig! Leaving me to imagine what other relics we could be sitting on. Though now the garden was blossoming, I was quite happy to just see what else appeared on the surface before disturbing it any further. Having lived in my previous property for a considerable period of time, I had nurtured it, adding plants and bulbs throughout the changing seasons to enjoy. Wondering now, if the new occupants had appreciated what might have been sleeping underground throughout the winter, just waiting for its right moment to burst into beauty, before remodelling it; reminded of the daffodils I'd planted as bulbs with the girls when they'd been little, as I caught sight of the ones outside. Realising, that just as we change, so do the properties we live in. Sadly, in Clether's case, it was a different story. But ultimately, all we can take with us are memories, something that Clether would hopefully realise and be able to replicate somehow in the new home he was building.
Oddly enough, or perhaps not, in his case, Ben had shared a similar conversation this evening after meeting with an

elderly lady with the intention of marketing her house. Apparently, having lived in the village all her life, able to remember the land Ben's house now sits on, before it was ever built on, explaining how she used to walk up the hill with her boyfriend at the time and sit under the tree that's now at the bottom of our garden!

'Really! So how old is she?'

'Oh, she must be in her nineties, her boyfriend went to war and never came back.'

'Oh, how sad,' I said. 'So, she's been on her own all this time?'

'No, she's got five great grandchildren. She's a widow now, which is one of the reasons she's considering moving to the new over fifties complex on the edge of town.'

'Really. I'm surprised, after living in a rural community all her life.'

'I think that's the appeal.'

'But there's actually a lot going on here, on a regular basis. Just have a look at the village newsletter. Stella's even started up a ballet class for adults.'

'You do remember how old I said she was?'

'I don't think they'll be auditioning for "Swan Lake" or anything. I got the impression it was more an alternative exercise class designed for the older woman.' Wondering who I was actually trying to convince.

'There's a huge difference between a fifty-year-old and a woman of ninety. And I think I remember reading they have a gym and pool at this complex. And like she says, you're never too old to try something new.'

'She sounds like a wise woman.'

'She is. It's not often you meet someone as interesting as she was, and with so much local knowledge.'

Ben continued, filling me in on his conversation, informing me of where her and her husband used to farm and all sorts of interesting facts that she could remember. Including, how she remembers the land Ben's house now sits on, was once farmed by Edward's parents, which would account for all the horseshoes we'd been finding.

'I'd have been happy to sit and listen to her all day, but I had to get back to the office. She did tell me, that even to this day, she sometimes walks along the bottom of the garden on her way to the graveyard, just so she can be reminded of her beloved Edward.'

'So, was Edward her husband?'

'No, the lad that was killed in the war.'

'I suppose that's alright,' I said.

'It is a public footpath.'

'No, I meant that she still thinks of him and puts flowers on his grave.'

'She didn't actually state who's grave she was visiting. Besides, if he didn't come home, he wouldn't be buried here.'

'I suppose, but there's always the war memorial. We should go and have a look for him.'

'What, now?'

'No, it's dark,' I stated the obvious, whilst reminded of all the atrocities the young men from our village once suffered. Whilst we who walk in their footsteps are afforded this green and pleasant land and how we should take the time to remember them and the sacrifices they made.

'She also told me that Edward once carved their initials into the bark of the tree, but she has never been brave enough to inspect it, respecting our privacy. Explaining, it's our tree now. And, if anyone had witnessed her examining it, she may have been carted off to another sort of establishment!'

'She sounds lovely!' I said, 'I'd love to meet her. Perhaps we should invite her round, if only so she can sit under the tree again. I don't even know what sort of tree it is.' I confessed, whilst realising how important it was to someone else. 'What's her name?'

'Isabelle.'

I'd never quite understood why people would ever want to revisit their old home once it was sold to someone else and they'd changed all the things that had once made it home; until I'd witnessed Stella's expression and realised how much it had meant to her to be reminded of something that had been so special to someone she loved and was no longer here to share things with. Ben, had instructed another colleague to value his old house, not wanting to evoke memories that he'd sooner forget. Of course, Clether's experience was something else completely.

'Let's see if she instructs me first,' Ben replied, not discounting the idea.

It was only after catching up with Stella the following day that I was reminded of Isabelle, reflecting on what Ben had told me and considering her intentions. Were all she might need was just someone to introduce her to what's available on her own doorstep rather than taking a leap in the dark and regretting it.

Unable to concentrate, I decided to take a break from work and make a drink downstairs. Noticing how warm it was, I decided to take it outside to enjoy. As I breathed in the clean, fresh air I immediately started to relax, my mind dispelling all thoughts of wedding plans or other people's quandaries; until I opened my eyes and noticed the tree at the corner of the garden, its buds already starting to unfurl, realising at once it was an oak, just like the one Freya used to climb as a child. Instinctively, I put down my cup and wandered over to it, remembering the inscription Ben had told me about, imagining, all these later it had possibly grown out, or weathered, like an inscription on an ancient headstone.

It took a while, but eventually I discovered a slightly distorted heart with both their initials inscribed inside. How romantic, I thought, that it still existed all these years later, long after he'd died, just like Isabelle's love for him appeared to have never died. As I turned to go back inside, I noticed a little sapling growing under the dappled shade of its branches, making a mental note to dig it up and give it to Isabelle. But all that would have to wait whilst I continued to share my love and start on my next order of invitations for a wedding not too far away, in September; the bride wanting, how she described, a home-grown celebration, especially, as her fiancée had been the boy next door. Not that her guests were all that local, I discovered on closer inspection. Realising they would need to be sent sooner rather than later. I'd almost finished Freya's, which I'd enjoyed just as much as when I'd created my first ever invitation for Beth's wedding, three years ago. Realising how far I'd come since then; not to mention how many invitations I'd created, that would be treasured by so many for years to come. The thought of which slightly overwhelmed me, so preferred not to think about it, instead to just enjoy what I did.

As often with the invitations, there were: save the date's, RSVP's and more often than not, a polite request for money; unlike Freya, who had already compiled an extensive list of all the household paraphernalia they might need to set up home, having only acquired the few basics to survive in their little shepherd's hut. Freya had also asked for each guest's favourite dance track to get them on the dance floor and so Clether could inform the band he had found for the evening. As yet, I still hadn't decided on what to list, realising it had been a long time since I had last danced with Ben.

The following morning, I could hardly wait to wake and open the curtains on a beautiful day. Ben had been a little less enthusiastic and had tried to lure me back to bed, but failed. Not that I wasn't tempted, but I had other things on my mind.

Once I'd replaced the ink cartridge in the printer, I was able to finish printing the invitations I'd started yesterday, eager to replicate a favourite design of mine that I considered to be the most romantic. Opening my tins of ribbon and lace was my favourite part and definitely worth waiting for, reminding me of when I was a child and used to always save the cherry on top of my fairy cake till last. But some things are worth waiting for. So instead, once I'd had my obligatory morning coffee and slice of toast whilst reading my emails, I headed outside to dig up the little sapling I had been wanting to do, ever since I first saw it.

Once potted, I gave it a little water and stood it in the sun, left wondering when I'd give it to Isabelle. Ben hadn't mentioned if she had instructed him to market her house yet, realising the enormity of such a decision, at not only her age but having lived in the same village all her life. I wasn't sure it would be at all easy, despite what Ben had told me. It's then I remembered the email I had opened containing the village newsletter and how it could potentially transform Isabelle's life.

Rather than wait for Ben to arrive home and being the impulsive person I was, I printed out the newsletter that was full of activities, including afternoon tea each Thursday, gardening club on a Wednesday evening, knit and natter - all in the village hall, just a stone's throw from her doorstep.
Unable to contain my excitement, I picked up the newsletter and pot from outside and before thinking about what I was going to say, headed out to knock on Isabelle's door. Only when she didn't answer, had I considered what to do next, deciding to post the newsletter and return later with the tree. Back home I continued to absorb myself in what I loved most about my work, applying the detail to the invitations, leaving them to dry before adding them to the box of finished stationary. Before I knew it, I heard Ben's car pull up on the driveway and then his key in the door.

'I'm home!' he shouted up the stairs, just in case I hadn't already realised.

'I'll be down in a minute,' I replied, clearing up. 'You're early,' I noted.

'It's been a long day,' Ben said, contradicting me. 'How's your day been?'

'Flown by!' I informed him, continuing to tell him about what I'd done, including posting a newsletter through Isabelle's letterbox.

'You can't go doing that, what I told you is confidential, she won't want everyone knowing her business.'

'It's care in the community,' I explained. 'What's the harm in that. Besides, she didn't need to tell you those things if she hadn't wanted to. She told you about the history of your tree that you shared with me, that's all. Surely now I live here, it's our tree.'

'You're right, there's no harm in that.' Ben agreed. 'And what you did was lovely. Though don't go making a habit of it, or you'll do me out of a job!'

'We could call and give her the tree together if you like, this evening,' I suggested. Ben agreeing to think about it, as well as a song to dance to at Freya's wedding.
Despite his earlier concerns over confidentiality, Ben continued to share interesting facts people had disclosed to

him about living where they do or in one case, the owner's obsession for model railways and miniature villages, which occupied an entire bedroom.

'No one is going to want to go back for a second viewing, I couldn't get away! He had to explain all about the intricacies of railway signalling. He could probably win "Mastermind" on that subject alone!'

'You have to remember, it's still his home,' I reminded him.

'And I was there to value the house, not the entire model village with a train line running through it! Anyway, enough about work, let's go and deliver that tree.'

'Only if you're sure?' I asked. 'I can go on my own another time if you'd prefer?'

'No, she'll love it.' Ben confessed.

Just as we were about to knock on Isabelle's door, she opened it, both surprising and delighting her with our gift, which she was very grateful to receive, explaining it was the best gift anyone had ever given her, whilst apologising for not being able to invite us in as she was just on her way over to the village hall, having heard about the gardening club.

'All this time I've lived here, and I never knew what went on across the road!' Admitting, she may not need Ben's services after all!

Just having got back from posting Freya's wedding invitations, I decided to enjoy the morning sun and sit outside a while before returning to my desk to pack up the other stationary I'd been working on that I'd decided to deliver in person, as it was only a few miles away, having already checked she'd be there. I rarely got to meet the bride, if ever, so it would be a privilege.

Unable to relax, I stood to go back inside, when I suddenly caught sight of Isabelle in the field behind the house, imagining she had been visiting the graveyard, calling to her as she passed.

'Hello dear,' she greeted. 'What a lovely day.'

'My thoughts exactly,' continuing to invite her into the garden for a sit down and a drink.

'This is very kind of you.' She thanked me, accepting a cup of tea. 'Who'd have thought I'd be sitting here, all these years later, as though it was only yesterday,' she said, expanding on what Ben had already told me and how Edward, who had been her childhood sweetheart had served in the territorial army before the second World War and then at the outbreak of war transferred to the regular army, being part of the expeditionary force that went to France in 1940 and the Dunkirk evacuation. Explaining he'd been stationed in England and Scotland for the next four years, during which time he was promoted firstly to Corporal and then to Sergeant, on two occasions!

'On two occasions?'
Isabelle smiled, as she recalled how he'd first been demoted after arriving back late from leave and caught breaking back into camp! The second time, he'd requested to be demoted back to Private, not wanting the responsibilities that had gone with the rank, preferring, to be just one of the lads!

'In October 1944,' Isabelle recalled, as if it was only yesterday, 'he'd embarked on a ship that took him to Belgium, and which landed very close to where he'd evacuated from Dunkirk four years earlier. During his voyage out he had written to me, saying how he was already missing home, but had a job to do. However,' she continued, with a sigh, 'he'd only been in Belgium six days before he died. The last letter I'd sent, in reply to the one he'd written on his voyage out, never reached him, and was returned unopened.'

'Oh, Isabelle,' I said, reaching to place my hand on top of her own, completely lost for words.

'Don't fret dear, it's all a long time ago now. I just had to learn to live without him. Anyway,' Isabelle said, finishing her cup of tea, 'as pleasant as it's been, I shan't detain you any longer with stories of Edward. He'd be flattered to think I'm still telling his tale. But don't they say, life's for living.'

'Don't be silly,' I replied. 'He deserves no less for what he did. His story is remarkable and should be shared. And it's an honour to meet you as well.' Realising how brave they had both had to be and how sad it was that she had lived without him for so long.

'Anyhow, how was the gardening club?'

'It was wonderful, I even came away with some young beans for my garden.'

'So do you think you'll go again?'

'Most definitely!'

'I have a friend who's starting a ballet class designed for adults, if you'd be interested,' I told her.

'Oh, I was never a ballerina,' Isabelle explained.

'You don't need to have been, it's more of a graceful exercise class,' I explained, as though I knew what I was talking about! And before I knew it, I'd volunteered to go along with her!

'In which case, we should give it a try. I've always said, you're never too old to try something new!'

Just wait till I tell Stella!

'I'm so glad I met your Ben,' Isabelle said, 'though I doubt I'll be instructing him, at least not anytime soon.'

Ben arrived home from work at the same time I'd pulled up on the driveway, having delivered the wedding stationary as promised. Elated at having met a recipient of my work who was so overjoyed with her order. It really did make all my hard work worthwhile. Not that it was particularly hard work; more meticulous, but definitely worth every minute. I certainly wouldn't want to do anything else; that's for sure. Ben had also had a productive day, managing to negotiate a sale on a property worth over a million pounds.

'We should celebrate,' Ben declared.

'Even though I lost you a sale?'

'What you did was wonderful. It also means Isabelle can get on and enjoy the rest of her life without all the upheaval of moving.'

'She did say, life was for living, and this way she gets to try new things as well.'

'Exactly. A new lease of life!'

Chapter 30

Something old, Something new

Spring had definitely begun to bloom and the little seedlings that had once adorned my windowsills had eventually made their transition into the ground outside, having become gradually accustomed to the prospect over the last week or so. I'd even had so many, I had been able to let Freya have some for a little patch they had cleared, having been inspired, but not yet having the time to plan what to sow.

Their barn almost resembled a home; the changes they had made over the last six months were truly remarkable. The stairs had now been instated, and the bathroom was being installed at the end of the week, before they left to attend Adam's wedding to Laura.

It still seemed odd that my daughters would be attending without me, not that I had any desire to witness my ex-husband's marriage to another woman; just that, the four of us had been a family once and done things together. I suppose, it's only natural to feel a little discombobulated at times, especially when something as significant as this happens, not to mention our daughter's wedding, which was already proving popular, by the number of acceptances I continued to receive. It had been odd sending one to Adam, especially as he would play a part in the ceremony, until I realised the invitation extended to his new wife and baby! Reminding myself that I would have Ben beside me, and I was the happiest and proudest mother Freya could wish for. Stella too, had been slightly overwhelmed when Freya had asked Ruby to be a bridesmaid. Though, as Freya had explained, it made perfect sense for Ruby to help Eliza and

Martha, who trusted her, to negotiate their way along the forest path. Luke had also been invited - though, how he would explain it to his parents, was yet to be determined!
Stella had been delighted when I had told her I would attend her ballet class, especially when I'd mentioned Isabelle. And despite our reservations, both Isabelle and I had been pleasantly surprised at just how much we had enjoyed our first tentative steps on the dance floor and at the barre, vowing to go again. I suppose, like Isabelle said, "you never know unless you try"! I had also gained an insight into Stella's world – although we were complete novices in comparison to some of the other students, despite the class being relatively new. Stella was obviously not only a great ballerina, but a wonderful teacher who was well respected in her field. Although, unlike us, she had been dancing all her life, which was apparent in her demeanour – something we could only strive to achieve.

Isabelle was also becoming a very keen gardener, not that her own garden said anything to the contrary. But every Wednesday evening she would shut her garden gate and head across the road to join the other green fingered enthusiasts for their weekly meeting. She had asked if I would like to join her, but on this occasion, I had declined. Especially as I got the impression, I might be playing gooseberry, after she'd told me all about Harry who she'd met there. I had however, said I would consider opening our garden to the public in the annual open village garden event, realising I may have to first persuade Ben! Wondering what else we might learn if we were to.

Ben, the thoughtful person he was, had had the foresight to plan the entire weekend off, knowing I would be upset and need distracting from my mind wandering, and creating wedding stationary, would be the last thing I would want to do. So, to my surprise, I found myself waking up in the most beautiful of surroundings, with Ben by my side. Arguably, he hadn't given me any indication of his plan so I could prepare! But then it wouldn't have been a surprise when he'd arrived home earlier than usual and asked me to pack a bag with something for every eventuality! Granted, it had been a long while since he'd lived with a woman and obviously didn't know me well enough to realise it just wasn't in my nature to pack lightly. Who knew what the weather might have in store at this time of year, assuming we were staying locally! let alone what wasn't in the wash!

Nevertheless, I had done as instructed, surprising myself, faced with such a predicament, managing to pack everything I'd considered relevant for what I assumed would be just the weekend, into a small case. The look on his face when I'd asked if I'd need my riding gear had said it all! Though, as Ben had never expressed a desire to ride and we only had the weekend together, it was unlikely to be on the cards. Though, he had advised to throw my walking boots and jacket in the car. Saying, that was all he would say! Fortunately, I'd had the foresight to change into something elegant rather than the jeans and sweatshirt I'd been working in all day. Which I later realised had been the right choice, as we'd arrived outside a beautifully lit country house hotel. Ben may not have had a lot of experience when it came to wooing women, but he certainly knew how to wow me!

I could have stayed where I was all morning, cocooned in Ben's arms, gazing out over the beautiful gardens, whilst wondering if Isabelle had considered what might be of interest in Ben's Garden, before suggesting we open it to the public. If this was anything to go by, it would be a huge disappointment to the other green fingered villagers, who were expected to pay for the privilege!

After we'd managed to prise ourselves out of bed and enjoyed a hot breakfast, we'd set out to explore what lay beyond the comfort of this magnificent retreat.

We hadn't had to walk too far before we'd found the heart of a quaint little village meandering down to the harbour. The weather couldn't have been more glorious, immediately reminded of Freya, Beth and of course Adam.

'How about we come back and explore somewhere for lunch later,' Ben suggested, breaking my thoughts.

'Sounds good to me,' I agreed, quickening my step beside him. Reminded of the breakfast we'd not long finished. Ben grabbed my hand as we continued on our way, letting the sun lift our spirits as we enjoyed a morning out together, instead of sat behind a desk; realising just how long it had actually been since we'd spent time exploring somewhere new together. Vowing to make the most of the time we had together in future, especially now the weather had improved.

The weekend had been wonderful and just what I'd needed, ending much too soon, especially as I was greeted by replies to the recent wedding invitations I'd sent out for Freya's wedding.

'They can wait until tomorrow,' Ben said, gathering them from the mat, realising what they were. 'It's been a long weekend, let's just go to bed.'
Ben had been right and we'd both slept well, woken by his alarm to signify the start of another working week, and that life goes on, for better or worse.
I'd felt the urge to prolong the feeling of escapism and just pick up my riding boots and drive to the stables; I wouldn't even have to encounter Freya as she wasn't due home until later, having extended their stay to catch up with relatives before their own big day. But, having been away all weekend, I felt obliged to pick up where I'd left off and at least complete the invitations I'd been working on. After all, I was taking time out to escort Isabelle dancing tomorrow morning!
Fortunately, I'd saved the mail from both today and yesterday to open later when I took a break. I always enjoyed receiving an envelope scrolled with familiar handwriting to celebrate an occasion. Naturally, there were going to be replies to Freya's wedding from people I hadn't yet had the pleasure of meeting, including Laura - who had taken it upon herself to reply on behalf of herself and Adam, which I hadn't been expecting! Though, something I needed to get my head around. After updating the guest list, I returned swiftly back to work, applying the final details to the invitations I'd been working on before wrapping them in tissue paper and ribbon, then placing them in a box along

with the other stationary I'd created, before sending them on their way to delight the guests of Rebecca and George.

The day had somehow flown by, and before I knew it, I was busy preparing dinner in the kitchen, eagerly anticipating Ben's arrival home, having missed him; despite being busy and having spent the entire weekend together.
As ever, Ben loved to share stories from his day, including a couple who had dismissed a house they had viewed because it didn't have the right Feng Sui!
And then agreeing to display some programmes for the local open gardens in a few weeks' time, organised by the local gardening club.

'Apparently, it was Isabelle's idea!' Ben informed me.

'I suppose it might even help promote the area. And it's all for a good cause.'

'Just as long as I don't have to participate!'

'Ah, I forgot to tell you,' I announced. 'I sort of gave Isabelle the impression we would be willing to.'

'You are kidding?'

'But Isabelle thinks it's a wonderful garden.'

'Only because of that blessed tree! Unless she's going to invite the tree hugging society, there's very little else of interest.'

'There are our vegetables,' I said, in their defence. 'There'll be flowers on the vegetables by then. Besides, I thought it might be more somewhere, to simply pause and reflect.'

'What, on what could be achieved?'

'No. On life. There's an abundance of nature out there,' I reminded him.

'Beyond the perimeter of the garden!'

'Surely, that's its unique appeal.'

'I agree, but doubt any green fingered enthusiast would. Surely, they'll want to see specimen plants and a riot of colour. Wouldn't it be better to just decline.'

'Most definitely not!' I declared, rising to the challenge.

I'd visited the local garden centre for some inspiration. It wasn't that Ben's garden -as I still perceived it, didn't have any plants, just that its main focal point was the tranquil view it offered - to detract from that would destroy the garden's appeal. So, instead of buying more plants to add colour, I'd opted for a bit of sculpture, in the form of two rusty copper hens - and some canes to support the now rambling peas and beans.

Only later, after catching up with Stella, did I learn of her slightly obsessive tendency towards collecting seed heads, that had appeared to have started as a child, having been introduced by her green fingered grandmother and which had apparently escalated over the years to now being unable to help herself whenever she got the opportunity to scavenge a seed head. Though, because of this, her garden now flourished year after year with a dazzling assortment of beautiful plants that she continued to collect seeds from; explaining, that Rob had even added to her collection, and that she even had plants grown from seeds he had collected, that may no longer exist in his garden; prompting me to consider reintroducing them to where they'd first originated! Needless to say, I got very little work done, in my bid to improve our haven of tranquillity and curtail the ever growing vegetables, that were attempting to creep further than intended!

Ben shared my satisfaction, and was pleasantly surprised by what I'd achieved, not forgetting the addition of Penny and Petunia, our little red hens!

Having devoted most of yesterday to other pursuits, I resisted the urge to contact Stella for her expertise on what I should sow and where, devoting the entire morning to a seating plan arrangement for an impending wedding, now that thirty eight guests had formerly accepted an invitation to what appeared to be a small but rather lavish affair to celebrate the wedding of Esme and George, who after twenty years of almost living separate lives - as I'd been informed, had now decided they could no longer exist without each other. It wasn't often that I got the pleasure of hearing the romance behind the stationary requests I received, so the odd time I did, made it more special. Despite their reluctance to tie the knot, they seemed to know exactly what they both wanted, from the style of wedding to the food on the plate, including a veritable feast with accompanying wines and champagne, all listed on individual menu cards for each guest, alongside a personal name card to be attached to a champagne flute. They had chosen what I considered to be the most romantic design in my portfolio: a theme of fine lace and white ribbon – letting my imagination portray the choice of gown. Sometimes I just couldn't help myself getting carried away. I had always been a self-confessed dreamer, especially when it came to romance. I'd even had an idea for another design to add to my collection – now that I'd discovered the beauty of botanicals. Their order of service was also going to be beautiful, including my favourite hymn: "Love Divine" whilst the signing of the register took place. Then, last but not least: "Mendelssohn's wedding march". From what I could remember from the initial invitations and the guest seating arrangement, it appeared to be adults only; in complete contrast to a request I'd received today for ninety two guests, plus an extra sixty evening guests – with even more refreshments! Imagining, the evening to be predominantly adults, once the young children had retired; not forgetting the older generation, who often retired early; reminding me of Beth's wedding and having to pause the onset of their first dance as a married couple, as Lucas's grandparents had already retired to their room and fallen into a deep slumber!

It seemed somehow odd receiving replies to Freya's wedding; not least because she was my daughter, although this was more a mixture of pride and realisation that she was now a young woman ready to embark on married life. But I still couldn't quite get used to opening up each envelope to reveal my own work! More worryingly, it was now only four months to the actual day! Reminding me of our appointment with the florist later in the week to discuss ideas. I appreciated Freya asking me along, not that I felt I had much to offer in that particular department, other than a few personal favourites I wish I'd chosen for my own wedding, instead having had Adam's mother's preferences imposed on me, which I'd accepted, respecting her professional criticisms on what I had imagined. Fortunately, Freya's grandmother had now retired from floristry and hadn't, as far as I'm aware, offered any suggestions on what was appropriate for her granddaughter, or indeed what her bridesmaids might carry. Not that Freya would tolerate someone else's preferences when it came to anything, especially something as special as her wedding day. She had, as I had suggested, created a mood board as well as a notebook, filled with snippets, photographs, business cards and materials to help her catalogue her ideas for both her wedding and life beyond, in her bespoke barn, which was also making marvellous advances, not that they seemed at all eager to leave the comfort of their little hut on wheels.

At least now, Freya had found her fairytale dress after searching online and all the charity and vintage shops she could find; unable to quite believe her luck, whilst out shopping in town recently, when she'd spotted a young woman carrying a large white box which looked suspiciously like it might contain a wedding dress, into a charity shop. So, not only to satisfy her curiosity, she had followed her inside and was pleasantly surprised when she'd revealed an exquisite dress, that she immediately knew she would love to wear herself. Freya, being the curious creature she was, and to satisfy her soul, had interrogated the woman donating the dress as to its origin and the reason she had decided to donate it, rather than keeping or selling it. Personally, I can't see the attraction of wearing a second-hand gown to your own wedding, or any occasion come to think of it; the idea, is all a bit creepy to me. But Freya was adamant that she wanted to wear a dress that had already been loved and had a story. I suppose, at least she got to find out the woman was happily married and hadn't been jilted at the alter!

Of course, as you might expect, despite having all the features Freya had been looking for, it didn't however fit in all the right places. But, as Clether's sister Stephanie was an experienced seamstress, she had offered to correct the few minor alterations required, promising to have it finished on time. All she needed now was a pair of shoes! Wondering if her love for something old would extend to her choice of ring, and whether Clether would choose to wear one.

A new day dawned, and as seemed customary these days, the postman delivered yet more replies accepting their invitations to Freya and Clether's wedding celebrations, reminding me of my plans to visit the stables – something I would regret if I left it much longer! But first I had an order for 'save the date' cards to quickly finish, and now that it seemed everyone had replied to Freya's wedding invitations, I could finalise the seating plan and make a start on place name settings.

Before I knew it, my tummy was starting to rumble, and the church clock was striking midday! It was easy to lose track of time when I was engrossed in what I loved doing, especially when it was for my own daughter's wedding day. So, without further ado, I quickly reheated and demolished the remains of last night's supper, omitting the last bit of wine that lingered in the bottle that Ben and I had enjoyed with our meal last night. Instead, pouring myself a glass of water before changing into something more appropriate and driving to the stables.

As it happened, Freya was just about to take her lunch break, which meant we could at least catch up properly, for what seemed the first time in a while. Freya reminding me she hadn't seen me since before her father's wedding.

Of course, she naturally had to show me some photos of the day, including his new baby daughter and wife!

It was, of course, nice to see Beth and her daughter too.

'It won't be long before your own day arrives,' I said, explaining to Freya how I'd begun work on her seating plan and addressing place names. At the same time, reminding her of our appointment with the florist tomorrow afternoon.

Then, right on cue, she burst into updating me on the progress of their barn - which along with the wedding, all seemed to be going to plan, and as if by magic, would occur simultaneously!

Bella, had been a little reluctant to leave the comfort of her stable where she'd been residing after just being shod, reminding me of Freya when she was little, and who also, so disliked wearing a new pair of shoes, even wellies! Until of course they were worn in, and her feet had grown!

'Come on,' I coaxed, 'the sooner we get you out, the better you'll feel.' Whilst donning her with her tack.
Sure enough, the sunshine and exercise did us both the world of good, lifting our spirits to face whatever else life decided to throw our way.

'You wouldn't like to take Jake out, would you?' Freya asked, after I'd left Bella grazing. 'He's been a little out of sorts since Mandy's been away.'

'I doubt I'd have the energy,' I sighed, apologetically. 'Apart from which, I really need to get back and get on with work,' I said, reminded of an email I'd received this morning from Ben's colleague Emma, informing me of their menu choices and order of service she now wanted printing, not forgetting their seating plan and place names.

'Not to worry,' Freya assured me. 'I'll ask Ruby later.'
We said our goodbyes, for now, suddenly realising just how lucky I was to be able to spend this time with her.
I'd actually made remarkable progress once I'd returned, surprising myself as to what I could achieve when I set my mind to it. Even the garden was flourishing – just as long as it stayed that way for a few more weeks and hadn't peaked too soon! Although, it would be nice if the slugs, or whoever else was helping themselves to my leafy vegetables would leave them alone. At this rate, I'd have nothing to show for all my patience and nurturing!
As if reading my mind, Ben had surprised me, arriving home with a selection of herbs – not for a culinary feast, but to plant in the garden to try and deter the culprits ravishing our crops. He had been quite upset seeing the destruction they had already managed to achieve and had obviously decided to take matters into his own hands, before it was too late. Stating, that we were going to have gone to all this effort and not have anything to show for it – other than a healthy slug colony!
It later transpired, that Imogen in his office had riled him, explaining the benefits of slugs, and how, in her opinion, they wouldn't nibble on leaves, unless they were already damaged!
Undefeated, he had decided to try and stop their invasion with pungent herbs to deter their incessant appetite.

I, on the other hand, had been more than a little dubious, but loved his enthusiasm! Especially when he had ventured outside before breakfast to see if his ploy had deterred the enemy!
Remarkably, it had seemed to have worked, and contrary to the statistics Imogen had quoted, the herbs had appeared to have warded them all away, as there wasn't a single trace of any further damage!

'You're a genius!' I confessed, as Ben led me out to show me. Who would think a few greens, could evoke such passion!
Ben's enthusiasm must have been infectious, as I couldn't wait to start where I had left off yesterday, finishing another batch of order of service, before grabbing some lunch and heading out to meet with Freya and the florist.

After a day of all things wedding related, Ben suggested we continue in the same vein and use his day off to shop for our outfits to wear to Freya and Clether's wedding, which seemed to be fast approaching. After all, I was mother of the bride, who after criticising the bride, had in fact now purchased her gown. So, it appeared I had no excuse. Not that I had been making excuses, it just hadn't crossed my mind! Whereas Ben, had fortunately realised that time was fast running out, and obviously wanted to make the right impression, especially now he realised he'd be sitting on the top table with every eye directed his way; the thought of which, made me rather proud!
Despite living in a little coastal village and hours away from the local city, we could in fact still find an outfit for any occasion, close to home, including a hat from a wonderful hat shop I remembered seeing when exploring a little market town recently, and had been excited to visit. But, as Ben suggested, it might be better to choose the dress first, or at least look. So, as luck would have it, we both found our ideal outfits in the same town, excluding the shoes, which considering Freya was marrying Clether in a forest, we decided to consider a suitable option later. We had of course, had to think a little 'outside the box' as it was, considering

the setting. But all things considered, were satisfied we'd chosen well, rewarding ourselves with a late lunch - sat outside, overlooking a beautiful stretch of river towards home. I did like it when plans worked out. It also meant we could enjoy the rest of the day together. Even if that meant overindulging ourselves. Surely, that was what days off were for!

Today, as planned I was catching up with Stella, which was a good thing, as all this talk about weddings, was actually impinging on my beauty sleep, having woken from a dream about a new stationary design including vegetables! Even Ben, who had discovered a new depth to even the humblest green bean, couldn't envisage the prospect! Although, I rather thought Freya might think I was on to something, especially after choosing brambles to adorn the other chosen flowers in her bouquet!

'At least they're not in her headdress!' Stella commented, when I explained what Freya had chosen.

'If only I'd discovered horticulture earlier, I could have saved a small fortune!'

'Perhaps you could add it to your repertoire,' Stella conceded, although the expression she bore, suggested otherwise!

'If only I had the time!' I considered. 'Though, Ben has definitely caught the gardening bug,' I explained to Stella. Informing her of his ploy to combat the slugs, which seemed to be doing the trick.

'You must ask him if he knows of anything that will stop ants. They seem to be lingering outside my back door,' Stella sighed, as we stepped into her garden, already a riot of colour and which she seemed very familiar with, including their Latin names! introducing me to a few personal favourites and old inhabitants from what was once Rob's garden, including "Lungwort" or "Boys and Girls" - a far more attractive description, depicting its tiny blue and pink bell shaped flowers. Explaining, as she dug up a clump for me to incorporate in my own garden, that what thrived in her garden would probably do the same in mine - especially as it once came from there!

Once Stella had filled a basket with several cuttings from her beautiful garden and extended my vocabulary and understanding – not only of Latin plant names, but French terms used in ballet, I left her to prepare her evening meal; promising to practice what she'd taught last week in class, before our next lesson. Reminded of Isabelle and how she always found the time to try new things.

Once our own supper had been prepared, I set about rehoming the plants I'd been given; deciding, the sooner I got them planted, the better chance they had of surviving. And, that evening may in fact be best, especially as there was a new moon, which is believed to stimulate growth. Then, as the moon wanes, it'll restore energy into the plant's roots.

Just as I'd finished watering the new plants, Ben appeared beside me with a few new plants of his own, that he'd been given from a client wanting to share a few favourites of hers with someone as avid as she was, before they were lost to someone who may not appreciate them quite so much, explaining how she was loathed to leave her garden that she'd established with her late husband over the last forty years. Admitting, he'd forgotten to mention the open garden event, where she could share it with other like-minded souls, as Isabelle had intended.

Chapter 31

Boys and Girls Come out to Play

The moon and the herbs had continued to work their magic on our now blossoming garden which we sat admiring as we enjoyed breakfast together, a few days ahead of sharing it with other green fingered villagers. The vegetables had not only conformed, but exceeded all expectations, just as the whole garden had, which was now a pleasure to behold. Only time would tell how many people would come to share in what we'd managed to create in such a short space of time – not that we'd be sharing that particular fact!
It was satisfying to think that not only the garden was thriving, but everything was falling into place in life, considering I hadn't even met Ben, this time last year!

Everything was on track for Freya's wedding – I'd even bought my shoes, bag, and the all important hat, which despite the venue, I considered obligatory, as mother of the bride. Apart from which, I relished the few occasions that allowed me to indulge in what my ancestors once considered customary and an important part of any outfit, irrespective of occasion. Something I knew my mother and no doubt Adam's mother would both be wearing.
Clether's mother, on the other hand, still hadn't been invited to her youngest son's wedding, not that I'd want to rearrange the seating plan to accommodate her, but just couldn't imagine not attending your own child's wedding day! But, realising it was an area of contention, kept quiet on the subject; realising, the top table could easily be extended to fit her in at the last minute, if Clether changed his mind. Freya had insisted on a customary top table, which despite

the obvious problems of Clether's parents being absent, meant Adam and I could balance it out without having to sit beside each other. Personally, I was uncomfortable sitting beside Clether, in what I assumed to be his mother's rightful place, but he had assured me it was what he and Freya both wanted, and that as the ceremony was unconventional, then there really wasn't any protocol they had to adhere to.

The weather was set to remain unchanged, which although dry, meant the plants needed more attention, my only hope being that the peas and beans, which contrary to my better judgement, I'd resisted picking – would retain their appearance. But, as Stella had reminded me, it was a domestic garden, not Chelsea Flower Show! And despite my best efforts, experience had taught me that nature always seemed to have her way, in whatever walk of life. Especially, when it came to delaying the aging process!

Ben had surpassed himself when it came to devising a plan to tidy the garden, by creating a new raised bed, incorporating all the garden debris underneath a layer of well-rotted compost, mixed with the all-important forkful of horse manure, before planting out some Kale I'd been nurturing from seed, that were now ready for the great outdoors.

What I was most looking forward to, was decorating the cakes I still had to bake, with the edible flowers I had also grown from seed. But, for now, I had a ballet lesson to attend and an order to complete before I could indulge anymore of my time in what had become a newfound passion, that both Ben and I enjoyed.

It appeared Stella's adult ballet classes were far more popular than she'd first considered, which even I had to admit I enjoyed, and despite having thought I wouldn't have the time, I felt even more invigorated to do other things. Even Isabelle had agreed and felt she'd suddenly been given a new lease of life. It also seemed, that not only Freya was getting to know Clether's family, but Stella was also being welcomed into the family. Stephanie, having introduced herself after her daughter's ballet class, had expressed a desire to return to teaching ballet. Which, according to Stella, couldn't have come at a better time, allowing her to grow the adult classes and concentrate on the older students, whilst Stephanie's expertise was with the other end of the spectrum.

Before we knew it, the day had finally arrived for us to dress the garden and furniture to add even more colour and put out the yellow balloons to signify our garden was open to the public to browse and hopefully enjoy, along with a slice of homemade cake, laced with cream and decorated with a variety of edible flowers – picked to perfection!

The vegetables had continued to flourish and were indeed ripe for the picking, just once we had shown the other inhabitants of our village what we had succeeded in growing. Even the sunflowers were making a bid to reach new heights, having established their roots and been given a little support.

It seemed, almost as soon as I'd put the kettle on, our first visitors were arriving, shortly followed by Ben's parents, keen to see what all the fuss was about, pleasantly surprised by the transformation since they'd last seen the garden, inspired to have a go at growing vegetables themselves and complimenting me on the delicious cake - that Ben was convinced was the only reason they'd come!

The visitors continued throughout the day, sharing their appreciation for not only our planting, but our idyllic position to just sit and relax, enjoying not only Ben's strategically placed bench, but the new additional seating we'd decided to buy to enjoy the beautiful palette nature had to offer beyond the boundary of the garden with our nearest and dearest.

Fortunately, there was a lull around midday which meant Ben and I could relax and grab some lunch, before what seemed like the entire gardening club descended upon us. Luckily, Isabelle had also arrived and was on hand to answer some of the questions that Ben and I couldn't, accepting my request to stay a little longer and enjoy the brief solitude at the bottom of the garden with a cup of tea and a well-earned slice of cake.

It seemed everyone was impressed with Ben's herbal remedy for deterring slugs, complimenting us on our healthy specimens, keen to share their experiences and what I considered might be secrets of the trade. Though, I suppose what else would they talk about on a Wednesday evening!

Isabelle appeared to be lost in thought for quite some time, whilst others came and went, including the woman Ben had told me about, who had instructed him to sell her house and begrudgingly her beloved garden that came with it, bringing with her yet another plant I was unfamiliar with, explaining it was an Aquilegia, an herbaceous perennial that would thrive in either full sun or partial shade and would produce seed heads after flowering that we could collect and scatter, or even share. Stella had also kindly donated lots of little envelopes filled with seeds to sell in aid of the church restoration fund.

The event was planned to span the entire weekend, so once four o'clock arrived I set about baking more cakes whilst Ben prepared us something to eat, resisting the urge to pick a few vegetables to add to the risotto!

We'd slept soundly, woken by the alarm, which we'd had the good sense to set, or we'd have still been asleep when our first visitors arrived! Who'd have thought so many people would be interested in looking at other people's gardens!

Stella, who'd been teaching ballet yesterday, arrived after lunch. Although familiar with the garden by now, never ceased to take advantage of an opportunity to enjoy time here, especially when there was tea and cake on offer!

    Freya had also taken the opportunity to enjoy her day off and accompany Stephanie, who had asked if she could come. Not that she was an especially keen gardener herself, having her hands full, but had wanted to show her daughters where she had played as a child and what remained of the garden her father had so lovingly tended.

Fortunately, it was quiet when they'd arrived, apart from Stella, who like Isabelle, was lost in thought at the bottom of the garden. So, Ben and I were able to welcome Stephanie to what had once been her garden and the memories it held. For a moment, she was captivated, until Martha spotted Stella and stole the moment.

Almost an hour later, Stephanie thanked us for letting her share such a special place with her own daughters and incorporating not only the plants Stella had explained had originated from what had once been her garden, but the vegetables that also reminded her of her childhood days, having shelled the peas and beans for dinner.

After every last crumb of cake had been consumed and the sun had begun its descent on another day, Ben and I sat in our favourite spot that we'd shared with so many grateful people over the course of the weekend, who'd also enlightened our lives – and if talking to plants really did work, then the garden would surely flourish.

Chapter 32

As Nature Intended

According to Freya, everything was still on track with the barn, which might even be ready before their nuptials, in now, less than two months' time, despite Clether being busy producing boards to satisfy his never-ending tribe of like-minded environmental surfing enthusiasts, who cared about the ocean they craved. Although, as he'd explained, some weren't too bothered about the natural beauty of the wood or where it had originated, or that it had been repurposed, more its organic feel and connection to the wave, giving them a sleeker ride. Though, I'm sure anyone who has ever met Clether, couldn't help but be inspired by his artistry and philosophy to create and even repurpose something that will last for generations to come, whilst also conserving the ecological balance. Freya had explained, that as well as repurposing an old headboard someone had brought in, he was still managing to not only find time to hand craft their kitchen but ride the waves until the sun went down. And, if I know Clether, he will be up with the lark and in the ocean again! It's no wonder they have managed to survive so long in such a confined space when they spend most of their lives outside! Ben however, who had apparently been a home bird, had also discovered a love for the outdoors - in particular, the garden, where he now spent most evenings. And who, if he wasn't watering the vegetables, was simply sat relaxing, revelling in all its beauty and tranquillity. We also never forgot what nature provided beyond the garden gate and often strolled down to the beach together whenever we got the opportunity and the tide allowed. More often than not, being the only ones on the beach, many people taking for granted, what despite being a little scramble to get down to and a climb back up to the lane, was almost on their doorstep. Occasionally, the odd surfer would pass us on his way down with his board tucked under his arm or we'd glimpse the odd walker or two who'd strayed from the coast path to relax for a while, but other than us and the unknown woman who swam on a regular basis, we had it all to ourselves, which made it all the more special.

Isabelle was also enjoying her new lease of life, as was her garden – filled to the brim with an array of colourful plants she'd either added or received from her fellow neighbours at the gardening club, attributing her sprightliness to her new exercise regime; as not only was she attending Stella's ballet class each week, but she was also practising each morning before breakfast. It wouldn't surprise me if she decided to include wild swimming into her regime! She certainly lived by her mantra, getting the most out of life – an inspiration to us all, not least Stella, who after hearing Isabelle's story, realised it was surely possible to overcome the tragic loss of a loved one, or at least, learn to live with it. There were obviously, always going to be reminders, she only needed to look at Ruby and Clether, who apparently looked more like his father than she could have ever imagined. But rather than dwelling on the past or what might have been, she had started to count her blessings and cherished the time she had spent with Rob and the memories she had of their time together.

Clether also seemed more accepting of the situation his father had created, grateful for what he had experienced with his father rather than what he had lost – especially after considering Ruby had never known her father. Perhaps in time, he could get to know her better, and who knows, even Stella. After all, it is what his father would have wanted, even if it had been a long time coming.

Ruby's relationship with not only Luke, but Stephanie and her daughters continued to thrive. Stephanie, seemingly having taken her under her wing whilst Ruby enjoyed spending time entertaining her daughters, who revelled in her attention. And, as word had got round as to how wonderful Ruby's babysitting services were, it wasn't long before she was inundated with requests!

After disclosing to my mother of Freya's decision to wear her old converse pumps under her wedding dress, she had persuaded her to accept a new pair as 'something new' and a gift from her. Although, Freya having insisted they weren't to be blue or white as her grandmother had imagined, but black! Her 'something borrowed' - and also blue, was a dress ring of mine, that Freya had always admired.

All that now remained was the long-awaited day and for Freya and Clether to agree on handles for their recently installed kitchen cupboards and a second coat of emulsion on the walls.

Chapter 33

Love and Marriage

As predicted, we awoke to beautiful sunshine on what was to be a very special day. Not only did we awake to sunshine, but to the sound of Megan, alerting her mother she was hungry!

Despite her grandmother's advice on upholding tradition and the consequences of not abiding, Freya had declined our invitation to stay and chosen to spend her last night before her wedding in the arms of Clether, explaining how special it was to be together on the eve of their wedding day, disputing any claims of bad luck or a failed or unhappy marriage – never being one to succumb to her grandmother's irrational beliefs. Although she had accepted her father's invitation to join him for breakfast at the hotel where he and his family were staying, before luxuriating in the facilities and suite he'd provided for her - just once she'd had her compulsory early morning ride – a prerequisite for Freya, any day of the week!

My parents had also declined, opting for a bit of peace and quiet, having experienced the delights of grandchildren before! Something Ben and I would no doubt be able to empathise with after this weekend.

Freya's initial wish had been to marry Clether as the sun rose, which despite strong opposition, may well have worked, wondering if perhaps Adam was already up with his baby daughter – until Ben wrapped his arm around me and reminded me how much I loved him.

By the time Ben and I surfaced, Megan was already having a nap outside in her pram, whilst we were instructed to keep an eye on her, but not to disturb her whilst Beth showered;

Lucas taking advantage of an extra couple of hours in bed! Realising Ben was as much use as I was if she was to wake, as she didn't recognise either of us!

Once everybody was refreshed and suitably attired, our overnight bags and the 'order of service' for each guest put into the car, we were ready to leave and enjoy the much-anticipated day, watching my much loved, youngest daughter, exchange vows with her beloved husband to be. I was unable to hide my excitement, imagining all the other emotions to manifest themselves when I saw Freya for the first time, not to mention as she walked arm in arm with her father, or when her eyes met Clether's for the first time. All of which gave me goosebumps.

Although I had questioned Freya's choice of venue, it was actually the most enchanting setting anyone could ask for; far from the madding crowd, festooned in nature. No church bells, just nature's own orchestra and an anxious groom, looking completely out of his comfort zone, despite being amongst so much wood!

It was obvious to anyone that his best man was an older but almost identical brother. What a pity that their parents weren't here to witness such a beautiful moment in life.

Luke was also present, amongst the small gathering of guests; though how he'd managed it, was a complete mystery!

Adam's parents, who were sat with Laura and her children, exchanged glances, acknowledging me, imagining we'd catch up later in the proceedings. The exact identity of Clether's other relations would also have to wait, as through the trees appeared a glimpse of Freya in the dappled sunlight, walking beside her father, just as she had dreamt of, ever since she was a little girl. Fortunately, there was a photographer, or the moment would have just become a sweet memory, along with the smile she gave Clether as he came into view and he pressed play on his chosen piece of music that depicted his love for her.

Even the birds quietened as she approached, as in reverence to the occasion and their profound love for one another. Her dress, which had been a complete mystery up until now, was absolutely stunning, as was her hair, which was flowing loosely, adorned with a crown of fresh flowers that were replicated in her bouquet; a sprig of which, adorned each corsage and buttonhole. If the sight of my daughter hadn't brought me to tears, the little bridesmaids would have - each and every one of them. Then last but not least, Ruby, who despite appearing in front of all her relations for the first time, her attention remained focused on Luke, who she obviously adored. Then, as Freya arrived beside Clether, his brother stopped the music and Adam gave his daughter's hand to Clether, kissing it first. Ben who had already taken hold of my hand, gave it a little squeeze which almost made me burst. And then, as they both made their vows and exchanged rings, the birds began to sing, before they kissed and another favourite piece of music played as they signed the register, witnessed by Beth and Clether's brother, his best man. Eliza presented the bride and groom with an old horseshoe - believed to bestow love, luck and fertility. And then, before the celebrations began - the all essential photographs, including our dysfunctional family! Ruby was quickly introduced to her half-brother, nieces and nephews, astounding a couple of elderly women, who I assumed to be Clether's grandmothers, whose photograph would have depicted their sheer bewilderment at what they'd just learnt. Of course, Luke could only look on, and perhaps wonder what his own parents might one day think.

Our own line up consisted of a variety of ensembles, Freya insisting on one of just her immediate family. Though, I for one, wouldn't be purchasing a copy!

The merriment continued long after the photographer had left and the wedding breakfast and speeches had been enjoyed - all of which had been well delivered and received, along with copious amounts of champagne, which even Ruby and Luke enjoyed!

Then, after a brief interlude and allocation of sleeping accommodation, including: shepherds huts, tents, and a tree house for the bride and groom – the party resumed, with Freya and Clether's first dance as husband and wife, before we all joined them on the dance floor to celebrate and lose our inhibitions. The young and old dwindled over the course of the evening, but not before the enormous hog roast over an open fire, which, despite having eaten a three course meal earlier in the day, was gratefully received, along with a local cider. Freya also got to dance with her father to her chosen track, played by the band and which Clether made even more special, as he took to the stage to perform. And the merriment wouldn't have been complete without Ben having requested our own special track from when we had first been together.

Stella had asked I look out for Ruby, whilst also realising my mind would be on other things, especially after a glass of Champagne, which I was only reminded of when Clether announced their carriage had arrived to whisk them home! I watched as Ruby and Luke embraced Freya and Clether, imagining the parties they'd attend together in the future and the bonds they'd form, and for the first time that day, Stella, and what might have been.

Epilogue

Following the wedding, Ruby had taken her bridesmaid's posy to place on her father's grave , making the same wish as she always made, before walking the short distance to look in on Stephanie and her daughters, where she was now welcomed and considered part of the family, spending more and more time together, learning more about the father she had never known as Stephanie shared her memories and photos of him with both her daughters and Ruby.

Unbeknown to Luke's parents, Luke continued to see Ruby, both at the stables and aided by Stephanie, especially as her daughters seemed as much enamored with Luke as Ruby portrayed.

Ben and I continued to add to our garden throughout the seasons, enjoying the fruits of our labour, continuing to find things emerging, that evoked memories with not only Clether, but Isabelle. Once, noticing what appeared to be an old, military button surface along with the new snowdrops we'd previously planted beneath the Oak tree. We'd decided to plant a new tree in our garden, not only to add to the diversity of the ever growing population of plants that encourage nature to flourish, but as a lasting memory to our love and contribution for generations to come. A legacy to celebrate a new chapter together in a garden with so many other peoples' memories.

My stationary business continued to thrive. Although, as yet, I still haven't incorporated a vegetable design!

The housing market continued to boom, especially when it came to second homes and the astronomical prices people were willing to pay. Only yesterday, Ben had sealed a deal on an all time high, exceeding two million pounds! Granted, it had a sea view and access to one of the most popular surfing beaches. But, as far as I was concerned, nothing could ever beat the seclusion of the beach we still enjoyed.

The tide was also turning on the sustainable and energy efficient aspects being incorporated in new build homes, including air source heat pumps, electric charging pods and solar panels becoming the norm. A far cry from a typical older house, but imagine in time, even these will incorporate renewable energy.

As promised, Clether had carried Freya over the threshold of the home they had crafted together, ready to embark on a new chapter of life as husband and wife, making memories to last a lifetime.

It seemed Stella would never really, ever recover from losing Rob, but took heart from all the good that was now part of their daughter's life and forever grateful for the time she and Rob had shared and the memories she would cherish as long as she lived. A lot like Isabelle, who continued to be an inspiration to everyone she knew, enjoying more time with Harry, who had introduced her to a local history group they now attended together in the village hall, across the road from where Isabelle still lived.

Printed in Dunstable, United Kingdom